# BROKEN KING

## KING BROTHERS
### BOOK THREE

K.M. SCOTT

# BROKEN KING

## Ronan

I had it all once. The beautiful girlfriend who loved me. A talent that was going to take me as far as I wanted to go.

I was living the dream.

But I lost her because I made a terrible mistake, and then one horrible night, I lost any chance to play ball again. Everything I thought I had going for me disappeared, leaving me with nothing to live for.

Now I'm left to pick up the pieces. I'd give anything for another chance with Kate, but can I truly expect anyone to love me now that I'm not who I used to be?

## Kate

He was the boy I fell in love with in high school, my first boyfriend. My first everything. I planned to spend the rest of my life being madly in love with him.

Until it all fell apart.

I never gave up hoping we might end up together, even though I moved on with my life. I heard he got drafted to a minor league baseball team, and even though we weren't together, I was proud of him for finally living his dream.

Now the boy I loved is a man in pain, and there's nothing I can do. I want to believe there's a second chance for us, but is it too late?

# BROKEN KING PLAYLIST

Open Arms-Journey
Black-Pearl Jam
A Thousand Years-Christina Perri
Heavy-Collective Soul
Someone You Loved-Lewis Capaldi
Second Chance-.38 Special
Blackbird-Beatles
Wouldn't It Be Good-Nik Kershaw
Would?-Alice In Chains
Won't Go Home Without You-Maroon 5
Need You Know-Lady A
Would I Lie To You-Charles & Eddie

# CHAPTER ONE

onan

THE SILENCE THREATENS TO DRIVE ME CRAZY, JUST as it does every night around this time. I lean over and pick up my phone off the nightstand. 3:22. God, I'd give anything to sleep through the night for once.

That hasn't happened since the accident. At first, the doctors thought I kept waking up because of pain. Then they guessed it was because I was having a hard time getting off the pain pills. That was three months ago.

Now they think my sleep is off because of anxiety.

They've been wrong every time. I can't sleep because I can't stop thinking about all I lost. It's got nothing to do with the drugs they pumped into me right after the accident or how fucking hard it was to break free from their hold, and it's certainly not because of anxiety.

What the hell do I have to be anxious about? I have my entire life in front of me. On top of that, I have more money than nearly every person on the planet. Even if I found a way to spend every last dime of my billions left to me when my parents died, my family would help me.

So you see, I have nothing to be worried about. At least, that's what everyone wants me to think.

That's what the shrink I see every week wants me to believe. She's very nice and doesn't speak in that irritating social worker voice so many in healthcare do, but she really has no clue how to help me.

The problem is to anyone looking in from the outside, my life isn't that bad. I'm wealthy and have people who care about me. The accident didn't hurt my looks, which wasn't obvious for the first few weeks after. I knew when Matthias and Ava walked into my hospital room that I was in rough shape. He tried to put on that stoic, miserable guy thing he sometimes still does, and she was all smiles and cheeriness, but I knew by the fear in their eyes that I looked bad. The cuts and bruises healed, though, so I look like I always have.

Like the youngest version of my brothers.

Except for one difference.

Nobody wants to think about that, though. Not that I want to either, but I can't escape it. They have no idea how much I wish I could wake up each day and be the person I was before. Then again, I don't sleep through the night, so it's not like I get even a few hours reprieve from the reality of what my life is now.

I look around the room for the bottle of pills Ava insists on moving further away from me every afternoon. It's only an inch or two difference each time, but every day they're in a new place. I think she's scared that if she doesn't do something, I'm going to become addicted to them. Or something worse. They're only sleeping pills, so it wouldn't be a big deal like the drugs they gave me in the hospital, but she's worried, so she does her little rearranging routine in my room every day right before dinner.

She means well. I know that. She's just afraid I might do something to hurt myself again. That's why she makes sure there are never more than a handful of pills in the bottle at any time. I have the feeling she thinks I haven't noticed these little tricks she's playing. Even though I haven't mentioned any of it to her, I know what she's up to.

Not that she's alone in her concern. Every time Matthias is in the same room as I am, his face tells the entire story of what he's thinking. Even when he tries to make it seem like he's happy, smiling like he's on top of the world, how he truly feels can be seen in his eyes. Same with Kellen and Marius. Everyone acts like they're walking on eggshells whenever I'm around, forcing smiles and acting like nothing happened.

But it did. And in that one moment when some stranger made the wrong choice, my life was changed forever.

That lady shrink keeps telling me to focus on the good I have in my life. Sometimes I can, but when I lie in this bed staring up at the ceiling in the middle of the night, I can't help but let my mind drift off to when I had everything.

It's been seven years, yet when I close my eyes, I'm right back there on a cold winter's night with everything in front of me. I had it all. The girl. The life. The dream.

*As I fuss with my tie trying to get the Windsor knot right, I walk into the game room to find my brothers all dressed for the party. Theo and Kellen take turns trying to beat Marius at a game of pool, and Matthias sits sulking on the sofa watching a football game.*

*"What's wrong with you? Why do you look like someone just killed your best friend?" I ask him.*

*He shoots me a glare that's typical of him lately, and Theo answers, "You know Matthias. He's always surly. He wishes he was anywhere else but here for this party tonight." Turning to face him, Theo asks, "Anywhere in particular you wish you were, Matthias?"*

*I don't know whatever inside joke my two oldest brothers have going on, but Matthias shoots him a vicious look that makes me think if someone doesn't change the subject, the two of them are going to be throwing punches any minute now.*

*"Can someone help me with this tie? I keep screwing it up," I say to no one in particular.*

*Marius looks up from eyeing up his shot and smiles. "Big night for you, huh, Ronan? The girlfriend's parents are finally coming over to meet us. We better be on our best behavior."*

*Kellen rolls his eyes and then shakes his head. "What's the big deal? It's Dad's usual holiday party."*

*Finally, Theo walks over to where I'm standing with both ends of my tie in my hands and takes them from me. "Here, I've got it."*

*I watch as he goes through the motions to get the Windsor knot right, his fingers moving fast as he slides the tie over and under, and when he's finished, I look up to see him smiling at me. He doesn't say anything, so I shake my head and ask, "What's so funny?"*

*As the youngest with four older brothers, I'm used to them busting my ass about everything from how I look to what I'm doing at any given moment. Marius and Theo especially enjoy teasing me about whatever they can.*

*Theo pats the finished Windsor knot. "Nothing. Like Marius said, tonight's a big night for you. Are you ready?"*

*Even as I'm secretly worried one of my brothers will do something to make this night a disaster, I shrug off Theo's mention of it being an important thing to me. "Dad has met Kate dozens of times. It's not a big deal."*

*My brother isn't buying my nonchalant attitude, though. "Yeah, but now she's bringing her parents to see us. You worried we're going to fuck things up?" he asks with a chuckle.*

*I glance around the game room and can't help but think one of my brothers is going to do something embarrassing tonight. Will it be Marius drinking too much and saying something stupid? Or Kellen acting like a fool for laughs? Or maybe Theo playing a practical joke?*

*Likely, it'll be Matthias who makes the worst impression since he looks downright miserable. Then again, knowing how he's felt all week since he missed going to the city with Theo, Marius, and Kellen, he'll probably just sit up here stewing in his bad mood during the whole party.*

*"Kate knows all of you too. It's really no big deal, Theo. Her parents already love me. You guys would have to do something really terrible to change that."*

*Theo's eyes light up, and he turns his head to look at*

5

Marius and Kellen. "Did you hear that? Ronan thinks we're going to do something really awful tonight."

As the three of them laugh and make plans to ruin the party, I try to explain what I mean. "I never said that. Theo, tell them the truth. I don't think you guys are necessarily going to do anything tonight."

Nobody is listening to me, so I look over at Matthias for help. "Dude, feel free to jump in here whenever you want."

He grimaces and shakes his head. "Don't get me involved in your little night of romance. I'm going to avoid this whole thing as much as possible."

"What's wrong with you? And it's not a night of romance. Has it ever occurred to you that you might be a happier person if you had someone?"

My oldest brother practically seethes at me before he storms out of the room, leaving me baffled at what just happened. Looking at my other three brothers as they shoot a game of pool, I wait for one of them to explain why Matthias is as miserable as cat shit.

When nobody says anything, I ask, "What was that about?"

Marius and Kellen shrug, but Theo laughs and says, "I think Matthias needs to get laid. That would put a smile on his face."

I don't have time for this, so I ignore him and walk downstairs to check on preparations for tonight's party. Kate texts me as I reach the first floor to tell me she can't wait to see me and her parents are excited to finally meet my father.

Smiling, I respond by telling her how it's going to be great and I'll see her soon and head down the hall to the kitchen to find Eleanor busy cooking. I sit down at the table and sneak a vanilla cookie dusted with red and green sugar, my mouth watering when the first taste of her delicious creation hits my tongue.

"Don't eat them," she scolds me, even though I could have sworn she never turned around from what she's cooking on the stove. "I only made enough for the party tonight."

"I only took one. I swear."

Eleanor turns around and smiles when she sees me. "Look at you! You look all grown up."

"I clean up nicely, don't you think?" I ask as my hand goes to my tie to loosen it just a little. "I had to get Theo to do this Windsor knot because I kept messing it up. It looks okay?"

"You look wonderful, Ronan. You and Kate are going to be the talk of the party. What is she wearing?" Eleanor asks before turning back to focus on the stove.

"She couldn't decide between a green dress and a red one, so I'm not sure," I answer just as Marius walks into the kitchen and grabs two cookies from the tray in front of me.

"You know what she's going to wear?" he asks with utter disgust.

Ever since he and that girlfriend of his broke up, he's been the most miserable bastard when it comes to women. Even Matthias isn't as negative about them as this brother.

"You know, it's normal for people to mention things like that," I say to him, but it's no use. He merely rolls his eyes and strolls out without saying another word.

Walking over to where I'm sitting, Eleanor sighs. "I worry he's going to become jaded if he keeps up like this."

I laugh at how she puts that. "Going to? I think it's too late for that. I swear every time he hears I even talked to Kate, he has to bust my chops."

"Don't listen to him, Ronan," she says sweetly. "What you and Kate have is a good thing. I only hope Marius sees that someday soon and finds someone who makes him happy."

I nod without saying anything else, but all I can think is that brother and Matthias are fighting to be the most jaded men ever when it comes to love. I doubt either of them will ever find anyone who wants to be around such moody bastards.

KATE AND HER PARENTS WALK INTO THE LIVING ROOM AND stop in front of the fifteen foot Christmas tree lit up with all white lights for the party. My father smiles at me across the room and begins to walk toward them, so I hurry over to join him. Kate looks beautiful in a dark green velvet dress she showed me last week when she bought it after exchanging a sweater her grandmother gave her. I've never seen her in it before tonight, but she's breathtaking.

Her mother's eyes light up when she sees me, like always. Mrs. Abbott has always liked me from the first time Kate introduced us right after we started dating earlier this year.

"Ronan, you look so handsome," she gushes as she hugs me.

"Thank you, Mrs. Abbott," I say when she steps back. "You look beautiful. Thank you for coming tonight. I know my father is eager to meet both you and Mr. Abbott."

Kate smiles as I compliment her mother, and out of the corner of my eye, I see her father nod his approval. My father joins us and shakes his hand, welcoming them to our house.

"I'm so happy to finally meet you. I have to tell you Kate is a lovely young lady. We love having her here whenever she comes to see Ronan."

Her parents beam their happiness at hearing my father's

words about Kate. "Oh, she raves about everyone here too," Mrs. Abbott gushes.

It's the perfect meeting between our parents, and as Kate takes her place beside me, I see she's happy. My father begins to guide them toward the bar on the other side of the room, so I take the chance to pull her aside into one of the alcoves where we can find a little privacy, even for a few moments.

She slides her hand down the length of my tie and smiles. "You look so handsome tonight, Ronan."

I lean down and kiss her on the lips, tasting that peppermint lip gloss she received for Christmas. "Thanks. You look great in that dress. I wish we didn't have to hang out here all night."

Kate blushes before rolling her eyes. "You have a one-track mind, Ronan King. Do you know that?"

Twirling the end of her dark brown hair around my forefinger, I smile at her description of me. "I'm a red-blooded boy in love with a beautiful girl. I'm supposed to think about sex twenty-four hours a day."

She slides her palm down my shirt and over the front of my pants, making me instantly hard. "Now you have to walk around this party with a hard-on," she says with a giggle.

I nuzzle her neck and groan against her soft skin, "Thank God I'm wearing black pants then."

The feel of her body next to mine and her hands stroking the back of my head makes my cock get even harder. If we keep it up, I'm not going to be able to stay at this party for long.

"I wish everyone would disappear so we could be alone," I whisper in her ear.

She begins to say something, but I feel a tap on my shoulder by someone interrupting us. I turn around to see Marius giving me a look of irritation.

"Dad's looking for you, so you and Katie better cut out whatever you two are doing and get back out there."

"How is it possible in a house this big I can't find anywhere to be alone?" I ask, knowing he won't give me an answer I want.

He walks away without responding, and I turn back to face Kate. "I guess we better go find our parents."

"Why is he always so surly? Or is it that he doesn't like me?" she asks as we make sure we look okay to join the party again.

"Marius doesn't like any women ever since that girlfriend of his broke up with him," I explain. "He and Matthias are in some kind of contest to see who can hate women more. I think he's winning, but never count my older brother out."

Ready to be around people again, we sneak one last kiss before I take her hand in mine. "Time to go hang with the parents. I'm sure my father has bored your mother and father senseless with his talk of business."

"Or my father has been droning on about the weird things he's seen as a plastic surgeon. My mother made him promise not to bore people with those stories like he always does when they go to parties, but it's like he can't stop himself."

Curious since I've never heard any of these stories, as we make our way toward where the three of them stand near the bar, I ask, "What kind of weird things?"

Kate rolls her eyes and laughs. "I try not to listen. It's all so gross to me. Do you know people's faces are actually nearly taken off in a facelift? Yuck. I'm never going to do that to myself."

"Well, if you ever change your mind, you know someone who will do it for you for nothing, I'm sure," I joke.

"No, thanks," she says, shaking her head as we stop next to our parents.

My father smiles when he sees us and asks, "Where have you two been hiding?"

Kate's parents look over at us with expressions that say they aren't anywhere as pleased about us disappearing, even for those few minutes. Hoping to smooth things over, I quickly answer, "We were helping Eleanor in the kitchen."

Of course, my father knows that's a lie. Eleanor has a staff of half a dozen people helping her with this party, so she doesn't need our assistance. Kate's parents buy the lie, though, and return to beaming smiles.

"You should be very proud of your son, Max," Mr. Abbott says. "He's a fine young man. He's got a great future ahead of him."

"Thank you," my father says, puffing out his chest with pride. "His mother would be so happy with how he's grown up."

I stare up in the darkness at the ceiling above me as those words repeat in my head. A fine young man. A great future ahead of him.

And in one horrible moment, it was all ripped away.

# CHAPTER TWO

onan

SOMEONE KNOCKING ON MY BEDROOM DOOR WAKES me, and before I can say come in, the door opens and Eleanor walks in. She's all smiles as always since I came back here.

As she sets a tray down with my breakfast of eggs and toast and a glass of orange juice, she looks over at me and says, "Good morning, Ronan. It's a beautiful summer day out. I hope I didn't wake you, but I didn't want you to miss the chance to get out there and enjoy yourself."

She knows as well as anyone else that I never leave this room. There's no reason to.

I sit up in bed, making sure I pull the sheets up to my waist so I don't give Eleanor a shock. "Thanks. I had a hard time sleeping last night, so I'll probably just stay in and catch up on getting some rest."

Her smile fades when I say that, but she quickly forces the corners of her mouth upward. "Oh, okay. Well, maybe you'll go out on the patio or hang out a little while at the pool today. You never know."

Yes, I do know. I don't want to go anywhere.

She leaves without another word, and I slide out of bed to get my breakfast. With the first bite of the scrambled eggs, I can't help but smile. I may be unhappy and hate everything, but I can't deny Eleanor makes the best eggs in the world.

Halfway through my meal, I hear voices outside in the hallway. Straining to listen, I recognize Matthias and Ava speaking to someone, likely Eleanor. I can't make out what they're saying, but the tone of their voices comes through loud and clear.

A second later, another knock on my bedroom door is followed by Ava poking her head into the room. Smiling, she says, "I wanted to make sure to say good morning before I take the baby to his doctor's appointment. Can I come in?"

For a second, I remember Mrs. Columbo, my sophomore English teacher constantly riding all of us about can and may and consider asking the questions she would have. Can you? Are you physically able?

Ava doesn't deserve that, though. She's been nothing short of terrific letting me stay here in what's her home now after what happened in the spring. I may not always like how sweet and chipper she is when she comes to see me, but I can't hold that against her.

That's just me being my miserable self.

"Sure," I answer with as much enthusiasm as I can muster, which doesn't amount to much.

She walks in with little Theo in her arms and sits down in the chair beside my bed. The baby seems particularly happy today. Poor guy doesn't know what's waiting for him at that doctor's appointment.

"It's a beautiful day outside," she says, leaving the last word of her sentence hanging, as if she wishes she could say what she's keeping to herself.

"I heard."

She nods and continues to smile, but in her eyes I can see she's disappointed I didn't answer with more enthusiasm for the weather report. What she and everyone else want is for me to happily tell them the beautiful summer weather has made me decide to leave this room for the first time in two months.

It's not going to happen, but she and the rest of my family get an A for effort.

We sit in silence as Theo coos, looking at me like he wants to ask why I won't leave this damn room. I'll explain it to you one day when you're older, little guy.

"Do you want me to pick you up anything when I go into town today?" Ava asks with such hopefulness in her voice I wish I could tell her I want something.

But what I want she can't get me. Nobody can.

I shake my head as my answer. It would be rude to tell her I just want to be left alone, but that's all I want to say right now.

We return to silence for a few moments until she stands up and says, "Okay. I have to get Theo and Matty to their appointment, and that involves two car seats, which never fail to be a production. Matthias and I hired someone to help since now that the new baby is here, it's a little bit much for me to handle. She's starting today, so I didn't want you to think someone broke in if you see her."

"Okay."

"Her name is Sabrina. She's going to be living here. All right, I need to get my little guys to the doctor's."

I nod, not caring about this new person or anything else.

Ava gives me one last smile before she heads out of my room with the baby, leaving me alone like I prefer. I sometimes wish she would give up on trying to cheer me up. Same with Eleanor. Just accept this is who I am now.

I've accepted my life. Why can't they?


EVERY ITEM HUNG IN THIS ROOM REMINDS ME OF the life I wanted and will never have. The picture of me on the All-Star Little League team that almost made it to Williamsport. We got so close. The whole team was disappointed, but we never had more fun than that year on our World Series run.

The New York Yankees pennant and ticket stub from my first baseball game when I was just ten. My mother wasn't feeling well that day, but she promised we'd go see the Yankees, so she drove all of us, along with Ava and Andrew, to the Bronx. We ate so many hot dogs Kellen got sick on the way home, but even that didn't ruin our time. The five of us talked about that day for months afterward.

My first baseball uniform shirt my mother framed for me right before she passed away. She hadn't been able to get out of bed all that week, but she worked through the pain to surprise me with that gift. I remember my father hanging it right where it is today. They were both so proud.

In the corner on top of my chest of drawers sits my first baseball glove. I wouldn't be able to fit even my fingers in it now, but when I was a little boy, that was my prized possession. Matthias and Theo showed me how to oil it, and I'd sit every night after dinner and finishing my homework rubbing that glove.

I close my eyes, unable to look at any of it for another second. All I ever worried about was not being able to make it to the major leagues because I dropped a fly ball or screwed up on a double play.

Now I can't even think of even being able to do either of those things.

As I slowly slip into my gloom, my door opens and I look to see it's Kellen and Matthias. They've already seen I'm not sleeping, so there's no escaping their visit.

"Still in bed? What is this like the fiftieth day in a row? Jesus, Ronan. You better get up or your legs will forget to work," Kellen says as he plops down in the chair next to my bed.

I don't even attempt to hide how much I don't want to listen to whatever it is he's come to tell me and turn my head to stare out the window. If he and Matthias cared at all about how I feel, they'd leave me alone.

My oldest brother takes his own approach to convince me to join the land of the living, walking around to the other side of my bed and blocking my view of the outside. "How are you today?" he asks hesitantly.

Glaring up at him, I sigh, already tired of the two of them. "I'm fine. I'd like to be alone. I was sleeping," I lie.

Matthias levels his gaze on me, obviously not believing anything I've said as he takes his position leaning against the window frame. "Kellen and I thought you might want to go swimming. He took the day off, and I'm working from home today, but I can blow off work for a few hours to hang out with you guys."

"No."

Dressed in a gray suit and black dress shirt with a pink and gray tie I'm sure Ava picked out, he doesn't look like he's working from home. At least Kellen seems like he may actually be here to enjoy himself. Then again, how hard would it be for him to change out of shorts and a t-shirt and back into a suit?

I watch as Matthias's expression morphs from slightly hopeful to discouraged in a flash, but Kellen isn't as easily persuaded. Beside me, he pushes on the pillows behind me like he always used to when I was sick as a little boy.

"Come on. Sitting here in this room day and night for weeks has got to be making you nuts. Nobody's saying you have to go out in public or anything. Just down to the pool. Maybe get in. I bet Ava will put those little swimmies things on Theo after she slathers him in sunscreen. It'll be fun!"

As much as I don't want to deal with him, I turn to

my right and stare into his eyes as I say, "What about no don't you understand?"

Even as he continues to play the clown, I see he understands this isn't going to happen today. If he was being honest with himself, he'd admit it's never going to happen again. I don't want to hang out at the pool. I don't want to do anything with anyone.

Why can't my family just leave me alone?

I close my eyes to avoid the look of pity I know they're both giving me. I don't want pity. I don't want anything.

I just want to be left alone.

Kellen taps me on my shoulder before standing up. "Okay, Ronan. If you change your mind, we'll be down at the pool trying to teach little Theo how to swim."

The sound of his footsteps tells me he leaves, but Matthias is still sitting against the window frame, which means he has something he wants to say. Terrific.

I wait, but he remains silent, so I finally open my eyes and there it is. Pity. Fuck, I hate that. Why does he have to look at me like I'm some pathetic creature he feels bad for?

"Since you're still here, I'm assuming you have something you want to say to me, so say it and let me be."

He folds his arms across his chest and sighs. "The doctor said you need to start getting out every so often."

"I go to my doctor's appointments every week, so I get out."

That answer doesn't satisfy him, unfortunately.

"We're not trying to torture you, Ronan. We're only doing what he says you need."

Sick and tired of hearing doctors say I should get out when they can't understand what I'm going through, I can't stop myself from barking, "What I fucking need is to be left alone! Why won't any of you accept that? I don't want to go anywhere. Just leave me alone!"

Matthias winces like I've just slapped him across the face and simply looks down at the floor. "Okay, Ronan."

He leaves me alone in my misery, but he doesn't make it far. Ava and Kellen are waiting for him out in the hallway.

"Did he say no to coming down to the pool?" Ava asks, sounding teary.

Matthias says something in a low voice I can't hear, but I can bet it's something like he wishes I'd snap out of it. He has no idea what I'm going through here. Snapping out of it isn't going to happen.

"I don't know what to say to him to get him to see life is still worth living," Kellen says in a rare moment of seriousness. "He can't just stay in that room for the rest of his life."

"He can stay here as long as he wants," Matthias says, "but the doctor told me he has to make some effort to at least try to get back to normal."

The three of them whisper something as I try to remember what normal felt like. It's all a blur now, the past where I was just like everyone else and had my whole life to look forward to a distant memory. Those days are gone.

"I just wish there was something we could do to make him see he has so much to look forward to," Ava says.

She's wrong. There's nothing to look forward to. There's only this room where I can hide out and never see the world again.

# CHAPTER THREE

ate

MY MOTHER SCOOPS UP MY CLOTHES OUT OF MY suitcase and starts to walk out of the living room before I can stop her. "Mom! I don't need you to wash my clothes. I just stopped by on my way to my apartment because I wanted to see you guys."

Michelle Abbott could never be confused with a mother who doesn't care. Too often, she cares too much, in my opinion. I'm a twenty-four year old woman who can do her own laundry, but to my mother, I'll always be her baby.

"It's no problem, honey. Sit with your sister and I'll be right back. Don't go into any detail about your trip before I return from the laundry room, okay?"

My sister Kelly gives me a disapproving look and then laughs. "Must be nice being the baby. I've been

23

here for weeks since Jason and I broke up, and never once has she offered to do my clothes."

She caught her husband cheating on her with the maid who was supposed to come in once a week and clean up after them. Somehow, they fell into bed that day nearly a month ago, and since then, Kelly has been staying back here at our childhood home while she gets her divorce started. Jason is about to learn the exact meaning of hell hath no fury like a woman scorned, poor fool.

"I don't want her to clean my clothes, you know. She's the one who's into that. I was just going to go home and throw everything into the wash, colors and whites all together."

My sister's eyes get wide, and then she throws her head back in laughter. "Don't tell Mom that, or she'll stroke out right here in front of us. Colors and whites in the same load? Oh, heavens no!"

I look around for any sign of my mother and lean in toward my sister to whisper, "I do that all the time. It's never turned anything pink or any other color."

Kelly smiles. "Me too."

"We better not let her find out, or she'll think she was a failure as a mother," I joke.

"Seriously. But forget the laundry. Tell me all about Europe. Did you and Jessie have a good time? I want to hear everything. I'm living vicariously through you, so don't leave out the tiniest detail."

"It was incredible! We had so much fun. My favorite part was France. Oh, you should have seen us. We saw the Eiffel Tower and the Louvre. We ate at this adorable outdoor café, and these two gorgeous guys came up to us and sat down at our table. Thank God I remembered some French from high school, or we wouldn't have been able to talk to one another at all. People say the French don't like Americans, but that's not true. All they wanted to talk about was American sports, especially baseball and basketball. I let Jessie handle that part of the conversation, but since she doesn't know much French, things got rocky fast."

As I finish, my sister's expression grows dark. "Speaking of baseball, did you hear about what happened with Ronan King?"

Why she uses his last name I don't understand since I've only known a single Ronan in my entire life. "What? We talked once a week the whole time I was gone. If something happened, why didn't you tell me?"

With sadness in her eyes, she explains, "I didn't want to ruin your trip. You waited two years for Jessie to be able to go."

Scared about what I'm going to hear but needing to know, I ask, "What happened to him?"

Kelly grimaces, and quietly says, "He was in a car accident on New Year's Eve. Seems some drunk lost control of his car and hit his. The car rolled a bunch of times, and he was trapped, pinned between the steering wheel and the seat until the ambulance got there. The drunk walked away from the mess he caused, but Ronan wasn't so lucky. Both his legs were broken, but even worse, he lost his right hand."

I can barely hold back the tears as I listen to all he went through. "Thank God he survived, but he lost his hand? I heard he got a position with a minor league team. What about that now?"

My sister shakes her head. "He can't play baseball anymore, Kate. That part of his life is over."

Hearing that makes my heart ache for Ronan. All he ever wanted was to play baseball in the major leagues. Oh, God. He must be devastated.

"Have you heard anything about how he's doing?"

Kelly's frown deepens. "It's not good. I heard his brother Matthias and his wife brought him to the family house because…"

She doesn't finish her sentence, but I have to know what happened. "Because of what? Is it that he can't walk?"

"No, his legs are fine. He's living there because they need to keep an eye on him."

That makes no sense. I know Ronan got a place in Rome when his father died, and I think he had his own apartment in Manhattan.

"Why? He's a grown man. Those brothers of his were always treating him like a child, even when he wasn't."

They always were unable to see he didn't want to be babied. I know he hated that.

Kelly reaches out and touches my arm. "No, it's nothing like that. They're having him stay there because he tried to kill himself."

I lower my head as tears begin to roll down my cheeks. "Oh, no. He must be so sad because of what happened. He always dreamed of being a ball player, and now that dream is gone."

My mother walks into the room, so I quickly dry

my eyes before looking up at her. "You know, you don't have to do my clothes, Mom. I can do them at my place."

"No, you can't, and what's wrong? Did something happen on your trip? Did some man try something he shouldn't have? When your father hears, he's going to tell me he was right about not wanting you to go on that trip all along."

I let out a heavy sigh and say, "No, nothing happened on the trip. Kelly was just telling me about what happened with Ronan. I wish one of you had told me before this."

"We didn't want to ruin the trip for you," she says sadly. "I always liked Ronan. He's had so much sadness in his life with losing his mother so young and then losing his father and brother before he graduated from college. That poor boy has had a lifetime's worth of misery. It doesn't seem fair that life should give him even more to deal with."

She and my sister talk about the accident, but all I can think of is I should go visit him. We broke up when the two of us were in college, but whatever hard feelings I had then are nothing compared to what he must be going through now.

I stand up and announce, "I'm going to the King estate to see him. I feel terrible that I didn't know until now, and he might think I heard and didn't even care enough to call him."

"Are you sure, honey? You two ended things pretty badly," my mother says. "I remember when you broke up. You were devastated and nearly failed out of school that semester."

Leave it to my mother to make this even worse than it already is.

"I didn't nearly fail out of school, Mom. Yes, I was upset, but that was a long time ago. I don't blame him for what happened to us anymore."

"I just worry about this idea. You loved him, Kate. I'm not sure those feelings ever went away for you, and he likely can't reciprocate even if he wants to now."

She's trying to help, but I can't think like that. Ronan was my first love. He was my first everything. I can't bear the thought of him struggling in life and not even try to see him to make sure he's okay. Whatever happened between us is water under the bridge.

"I'll be fine, Mom. Maybe seeing me will remind him of the good times we had together. I just want to let him know I'm here as a friend. I'd want that if I was going through tough times."

Before my sister or mother try any more to talk me out of going to see him, I grab my purse and hurry upstairs to my old room. I don't want to rehash the day I broke up with Ronan, but I can't stop the memories as they come flooding back.

Just like then, they take my breath away.

*Ronan walks through the door of Beanz, our favorite coffee shop, the place where we had our first date almost two years ago to the day. The last time I saw him was during the holidays. We promised one another that we'd make sure to spend our spring break together since both his university and mine have the same week off.*

*He smiles when he sees me, and even though we've dated for years, my heart still does a little flutter when I first lay eyes on him. It's been like that ever since that first day he walked up to*

*me in high school and asked me out in spring of our junior
year. We've been inseparable from that moment, except for the
past six months after he chose to go out of state for school and I
stayed home for college.*

*I watch as he walks over to the table where we had our first
date. We've always joked this is our table, like no one else has
ever had anything as wonderful happen as we did that first
night. He looks as handsome as he did then. Maybe a little
bigger since he's been playing ball even more while he's been
away at school. He's still the most gorgeous guy I've ever
known, though.*

*"Hey, I should have known you'd pick this table if you
could get it," he says with a smile, but I sense something
different about him.*

*"Of course. It's almost our second anniversary. I'm just
glad we both have spring break at the same time."*

*Ronan sits down and looks around the coffee shop before
staring up at the board with all of today's coffee and snack
choices written in chalk. "I haven't had a latte since I went
away. I could go for one, though. What did you get?"*

*I lift up my cup and smile. "Same as always. Latte with a
pump of caramel with whipped cream on top."*

*He turns to look at my coffee and shakes his head. "Same
old Kate with her dessert in a cup. Want anything while I'm up
there?"*

*"No, I'm good. I went out to dinner with my parents before
I came here, so I'm pretty stuffed."*

*With a chuckle, he points at my drink. "Except for that,
right?"*

*"There's always room for coffee. You know that."*

*He nods and then walks up to the counter as I watch his
every move. I've never been able to be around Ronan King*

*without admiring him. I'd never dreamed he'd ever want to go out with me. Even though we attended the same private school, Ronan comes from a much wealthier family than mine. My father is only a plastic surgeon, not a billionaire owner of a multinational company like his father. Even with my mother's income from her real estate business, we don't come anywhere close to the level of the Kings. Every girl in school wanted to be with him, but he chose me that April afternoon when he stopped at my locker to ask me out.*

*We were together day and night from that moment on until we went to different schools last fall, but we've talked every day, so it hasn't been too bad. I've missed him so much and can't wait to spend this week together like we have planned. My friends may all be thrilled to hang out on the beach in Fort Lauderdale for the next seven days, but I wouldn't give up my time with Ronan for anything.*

*Not even a week full of sun and fun.*

*Lost in thought, I don't see him come back until he taps on the table in front of me. I look up and see him staring at me, likely because he said something and I didn't hear him.*

*"What do you think about going for a walk? It's not too chilly out tonight."*

*I stand up and grab my bag off the back of the chair before taking my cup with me. "Sure!"*

*It's just like our first date when after we sat and talked for an hour or so he suggested we go for a walk. That's when we kissed for the first time on the path that leads through the park. He's so romantic to remember that.*

*As we walk toward the park, we talk about school and how he made the baseball team at his university. I tell him about my classes and how I think I'll make the Dean's List for the second semester in a row.*

"You've always been smart, Kate. I knew you'd do well," he says as he takes my hand.

"I thought college would be so much harder than high school. I feel like going to see Mr. Harvey to tell him all those scary stories of his weren't the truth. You know the ones he told us about how hard college was going to be if we didn't study."

Ronan squeezes my hand and chuckles. "Those stories weren't for people like you. They were for jocks like me."

I've never been okay with him talking about himself like he's some stupid athlete who can't do much else than play ball. Ronan's always been much smarter than the usual guys who spend all their time on the field.

"You did great last semester, so I'm not hearing anything about you being a stupid jock. I bet you're going to hit the Dean's List this semester."

Underneath one of the new lights the city put up on the pathway last summer sits a bench, so he guides me over to it. "I thought we could talk here," he says quietly.

He's acting strange, almost nervous, tonight. Then it dawns on me. Oh my God! Is he planning to propose right here, right now? We talked about getting married someday after I finish college and he's set up playing ball on a team somewhere. I'd have to relocate since it's highly unlikely he'll get to play for a New York team, but I don't mind. With my teaching degree, I'll be able to go practically anywhere.

My heart begins to race, so I take a deep breath in as we sit down. I wish I didn't have so much coffee. That's probably making me more nervous.

It's okay, though. This is Ronan with me. My Ronan. There's no need to be worried or scared.

After taking another sip of my coffee, I turn my body toward him and ask, "So what did you want to talk about?"

*My hands are shaking, but I don't think I've ever been happier in my life. Of course, I'll say yes. I've loved Ronan for what feels like my entire life. I can't imagine my future without him.*

*"It's a beautiful night, isn't it?" he says, but he's looking away from me.*

*"It is. Is something wrong, Ronan? What are you looking at?"*

*He quickly turns to face me and shrugs. "Nothing. Everything's okay." For a moment, he stops and then adds, "Well, there's something I wanted to talk to you about."*

*I can't keep the smile off my face at hearing that. "I'm all ears. What's up?" I ask as I look down at my left hand and wiggle my fingers.*

*An engagement ring is going to look so perfect on me.*

*"Something happened, Kate."*

*His words come out like they're being dragged from his mouth. I don't understand. Did something happen with his father or one of his brothers?*

*"What? What's wrong? Is it something bad? I hope your family is okay."*

*I wait for him to answer, but he doesn't say anything. He simply lowers his gaze to the ground. What could be going on that's so terrible he's acting like this?*

*Sure it can't be that bad, I take his hand and give it a gentle, sympathetic squeeze. "Whatever it is, I'm here for you, Ronan. You can tell me. Whatever you need, you can count on me."*

*He clears his throat but still doesn't say anything. I wait to hear what's troubling him, worried more with each second that passes that he still doesn't tell me.*

*I bring his hand to my lips and press a tiny kiss on his*

knuckles. "It's okay. If you need some time, we can sit here all night."

Ronan swallows hard, and I see his Adam's apple bob up and down. I've always loved that, even though I have no idea why. Something about it seems so masculine.

As I think about how even such a minor thing about him makes me smile, he finally speaks, and in a flat voice devoid of any emotion, he quietly says, "I slept with someone, Kate."

At first, his words don't register in my mind. I can't comprehend them, even though they're only six short syllables.

I slept with someone, Kate.

When I finally realize what he meant, I shake my head. It's all I can do. I can't think of anything else to do. There are no words in my head I wish I could say. There's nothing else my body seems to be able to do but that one motion of shaking my head over and over.

Now he can't seem to stop talking. He turns his body toward me, and I see worry written all over his face.

"It didn't mean a thing. I swear. I don't know how it happened. I was at this party one night right after I got back to school from winter break, and we were all just having a good time. One thing lead to another, and I ended up alone with someone when everyone else passed out."

He stops, I assume to let me say something about what he just confessed, but I have no words in my head. All I feel is sick, like my entire body aches.

Ronan takes my other hand in his. In his eyes, I see how upset this had made him. "It was just one time. I swear. I've felt like shit ever since. I should have told you before this, but I didn't want to do it over the phone or in a text. Say something. Say anything. Just don't stay quiet. Tell me I'm a bastard. Tell me it's going to take me doing something pretty damn incredible to forgive me. I get that. I promise I'm going to do so many wonderful things from now on that you'll be able to forget this stupid mistake."

He finally stops talking, but I still don't know what to say. He cheated on me. He slept with some girl at his school. How could he do that to us?

Then all I want to know is who. Who was this girl he forgot all about me for that night? We've spoken every night since winter break, so who was she that made him able to simply forget he loved me?

"What girl, Ronan? What's her name?"

He winces, as if telling me her name hurts him. "Amanda Isaacson."

In my mind, I repeat her name as my stomach roils, threatening to make me vomit all over him and me. Amanda Isaacson, the cheerleader from high school who's always wanted to have Ronan all to herself. She told me those exact words when she heard we'd begun dating.

Amanda Isaacson, the only child of the man who owns half of the island of Manhattan. The one person from high school who comes from a family as wealthy as the Kings.

Beautiful Amanda with the blond hair and the nose job her father got her for her sixteenth birthday and the big fake boobs he got her for graduation.

I tug my hands from his hold and stand up, still not sure what to say. But now that I know who he cheated on me with, words begin to form. If I should say them is another story because all I've got is hurt fueling my thoughts.

Ronan looks up at me with those soulful brown eyes I've always loved, and in them I see worry but even more, I see fear. "Please, Kate. It meant nothing to me. I know I'm going to have to do a ton to make it up to you, but I'm ready to make *this right. Just give me the chance. Please. Don't let this ruin everything we have."*

*Tears begin to burn at the back of my eyes, but I refuse to cry. "We have nothing, Ronan. Whatever we had, you killed it that night you slept with her."*

*Jumping up from the park bench, he shakes his head wildly as he tries to get me to give him his hand again, but I won't. "No! Trust me. It meant nothing. I was drunk. She was there. That was it. Please, Kate! Just let me fix this, and we'll be good like we've always been. Nothing's changed between us. I still love you, and I know you love me. We've got our future together all planned out. I'll be playing ball somewhere, and you'll be right there with me teaching kids like we've always dreamed. Don't do this, Kate. Don't give up on us because of one stupid mistake."*

*As much as I swore to myself I wouldn't cry, I can't stop the tears as they stream down my cheeks. "It meant nothing? Nice. So you got drunk, and the one girl who's always wanted to get with you is the person you cheat on me with? I told you what she said to me when she heard we started dating, and still you decided to go with her? It wasn't nothing, Ronan. You broke us. You broke us, Ronan! I loved you more than I ever thought possible, and you broke us. And for what? To sleep with the one person I always worried you'd choose over me."*

*He tries to explain himself more, but I can't stand here and listen to any more about him cheating on me. I run away, unsure where I want to go but knowing I can't be anywhere near him anymore. My tears make seeing next to impossible, but it doesn't matter.*

*I just need to get away from him, from the hurt seeing him now makes me feel.*

The pain of that night washes over me again, and I

collapse onto my bed. I shouldn't feel like my heart is breaking all over again, but I do. Maybe my mother's right. Maybe I can't be around Ronan now.

No, I can't think of how hard it'll be to see him again. Whatever pain the memory of that night brings me is nothing compared to what he must be going through. He's lost the one thing he always dreamed of. That's so much worse than anything I might go through talking to him now.

# CHAPTER FOUR

onan

ANOTHER KNOCK ON MY DOOR, THE THIRD OR MAYBE the fourth today, makes me want to throw something in that direction. Too bad my fucking hand is gone. Whoever it is that insists on bothering me is lucky I can't do a damn thing with the one that's left.

I don't bother yelling for them not to come in. They're going to anyway, so why expend the energy?

The door creaks as it opens, but I'm not looking at who's coming in. It's probably Ava or Eleanor, and neither of them require me to acknowledge them. I glance at the clock on the nightstand and see it's nearly dinnertime. So that's why they feel the need to interrupt my day again.

"I have a surprise for you, Ronan," Ava says in that sweet voice I shouldn't hate since she means well.

Still, I don't turn to look at her. I don't give a fuck about her surprise. The last time she said that she came in with a birthday cake to celebrate my birthday six months too early. She said it was to cheer me up, but all I could think was she doesn't understand how calendars or birthdays work. When I told her I wish I'd never have another birthday again, she practically burst into tears. Kellen claims it was because she was pregnant. Whatever the reason, the whole thing got me a visit from Matthias I could have done without since I don't care why she cried.

"Okay, I'll just leave you here with your lovely surprise," Ava says before I hear the door close.

I don't give a damn what the surprise is, but I turn my head to see it anyway and instead see Kate. What the fuck is she doing here?

"Hi, Ronan," my ex-girlfriend shyly says, her expression full of the one thing I never want to see again.

Pity. I could handle anything else but fucking pity.

Hating that I see that in her, I turn away and go back to staring out at the summer day outside my window. I swear I hear kids playing somewhere, but that's not possible since the grounds this house sits on are at least a mile away in every direction from other people and Matthias and Ava's kids are too small to be outside making that noise.

I used to love to play on the grounds when I was small. Kellen and I would convince Theo to chase us around the backyard, and sometimes he'd scare us so we'd run to the part of the estate we were never supposed to go to. He never cared. Rules were meant to be broken, according to him. Anyway, if our parents said anything, he'd blame it on me. Being the youngest, I always ensured he never got into trouble because our parents rarely punished me for anything.

Those were the days.

"I'm sorry I didn't come over to see you before, Ronan, but I just got home from being out of the country since December and didn't hear what happened until today."

Kate's careful not to say what she didn't find out until today, but even unspoken, the words echo throughout the room. That I lost my hand and now I have nothing to live for. She should have just said it. At least that would be a change from everyone else who works overtime walking on eggshells around me and acting like everything's going to be fine.

It isn't. It won't be ever again. Why no one can see that I'll never understand.

When I don't respond to her attempt to start a conversation, she walks around my bed and stands in my line of sight. "I'm sorry I wasn't around until now. This must be so hard for you," she says, and once more, all I see and now hear is fucking pity.

Finally, I meet her gaze and see tears in her blue eyes. I loved looking into her eyes when we were together. They're what Eleanor says is cornflower blue. I'm not sure I've ever seen that particular shade of blue she's talking about, but Kate's blue eyes are soft, like they never held any hint of judgment in them.

Never once until that night I had to tell her I fucked up.

She shouldn't be here. She had every right to leave

me after that. I cheated on her, like some asshole who didn't know how good he had it. She should hate me.

"You shouldn't have come here," I say through gritted teeth as my anger threatens to explode out of me like it hasn't since that day Matthias, Marius, and Kellen insisted I needed to come live here instead of at my apartment.

If I'd finished myself off like I wanted to, I'd be free of them and Kate.

She takes a step toward the bed and stops. I can smell her perfume. It's the same stuff she used to wear when we dated. I can't remember the name of it, but I'd recognize that scent anywhere. Light and flowery, it reminds me of spring and the two of us happy together.

"I know we haven't spoken in a while, but I'm always going to be here for you, Ronan. You were a huge part of my life for a long time. As soon as my sister told me what happened, I had to come over to see you."

So, she wants to talk? Fine. We'll talk. Just a nice chat between two people who once cared about one another.

"Why? What good do you think it does coming to see me? Did you want to see if what you heard was real? Well, then fine. Take a look."

I lift up my right arm and show her how my hand and half my forearm are gone now. I see the horror fill her eyes, just like it always does with everyone when they see me now.

"Nice, huh? I go from having it all to having no point in fucking living all in one night. Take a good look at it, Kate. This is what you came over to see, isn't it?"

My words are intentionally sharp and hurtful, but I regret not a single syllable. If she doesn't like hearing what I have to say, she can leave. Nobody asked her to come here today.

"Don't say that. You have a million reasons to live. And I don't care about looking at what you lost. That's not why I came here."

She forgets I know her almost as well as I know myself. I know exactly what brought her here.

Pity.

Kate can't help herself. I've seen her rescue kittens from rainstorms and little kids who got lost in the park. Every time she tried to save someone, she wore the same expression she does now, and it's nothing but pure fucking pity.

I look past her and shake my head. "I don't need you here. I don't need anyone. Just leave me alone. Why does everyone think I want to see people? What fucking good does that do? Do you have a spare arm and hand? Because if you don't, then go the fuck home and live your life, Kate."

She sniffles and then clears her throat. Jesus, if she starts crying, I'm going to fucking lose it.

Thankfully, I don't hear any sobbing, but when I look at her again, I see tears in her eyes. Great. Sorry, sweetheart. I'm not the guy who can help you see the good in life or tell you everything's going to be okay anymore because it's not.

"I didn't mean to upset you, Ronan. I just wanted

to come by and tell you I'm around if you want to talk or anything."

"Well, I don't."

Still, that doesn't make her leave. Kate always was too kind.

She reaches out to touch my left hand, but I snatch it back before she can reach me. "Don't touch me! Just fucking go! Leave me alone and don't come back here!"

That finally does the trick, and she runs from the room crying. Good. Now she'll see there's no point in coming here with her pity and her hope that she can cheer me up.

Alone again, I close my eyes and push away the first hints of regret that begin to crop up inside my brain. I have nothing to regret, so fuck that. Nobody understands. They would if they lost the only part of them that ever meant anything. If that happened, they'd want to die just like I do.

Why did Marius have to find me at my apartment that day? I would have been out of my misery and all the pain. Why couldn't he let me have that? Why did he have to be so goddamned selfish and save me when all I wanted was to die?

I don't want to think of anything, but my brain has a different idea and the memory of that holiday party when Kate's parents finally met my father and brothers floods my mind. Why does that keep coming back to haunt me? What good does it do to remember how happy I was with her then?

*Kate squeezes my hand, and I look around the party to see no one seems to be paying attention to us. Good. Now's our* chance to sneak away and have our own private party upstairs.

Leaning down, I whisper in her ear, "I think we can make our getaway. Let's go up to my room. We can get some privacy there. All this smiling for our parents is making my cheeks hurt."

She smiles up at me and nods, so I slowly begin backing up toward the door at the far end of the living room. My father is regaling a group of people, including her mother and father, with some story of when the five of us kids were young. He's probably telling the one about how Theo convinced Kellen and me to stand still while he covered us in snow to be his own personal snowmen. He always loves telling people that one.

"What if someone see us?" Kate whispers as we take a few more steps closer to the door.

With a laugh, I answer, "I'll tell them I'm showing you where the bathroom is."

Kate rolls her eyes at what might be the lamest excuse I could think up. "Yeah, like anyone is going to believe that. You're practically dragging me away like a caveman."

I wink at her mention of that and say, "I'm not pulling you out of the room by your hair. I'm just being a gentleman showing you where the ladies' room is. Now let's go before one of my brothers screws this up for us."

Kellen eyes me making my way out of the room and gives me a knowing look. Now I just hope he doesn't ruin everything by announcing to my father that we're leaving.

We take a few final steps out into the hallway, and we're finally home free. I tilt my head toward the stairs and pull Kate along. She catches up easily, and then the two of us run upstairs to the second floor, hand-in-hand giggling the whole way.

When we finally reach my room, I hurry her inside and lock the door. "I thought maybe Kellen would rat us out, but he doesn't seem to be into busting balls tonight. I'm surprised since he and Marius have been all about the women hating lately."

Kate smiles as she looks up at the framed picture of me when I was in Little League hanging on the wall opposite my bed. "You were so cute! I can't get over how adorable you were back then."

I come up behind her, wrapping my arms around her waist and leaning down so my chin rests on her left shoulder. She smells so incredible tonight, even though I know she's wearing that same perfume she always wears.

"Even more adorable than now?" I whisper in her ear.

She turns in my hold and looks up at me. "Ten-year-old boys are adorable. Now you're sexy and hot. But you know that, so why are you fishing for compliments?"

I shrug, not realizing that was what it seemed like I was doing. "I wasn't. I guess I just like hearing that you think I'm hot."

As she runs her hands over my stomach, she smiles, and I swear she's never been more beautiful than she is right now. "I tell you all the time. You're going to get a big head if I tell you any more often."

I look down at where her hands are brushing up against the top of my pants and grin. "You keep doing what you're doing, and I'm going to definitely get a big head."

She blushes, like she always does when I say things like that. "What if someone in your family or my parents hear you?"

Leaning down, I pepper her neck with soft kisses as I whisper, "They're all downstairs being bored to tears by my father's stories about my brothers and me, or even worse, his stories about work. Nobody is going to hear us up here."

Her hands slide over my shoulders and down over my back until they come to rest on my sides. "We can't do anything here, Ronan. I'd be too afraid one of your brothers will interrupt us. You know how they are."

I lift my head and sigh. She's not wrong. I swear to God every time I have Kate here at the house, one of my brothers or a combination of them comes banging on the door. One time, Kellen and Theo even burst in without even knocking. They have no appreciation for what it's like to want to be alone with the girl you love.

"Yeah, but we can at least spend some time together alone. I've wanted to kiss you all night."

I don't give her a chance to say anything to that before I press my lips to hers in a kiss that I hope will let her know how much I love her. She kisses me back, but I sense the hesitation in her because of her fear of what my brothers might do.

"You know what? I wish we were at your house instead of here."

Her blue eyes get big, and she shakes her head like she can't believe I said that. "My house is nothing compared to this one. Why would you want to be there?"

Sliding my hands along her sides, I let them come to rest on her hips. "Because we can be alone. This house has too many people in it."

"Well, the only person I care about is you, Ronan King. Anyway, we're going to hang out at Courtney's house for New Year's night, and none of her family is going to be at her house."

The thought of the two of us having to go to Courtney's house to have sex isn't exactly my idea of a perfect time, but *beggars can't be choosers. Her parents aren't going out for New Year's, and there will no doubt be too many Kings in this house for us to have any privacy.*

*So Courtney's it is.*

"Or we could get a hotel room, just the two of us, and celebrate the new year together that way," she suggests in that coy way I always adore.

That perks me up, and I immediately begin planning our time together three days from now. "I like that idea. What do you say to that hotel in Scarsdale where everyone ended up at after prom?"

"I don't care where we go. As long as you're there, that's all I need."

Kate makes me happier than I ever thought I could be. Maybe I should surprise her with a room in the city. That might be difficult since there's probably not a room to be had at any hotel now for New Year's Eve, but I think I'm going to try anyway.

*She deserves at least that.*

"I love you, Kate."

With a big smile, she stands on her tiptoes and kisses me before whispering against my lips, "I love you too, Ronan."

I lift her up and walk toward the wall where there aren't any pictures. Gently, I press her against it as I kiss her, my cock aching to be inside her. Everyone is downstairs focused on having a good time, so why shouldn't we have our own up here?

"Ronan, what if anyone…"

She doesn't get to finish her question before I move her panties aside and slide a finger inside her pussy. Wet and ready for me, she moans against my lips as I attempt to unzip my pants while trying to hold her up with my other hand.

*Excited, Kate changes her tune and moans as I get my hard cock out. "Hurry before someone comes up."*

*I move my hands under her so I can hold her up while we fuck. She kisses me long and deep while she grinds against the front of my pants, ratcheting up my need for her.*

*Knowing we may not have much time, I thrust into her, and she takes all of me down to my balls. She feels so fucking good. I wish we had all night because we'd be able to take our time and do it right, but knowing my family, I'm betting at least one of my brothers will be interrupting us at any moment.*

*Kate looks over toward the door, so I gently take her chin between my fingers and direct her attention back to me. "Don't worry about anyone bothering us. We're okay."*

*She nods and kisses me. "I'm just afraid one of your brothers…"*

*With each thrust into her, I swear I'm in heaven. I squeeze her beautiful ass and dip my head so I can kiss her neck. My nose fills with the scent of her perfume that never fails to remind me of springtime when we first started going out. Soft and flowery, it's a smell I'll always connect to how much I love her.*

*Kate scratches her fingernails across the top of my back and says, "Oh, God…don't stop…Please don't stop!"*

*Her pussy tightens around my cock, and I'm sure she'll come at any moment. God, she feels so good. I'm almost there. Just a few more thrusts into her and I'll come.*

*Suddenly, my bedroom door flies open and slams off the wall behind it, startling us. Theo and Kellen come walking in like they have any fucking business being in my room.*

*I quickly set Kate on her feet even as she's in mid-orgasm and push her behind me. My brothers stand in front of us staring, and a quick glance at what their gazes are focused on reminds me my dick is out.*

*"What? Why the hell are you two in my room?" I bark as I stuff my cock back in my pants and pull up my zipper.*

*"Did we interrupt anything?" Theo asks before trying to look around me. "Kate, you might want to fix your dress."*

*"Getting busy? You two are bad," Kellen says with a laugh.*

*"Get out!" I snap before marching toward them.*

*They run out, laughing like the jackasses they are. I slam the door closed and turn around to see Kate hurrying into the bathroom. I follow her in there to make sure I look okay and not like I was just having sex, and I find her standing in front of the mirror.*

*"I'm sorry," I say as I walk behind her and wrap my arms around her waist. "My brothers are assholes."*

*Worry fills her eyes as she stares at me in the mirror. "You don't think they saw anything, do you?"*

*Even as I shake my head and reassure her they saw nothing, I honestly have no idea. I don't care either. Kate does, though, so I know I have to make her think they couldn't have seen a thing.*

*"Forget them. I'm sorry they came in."*

*Kate turns around and tucks my shirt into my pants before kissing me sweetly. "Maybe we should just go downstairs and rejoin the party. We have New Year's Eve in only a few days, so we can wait, right?"*

*I don't have any choice but to agree with her. "Yeah, New Year's."*

*Leave it to my brothers to ruin our good time.*

Shaking my head, I get rid of that memory as I remind myself of the night I had to tell her I slept with that girl. I'd never made Kate cry before then, and she had no idea how bad I felt watching her react to that terrible news. Not that I didn't deserve to feel like shit. I knew what I did fucked everything up.

I push my feelings down and replace them with the anger that's never far away. It's good I made her cry then and gave her a reason to break up with me. That way she can understand there's no place in my world for her.

A broken person like me has no business being with the likes of Kate.

# CHAPTER FIVE

Kate

AVA CATCHES ME AT THE BOTTOM OF THE STAIRS AND grabs my arm. "Hey, what's wrong? Don't run. You'll get hurt. You can't see straight because you're crying."

I stop, nodding since she's right. I'm lucky I didn't break my neck running down the stairs. "I know. I'm sorry. I don't mean to be a blubbering mess. I just thought he'd be—"

I'm not sure how to finish my sentence, so I left it drift off to nothingness. I don't know what I expected to find when I saw Ronan today. The boy I loved all that time ago? The man he grew into? I don't know. I guess I just thought maybe he'd be happy to see me.

Matthias walks down the hallway toward us, his face pure worry. God, now he's going to see I'm crying too.

"Everything okay?" he asks his wife before looking at me. "Oh, hi, Kate. Did you come to see Ronan?"

His voice sounds so hopeful, but his optimism disappears when he sees how upset I am. "Oh. Yeah, I guess you saw him."

Ava takes me by the hand and begins to lead me to the kitchen. "It's okay, honey. Kate and I are going to have something to drink and maybe one of those little cakes Eleanor made this morning. We didn't mean to interrupt your work."

Before he can say another word, she picks up the pace so we're out of earshot in seconds. Turning to look at me, she sighs. "Men don't really understand the crying thing. Better for us to hang out with Eleanor. She gets it."

We walk into the kitchen, and I see it's the same warm place it was when Ronan and I dated. Ava points at the table and says, "Take a seat. I just put the boys down for their naps, and if they wake up, Sabrina, the girl we hired to help out around here, will check on them. So I have time to chat. Do you like tea or coffee, or would you prefer something cold, like a water or soda? We've got it all."

"Um, a water or soda would be great. Thanks."

Eleanor notices me and smiles like I'm an old friend. "Kate! It's so good to see you again. How have you been?"

"I've been good," I answer half-heartedly, sounding nothing close to good.

"She was up with Ronan," Ava says, and that's all the explanation the housekeeper needs.

"Oh," Eleanor says before letting out a heavy sigh.

"Yeah, so I thought she might like something to eat. Maybe one of those little coffee cakes you made this morning. I know I can go for one."

The older woman's face lights up, and she hurries over to the island where a platter of her cakes sits next to a basket of lemons. "You handle the drinks, and I'll get the cakes."

They're both so welcoming and sweet, but all I want to do is break down and cry after seeing Ronan. He's so bitter and angry. I can understand why, but I didn't expect him to lash out at me like that. It's like he has no memory of ever loving me at all.

And he doesn't even look like himself. In all the time I was with him, he never let his beard get so unkempt. He looked like he doesn't even want to take care of himself. That was never the Ronan I knew.

Ava sets a glass of soda down in front of me, and Eleanor follows with a plate with two mini coffee cakes that smell like pure heaven. She always made the most incredible desserts.

"These look great. My mouth is watering from the smell of butter and cinnamon. Thank you."

The two of them smile and proceed to sit down at the table with me. Ava takes a seat across from me, and Eleanor sits down beside me.

As we begin to eat the treats, I can feel myself grow happier with each nibble. Ava reaches out and pats my hand.

"I'm sorry it was so jarring to see him like that. I didn't want to give you any advance warning just in case he acted like his old self with you. I guess I was hopeful because it was you."

Nodding, I let out a sigh. "I knew what happened to him, but that's not Ronan up there. Not the person I knew and loved. This Ronan is so angry. I've never seen him like that."

"The doctor says he's still mourning the loss of his hand," Ava explains. "Like with any other kind of loss, there are phases. I have to admit, though, that I'm getting a little worried he's stuck in the anger stage. We've all tried anything we can think of, but he's getting worse, not better."

God, I hate hearing that. Ronan has had to deal with so much loss in his life already and now this.

"I still see that wonderful boy I knew in him," Eleanor says, almost as if she's trying to convince herself along with the two of us that Ronan is still Ronan. "It's just hidden under all those layers of unhappiness."

She looks genuinely sad, but that's not a surprise. Eleanor has been practically a mother to all the King boys after they lost their own mother so young. Ronan was only ten when she died, so he's lived longer without her than with her. Eleanor has been the only maternal figure in his life since then.

I don't know what to say because everything I'm thinking threatens to make me burst into tears. Seeing him like he is broke my heart, and I don't know what to do now.

After we sit in silence for a few minutes as we finish our coffee cakes, Ava sets her jaw and takes a deep breath in, letting it out in a rush. "Well, we can't give up on him. It's hard, but the Ronan we all know and love is still in there."

While she seems optimistic, I don't know if seeing me is going to help or hurt him. She senses my apprehension when I don't say anything and pats my hand sympathetically.

"Please don't think you did anything wrong up there. You wanted to see someone you cared about for a long time. That's a genuinely good thing."

I hang my head, too sad to look at her. "I never stopped loving Ronan. We broke up, but that didn't change how I feel."

"That's good!" Eleanor says excitedly.

Turning to look at her, I see her smiling. "It didn't seem very good a few minutes ago. Maybe it's my fault. The last time I spoke to him after we broke up, I told him I didn't think I'd ever forgive him for what he did. Is it possible he's angry about that instead of my coming to see him?"

"No matter what happened between you two, I know he loved you," she says so sweetly that I nearly burst into tears. "People in love say things sometimes that they regret."

Unsure whether she's referring to me or Ronan, I explain, "I said I didn't know if I could forgive him because of something he did. Now I wish I had never said that."

"Oh, trust me. He wasn't like that because you told him how you were feeling a couple years ago. That up there is because he's angry at the world, angry at what happened, but most of all, angry the accident stole his dreams from him. The job for all of us who care for him is to help him see there's so much of life still open to him. He just has to look for it."

"Do you think it would be good if I stay away for a while? I feel like I upset him so much I might have hurt any chances he'll want to see me again anytime soon."

Ava and Eleanor exchange glances before Ava says, "I'll tell you what. Please keep coming to visit. Hopefully, he'll see you here, and you two can talk again."

"And I'll make sure to have goodies whenever you come by," the housekeeper says, gently patting my arm.

"Thank you. I just want him to get better. Even if we're never really friends or anything else to one another, I just want Ronan to be happy. I always have."

Ava nods. "I know. It's hard now, but I have to believe things are going to get better. I'll keep trying. Matthias isn't going to give up either, and I know Eleanor and his other brothers won't give up. Ronan loved you, Kate. I'd be so happy if you'd come over whenever you want and see us, and if he's willing to see you, that's good for both of you. Just give him time."

"Is he like that when his other friends come to see him?"

I watch as Ava and Eleanor look at each other with sadness. Ava sighs and says, "Nobody's come to see Ronan in a long time. I think some people visited him in the hospital, but after that, they sort of disappeared. When he first got here, one or two guys came by, but he sent them away. Since then, there's been nobody."

Eleanor shakes her head, and I swear she's trying

to fight back tears. "It's not right. When people are down, that's when they need others the most."

How could this be? "Ronan had lots of friends in high school and college. How is it possible nobody cares about what's happened to him?"

Ava shrugs. "People have their own lives, and when someone tells you to never come back, people tend to listen. He's got us, his family, and hopefully, Kate, you'll come by again."

My emotions can't stop twisting into tight knots in my stomach after all I've heard and seen today. I know Ava's right that he needs time, but what if my being around makes things worse?

Do I remind him of a time he wants to forget?

"I better go," I say as I stand to leave. Grabbing my bag, I thank Ava and Eleanor for the wonderful coffee cakes. "I'll be happy to come over whenever you think is good."

"That'll work. Let's exchange numbers so you know who I am when I text you."

After we both put one another's phone numbers into our cell phones, I thank them both again and leave by the kitchen door like I did so many times when I'd be here with Ronan. I loved coming here when we were together. Unlike my house, which always seemed so quiet and reserved, the King house with its five boys, Mr. King, Eleanor, and the staff never had a calm moment. There was always someone coming or going, and when the brothers would all be home at the same time, it was near bedlam.

And I never felt more at home anywhere but here.

As I walk to my car, I turn and look up toward his

bedroom windows. The boy I loved sits up there lost in his misery, and I wish more than anything I could do something to help.

When he doesn't appear in the windows looking out at me after a minute or so, I continue walking to my car while I think back on all the wonderful times Ronan and I had. Until that night he told me he cheated on me, we were happy. I know that. He was my first love, and I was his. We were going to be together forever.

Maybe that was our immaturity talking, but I believed him when he said he'd love me for the rest of time. I'd never met anyone like Ronan, and when we got together, he turned my world upside down. He made me feel special, and I couldn't imagine life without him.

I settle into the driver's seat and glance up once more at his windows. If only he and I were together, maybe he wouldn't have been on that road on New Year's Eve. Maybe he would have been with me because I wouldn't have gone to Europe right after Christmas.

So many if onlys and maybes.

# CHAPTER SIX

onan

I WATCH KATE WALK TO HER CAR, MAKING SURE TO hide behind the curtains when she looks up. She looks exactly the same as I remember her. Beautiful and sweet, just like she was when she was mine.

Life after me has been good to her. I wish I could be happy about that, but all I feel is jealousy. I want to be happy like her. Like anyone. I just can't.

She drives away, leaving me standing in front of my bedroom windows staring out at a sunny day that will be another one I spend in this room. As much as I know Matthias and Ava think they're helping, I hate this place now. It only serves to remind me of what I used to be, and that's the last goddamned thing I need to focus on.

On my way back to bed, I catch a glimpse of that

picture of me playing shortstop in that game in college where I hit a homerun. Never as great a hitter as I was a fielder, watching that ball sail over the back fence was the greatest feeling in the world.

What I'd give now to feel even half that good.

That picture only reminds me of what I'll never have, and I hate that. I shouldn't have to see what could have fucking been every time I open my eyes.

Full of rage, I clumsily grab the picture frame and tear it off the wall, my left hand barely able to hold onto it as I decide where to hide it so I never have to see it again. It falls from my grasp since my left hand isn't nearly as strong as it needs to be, and I watch as the glass covering the picture shatters at my feet.

"Hey, you okay?" a voice asks behind me, and I look back to see a strange woman with blond hair up in a ponytail and what looks like some white stain on her black t-shirt that travels all the way down to her jeans.

"Go away."

She grimaces at me and rolls her eyes. "Okay. I'll take that as a yes."

When she does as I order her to, I'm relieved. I don't need some stranger chatting me up. I barely tolerate my own family talking to me.

I stare down at the broken glass and the disheveled picture and wood frame sitting in pieces and shake my head. Whatever made me think I was going to be a major league player?

"So, Ava asked me if I'd give her a hand cleaning this up since she's feeding the boys," the woman announces when she walks into my room uninvited with a broom and dustpan in her hands.

"What about go away can't you comprehend?" I snap.

She looks me up and down and shrugs. "Nothing. Doesn't change the fact that I need to clean this mess up. Be careful. I see you aren't wearing shoes."

I look down my body and see a hint of blood just below where my gray sweatpants end. Wonderful. I've already cut my right foot on the glass.

Hobbling into my bathroom, I sit down on the side of the tub and then realize I didn't grab a Band-Aid first. Could this fucking day get any worse? Frustrated, I stand up and hobble on one foot over to the linen closet where they're kept.

Once more, I sit down on the edge of the bathtub and try to open the bandage wrapper, but since I only have one goddamned hand, it doesn't happen. This is why I don't get out of bed. How the fuck am I supposed to get the Band-Aid on if I can't even open the paper over it?

"Here, let me help," the strange woman says as she walks toward me.

Who the fuck is this person, and why does she think it's okay to intrude on me when I'm in the fucking bathroom? My fucking bathroom.

"You don't take a hint very well, do you?" I say as she snatches the Band-Aid out of my grasp.

She easily tears off the paper and the plastic on the back of the bandage. "There you go. One Band-Aid all ready to go."

I try my best to put it over the cut on the top of my foot, but I can't because my left hand seems to have a mind of its own. Utterly disgusted, I toss the useless

Band-Aid onto the floor and stand up to get another one.

"Okay, see, there's the problem. You can't expect it to work on the floor. Let me get you another one, and this time I'll help. Hang on. In fact, sit back down, okay?" the woman says like I'm aggravating her.

I'm not the one who's intruding on another person's privacy.

A couple seconds later, she turns back toward me with the bandage hanging off her hand. I watch as she grabs a white washcloth and wets it under the warm water.

"First off, you should clean the cut, so that's what I'm going to do. Then I'll dry it off and put the Band-Aid on, and you'll be as good as new."

As she does exactly as she said, I grumble, "I could have done all that myself. I'm not an idiot."

She doesn't respond to that, and when she gets the bandage onto my skin and actually covering the cut, she stands up and smiles at me. "All good! Need anything else?"

"I didn't need that," I say as I stand up from the side of the tub.

"You're welcome."

Glaring at her, I answer, "I didn't say thank you."

That stops her, and finally, her helpful façade disappears. "What is your problem anyway? I saw you needed help, so I helped. What's wrong with that?"

I push past her to walk out into the bedroom and step on another sliver of glass, this time cutting the side of my foot. As much as I don't want her to see me react, I let out a tiny cry, mostly of disgust that I have to do that whole fucking Band-Aid routine again.

Spinning around, I walk back into the bathroom and grab the box of Band-Aids. She stands in front of me, blocking my way.

"Everyone else here is nice. What's wrong with you to make you so curmudgeonly?"

Jesus, is she here to make my day even worse?

"I'm a little young to be curmudgeonly," I answer. "Now can you move so I can sit down and put another goddamned Band-Aid on?"

"I'll make you a deal. If you promise to be nice, I'll help you this time too. If not, then you're just going to have to bleed out here because I'm not budging."

Her words make me wish I'd never gotten out of bed today. "Who are you?"

That makes her smile, and as I'm noticing how much her brown eyes light up when she's happy, she takes the box of Band-Aids out of my hand. "Sabrina. Nice to meet you. And you are?"

I don't know why I don't push her out of my bathroom and slam the door shut, but I answer her question, if only to get things moving so she'll leave me the hell alone. "Ronan."

"Nice to meet you, Ronan. Now sit down on the tub, and we'll clean this one up too. By the way, walking around in bare feet when there's glass around isn't a smart idea. You might get really hurt."

As I sit down again, I mumble, "I've already been really hurt."

She crouches down in front of me and shakes her

head. "This isn't that bad. I'll have this cleaned up and bandaged in no time."

I hold my right arm up for her to see. "That's not what I meant."

While she repeats on the side of my foot what she just finished on the top a couple minutes ago, she hums. "I'm guessing you weren't born like that by the way you said you were already hurt."

Shaking my head, I stare at where my hand should be. "No."

When she finishes with the second cut on my foot, she stands up with the wrapper and the washcloth stained with my blood. Looking at me, she says, "Good thing you have another one."

"Another one?" I ask, confused as to what she means.

She points at my left hand. "Another hand. You had two, and now you have one."

"That's not how it works."

"I think it is."

I can't decide if this person is merely frustrating my efforts to be miserable or seriously is trying to be an asshole about my lost hand. Who the hell says that kind of thing to someone who's lost a fucking part of their body?

Once more, I push past her and walk back out into my room, but this time I make sure to stay far away from the broken glass from the picture frame. "Exactly what is your reason for being in my house? It's quite clear you're not a nurse. You have no bedside manner at all."

Behind me, she laughs, and I turn around to see her

sweeping up the last of the glass into the dustpan. "What was funny about that? If you are a nurse, you suck at it."

Finished with cleaning up, she stands to her full height, which can't be more than five and a half feet tall. Jutting her hip out, she's full of attitude when she snaps back at me, "I never said I was a nurse. I'm here to help Ava with those beautiful little babies. I was just trying to be nice to someone who looked like they needed it. I get you're all about being miserable, or better yet, curmudgeonly, but maybe you could be thankful for the help."

Maybe she can go fuck herself with that thankful bullshit. I didn't ask for her help. I could have gotten that Band-Aid on quite nicely myself. And if she hadn't been in the way, I never would have cut my foot a second time.

I consider telling her all of that as I sit back down on my bed, but I don't bother.

"Nice meeting you, Ronan. Let's hope our next time chatting is nicer," she says as she walks out of my room.

"I've got a better idea. How about we never talk again? That means stay away from me. Got it?"

She doesn't answer me. That's okay. I don't need to talk to her anymore anyway.

At dinnertime, Eleanor brings me a tray with food and a glass of Coke like every night. I pretend to be asleep so I don't have to talk to her, but when I hear the door close, I quickly sit up and inspect what she brought me to eat.

A pork chop, her homemade stuffing, and green beans with a side of applesauce.

Memories of her making this for all of us when I was a little boy flood my mind, particularly the one time that sticks out among all the others. It was right around when we all found out my mother was sick. The entire house felt like a funeral home, but my mother didn't want us to be mourning her while she was still alive, so she pulled herself out of bed and made her way down to the kitchen to help Eleanor make dinner.

That night, we ate my father's favorite meal, pork chops with applesauce and gravy. I never liked gravy, but the pork tasted so good when I dunked it into the applesauce. The seven of us sat around the kitchen table and talked about our day at school and what homework we had like any other family.

Except we weren't any other family. We were a family slowly losing our mother and wife.

We never had another family dinner like that again. My mother died a month later, and after she was gone, my father could barely bring himself to eat, much less sit around the table like everything was normal.

Because it wasn't. Not for him, and not for us.

Dinner turns out to be delicious, and I enjoy it more than I expected after the shitty day I had. I know Ava needs help since she and Matthias have two children who are so young, but does that mean I have to deal with this Sabrina person sticking her nose into my business?

I need to have a talk with her or my brother and make it clear if they're going to insist I stay here with them, then they need to keep their little babysitter out of my way. Since there's no time like the present, I slip on my slides and head downstairs where I hear voices that sound like they're all in the kitchen eating dinner.

When I turn the corner into the kitchen, I find Ava and Matthias sitting alone with little Theo in his high chair. Everyone looks surprised to see me, but they hurriedly attempt to make me feel welcome.

"Ronan, I didn't realize you were going to come out of your room today," Ava says in that chipper voice I know she's forcing because she wants me to be happy. "I wouldn't have had Eleanor bring you up a plate if I knew. Come! Sit down with us. Matty is upstairs since he ate already, but Theo is here with us."

My brother simply looks at me like he always has. I'm just his youngest brother interrupting his dinner with his wife and son. I don't think he resents me for that. He just isn't as cheery as Ava.

I sit down next to him and say, "We need to talk about whoever that Sabrina person is."

Matthias looks confused, but Ava quickly says, "Oh, she's been a godsend already, and it's only been one day. She's living here, so I'm sure you'll get to see her."

Turning to look at Ava, I don't try to hide my disgust when I say, "I already met her. She walked into my room uninvited and proceeded to get in the way."

"Oh, I'm sorry, Ronan. She probably didn't know you were there. I'll talk to her."

"She knew just fine I was there. She said you

wanted her to clean up the mess I made when I dropped a picture and the glass broke all over the floor."

For a second, Ava doesn't seem to know what I'm talking about, but then I see recognition in her eyes. "Oh, that's right. Yeah, I asked her to help because Eleanor and I were busy down here. She didn't mean any harm. I'm sorry if you didn't like her helping."

Great. Now I sound like an asshole because I'm complaining about someone helping Ava.

"It's not that I don't like her helping you. I didn't like her barging into my room."

Before I can continue, the baby screams and throws some kind of cookie that looks like he's been gumming it to death for hours. The soggy brown thing lands on the table between my brother and me, and immediately, his attention is on that and not on the issue I want to discuss.

Matthias laughs and picks it up with a napkin. "Sorry, Ronan. What were you saying? Theo distracted me. Something about your room?"

"Yeah. Keep your babysitter out of my room," I say as I stand up to leave.

Both Matthias and Ava stare up at me with that same look in their eyes I've seen nearly every moment I've been back here. It's a mixture of pity and concern with a tiny hint of frustration rolled in.

"I'm sure she didn't mean any harm, Ronan, but Ava and I will explain to her that you don't want to be bothered. I'm sure she'll understand."

Now the frustration comes through loud and clear in his voice, even as he works to keep his expression looking like he's happy. Terrific. Like I'm the bad guy because I don't want strangers waltzing into my damn room whenever they please.

"And if you're thinking of having anyone else over to bother me, Kate, for example, forget it. I don't need anyone coming to see me thinking they're going to cheer me up. Okay?"

I see in Ava's expression she's dying to tell me that Kate meant no harm and she only wanted to make sure I was okay, but she doesn't say a word about that. Only Matthias speaks, and I get the sense he just wants me to go away at this moment so he can go back to enjoying his dinner with Ava and the baby.

"Got it. No more visits from anyone. I hope you'll understand if we have guests here to visit us, but I'll make sure nobody bothers you again."

He says that, but I'll bet money before the week is out, he or one of my other brothers will be marching into my room doing their best cheering up routine like they have since I came to stay here. I'd tell him to make sure he doesn't let Kellen or Marius bother me either, but I know that won't happen.

Even though I've told them dozens of times I don't want visitors or anyone coming to see me, they insist on popping in. They think they're helping. They're not. All their visits do is remind me that I used to be like them and now I'm not.

I used to be normal. Now I'm just broken.

# CHAPTER SEVEN

ate

JESSIE WAVES HER HAND IN THE AIR TO GET MY attention, so I walk down the sidewalk to where she's sitting outside on this beautiful June day. After spending nearly six months together touring Europe, I was worried we might never want to speak to one another again, but thankfully, our trip only made our friendship stronger.

"I ordered you a diet Coke. Why do you look like you just lost your favorite purse? What's wrong?" she asks as she removes her bag from my chair so I can sit.

"Nothing. Well, nothing I want to talk about. What's new?" I ask and then burst into laughter. "That was stupid. I just spent half a year with you, and I've only been away from you for like twenty-four hours."

She smiles, making her slightly round face grow

wider. "Just something we always say. But seriously, what's wrong? Did your parents not like the gift you bought them from our trip?"

I wave away that idea and pick up the menu from my plate. "No, they loved the dish from Spain, just like I knew they would. It's something else. Ronan."

Jessie's eyes get wide. "The Ronan, as in your first love and the only guy you've ever wanted to be with in your entire life? That Ronan?"

Clearly, I've talked about him more than I thought.

"Yeah, I guess. Ronan King. My first boyfriend. He was in an accident while we were gone. On New Year's Eve, in fact. Some drunk driver hit him and messed him up pretty badly."

"Head injury? Jeez, that's rough. I had a cousin who was in a bad car accident, and when he came out of the coma, he was never the same again."

I think about what she's saying and shake my head. "I don't think he was in a coma. Actually, I don't know. By the way he was acting today when I saw him, maybe. He didn't even seem like the same person I knew and loved once upon a time."

That makes her smile. "I love how you get so romantic whenever you talk about him. Once upon a time. It sounds like a fairy tale."

I scan the menu to find something I might like before the server comes over. "It was like a fairy tale being with Ronan. He was sweet and sexy, and I thought we'd be together forever."

Jessie's heard the story of how things ended with Ronan, so she finishes my thought for me. "And then he cheated on you, broke your heart, and you've never found another guy you love like him again. I know."

"Well, it's worse now. He lost his right hand in that car accident, and now he's so unhappy. It was like I didn't even recognize him today. He didn't want to see me and told me to go away. The Ronan I knew would have never said that to me."

My friend, never someone to waste a tear on any man, pushes her fingertips against my arm. "Hey, you're really bothered by this. I thought this guy was ancient history."

I shrug and nod, but I'm not sure that's how I'd classify Ronan. "He is. Or not. I don't know. Ronan is Ronan. He was my first everything. First boyfriend. First love. First guy I ever slept with. I grew up when I was with him."

"Thank God you didn't say your first kiss or I would have had to take you to have your head examined since you told me one time you two didn't start dating until you were like seventeen. A girl has to have her first kiss before then."

Obviously, Jessie isn't a romantic.

After taking a sip of water, I explain who my first kiss was from. "No, it wasn't Ronan. It was Danny Canton. He gave me my first kiss. I was fifteen, which I'm sure you're going to say was way too late in life to be getting a first anything. Whatever. He was my first kiss, and unfortunately, he wasn't very good."

"Too dry or too wet? Or no, the worst is too much tongue and they try to force it down your throat like they're one of those jackbooted thugs who would force feed the suffragettes. Bastards!"

Knowing I need to stop her before she goes off on a tangent about what seems to be her new, favorite topic, I quickly shake my head. "No, no. It wasn't like that. It wasn't too dry or too wet, and I don't think Danny even tried to stick his tongue in my mouth. It wasn't much of anything. Just sort of meh. I think he may have had bad breath."

Jessie levels her gaze on me like she hates this story more than she hates liver. "Please tell me your second kiss was better than that. Jesus, that's an awful story."

Although the memory of my first kiss has always stayed with me, the same can't be said for my second kiss or any of the others before I met Ronan. "I don't remember. All I remember about kissing boys in high school was poor Danny that night after the homecoming football game behind the food stand since he'd worked it that night and then Ronan. Everyone in between is just a blur."

"A horrible blur, I'm sure. See, that's the problem with those private school guys. They act like they're all sexy and badass, but they aren't. All they have is money going for them."

The server comes over to our table and sets down our drinks before taking our order. At least that gives me a reprieve from my friend's attacks on my nonexistent love life for the majority of high school. I don't remember her ever telling me about her first kiss, but I'm guessing it's a much better story than mine.

Considering how comfortable she is with men, I'm willing to bet all of her kissing stories are better than mine. Well, none of them involve Ronan. He wasn't like the other guys in high school.

"So, where are we going after dinner tonight?" she asks. "I was thinking that place that just opened up near my apartment."

I nod, lost in thought about how terrible Ronan looked today. If only there was something I could do, but he doesn't even want to see me.

"Hello? Earth to Kate. Come in, Kate."

Jessie's in rare form today. I force a smile and turn to see her expression one of complete judgment. "What? I'm sorry. I was lost in thought there. What did you say?"

She folds her arms across her chest and lets out a sigh that sounds like a huff or a harrumph. "Okay, what is this about? Are we still on Mr. Dreamy from high school?"

"We dated after high school, you know," I say, but my attempt to correct her falls flat.

"Fine, you dated after high school. How is it you haven't talked about this guy but a handful of times in the past six months when I was with you twenty-four seven, and now you can't even have a normal conversation without getting lost in thought about Ronan?"

She's right. I hadn't thought about Ronan King in forever, it seems. I think I only mentioned him once or twice when we were in Italy, and we just spent six months together, day in and day out.

"I don't know," I answer, staring off in the distance. "He's hurting, and I don't like that."

That gets me another harrumph. "Sounds like the

problem is you do like him. So what are you going to do about it?"

Jessie is very much one of those people who always feels there's something to do about any situation. Whatever the issue is, some kind of activity or movement is always called for, according to her.

I'm just not sure that's the case in this situation.

"What is there to do about it? He wouldn't even talk to me. I ran out of the room crying."

"That cad!" she says far too loudly, making the four people at the table next to us turn and give us dirty looks.

Leaning over toward her, I grab her arm. "Shhhh! And who says cad anymore? It's the twenty-first century, Jessie."

But nothing I say stops her, and she raises her voice again to say, "First of all, cad is a great word and should have never gone out of style. Second of all, we're on a busy street in Brooklyn, for God's sake! Why do I need to keep my voice down?"

Humiliation covers me, and I turn my head so none of the other diners can see my face. "If I promise to go where you want, will you please keep quiet? They're going to throw us out of here if you don't."

She rolls her eyes but agrees to do as I ask. "Fine, but exactly where are they going to throw us out of? They already have us on the sidewalk, Kate, and paying the same price as if we were sitting inside, I might add."

I can practically feel the angry glares coming from the people around us. I love Jessie and how strong she is, but when she decides she has something to say, God help anyone who isn't interested in hearing it.

"Please. Everyone is looking at us," I say, nearly begging her to keep cool.

She waves off that silly idea and shakes her head. "Nobody cares, honey. This is New York. I could run down the street screaming at the top of my lungs, and I bet not a single person would stop me."

I cautiously turn my head to see if she's right that nobody's looking at us, and thankfully, I see everyone sitting outside of the restaurant has returned to their meals and their own conversations. I breathe a sigh of relief and slowly sit up in my chair.

"Okay, I need you to promise me that you won't get loud like that again. I'll do whatever you want. Just keep it down, okay?"

"I think you should go see him again."

Clearly, we've moved on from the public embarrassment portion of our time here and now we're talking about Ronan again. Odd since I didn't think she wanted to discuss that topic anymore.

"Jessie, he told me to go away. He wasn't trying to be subtle. He doesn't want to see me."

She twists her face into a strange expression and doesn't say anything for a long moment. Then she asks, "Do you think this is because you broke up with him? Men do have a hard time with rejection."

It doesn't take me long to decide that isn't the problem. "No. He's not like that. He understood why I broke up with him. I saw him a few times before the accident, and he was always the same sweet guy I always knew. He got that he hurt me when he slept with that girl."

"Okay, it's not a rejection thing. So what is it?"

I hold up my right hand in front of her. "He lost his hand, Jess. The guy wanted to be a baseball player. He was a great shortstop. All he ever wanted to do was play professional baseball, and he lost his hand in that accident. His dream job isn't a possibility anymore. That's why he's unhappy."

She doesn't seem impressed with my explanation. "Okay, I get that he can't do what he always wanted to do, but the guy's a billionaire, isn't he? Or am I getting him confused with someone else?"

"He is. Ronan's family is wealthy, and he is too. I don't think that matters when all you ever wanted to do was play ball, and now you can't. Money doesn't buy happiness."

That gets me a look that tells me she thinks that's ridiculous. "Only people with money think that. The rest of us know the real truth. If you've got money, you've got it all. So Mr. Moneybags isn't happy. I think the answer is you have to change that."

Already tired of this conversation, I look around for the server and pray to God he's bringing our food soon. Jessie isn't done with her comments, though, unfortunately.

"Here's the thing. You have to show Mr. Moneybags that the hand thing isn't the end of the world. Make him realize there are a million other things he can do, including you."

Since there's no sign of our server or our food, I reluctantly rejoin the conversation. "Please don't call him Mr. Moneybags. His name is Ronan, and money never meant anything to him."

"Again, because he's always had it."

She's wearing me down, but I won't give in on this one point. "Yes, he has, but Ronan isn't like other guys with money. He's down-to-earth and sweet."

Well, he used to be when I knew him. Now I don't know what to say he is, other than angry and devastated, which I completely understand.

"Fine. He's a wonderful guy, except for the fact that he told you to go away and made you cry. I still say you just have to show him that there are wonderful things to be had in life without a hand."

As much as I don't want to extend this conversation, I can't help but ask the obvious. "How am I supposed to do that when he doesn't want to see me?"

That finally makes her stop, and for a few precious moments, she isn't acting like getting Ronan to see he still has so much to be grateful for is going to be a walk in the park. It also gives me a chance to remember that Ava told me I could come over to see her anytime I wanted.

"His sister-in-law who owns the house where he's staying did say she'd be happy to have me come visit whenever I wanted to."

That one, simple statement makes Jessie excited, and she points at me wearing a huge grin. "That's it! Just make a habit of going to the house to see her, and hopefully, you'll get to spend time with him. That's all it's going to take, I bet. The guy was crazy about you, and you're still wonderful, so it won't take long before he's forgetting the go away nonsense and asking you to hang out. From there, it's easy peasy."

I've always admired how positive Jessie can be when she decides on a course of action. If only I could be that way, but all I can think of is how miserable Ronan was when I saw him.

"Thank God, here comes the food," she announces, and a second later, I see the server coming toward us with my chicken salad sandwich and her vegetarian plate.

As much as I sometimes have a hard time with how strong her opinions can be, I think Jessie's got the right idea. I'm going to make arrangements to go back to the King estate this week, and hopefully, I'll get a chance to see Ronan again.

Now I just have to figure out what to say to him if he decides to talk to me.

# CHAPTER EIGHT

onan

THIS HOUSE GETS LOUDER EVERY DAMN DAY. I swear it's noisier than when my brothers and I lived here as kids with our parents. How that's possible is beyond me since it's literally half the number of people here now, and two of them don't even know how to speak yet.

Then again, maybe Theo knows how to talk by now. I'm not sure. I haven't spent more than a few seconds around him since I came here to stay, so he could be reciting the goddamned Gettysburg Address by now and I wouldn't know.

I glance over at the window and see it's another beautiful sunny day. Not that what it looks like outside matters to me. I don't go out, so what the fuck do I care what it looks like out there?

Since I don't need to have the weather reminding me of that fact, I should ask Eleanor to put up those room darkening curtains Marius had in his room when he was going through that phase of his when he would only leave his room at night. It didn't last long. Maybe eight months right after high school. He claimed it helped him focus on his art, but I always suspected it had something to do with that girlfriend of his at the time who he spent all night talking to on the phone.

My door opens, again without anyone knocking, and I see Eleanor come in with my lunch. All smiles, like I'm sure she thinks is necessary, she sets the tray with what looks like some kind of sandwich and potato chips along with a glass of soda on my dresser and turns to face me.

"I made you a ham and cheese sandwich, just like you used to love when you were a boy."

Since I doubt she needs me to compliment her on that, I don't say a word. Eleanor's a good person, but her tendency to be so damn happy around me gets under my skin sometimes.

"Okay, well, I need to get back downstairs since Ava and Matthias decided to have lunch with the boys today out at the pool. They're getting ready right now with their sunscreen and hats to shield them from the sun. I want to make sure they have everything they need."

Again, nothing I feel the need to respond to, but as she walks toward the door, I do have one question I need answered to satisfy my curiosity. "Is Theo talking yet?"

Eleanor stops and gives me an odd look. "The

baby? Oh, not yet, but I think any day now," she answers with far more enthusiasm than I expected.

I nod, not knowing what else to say to that. So the kid isn't speaking yet. I guess that's normal since he's not even a year old?

"I'm sure you'd have a great time if you came outside and spent some time with him. He's a lovely child. In many ways, he reminds me of you, Ronan. Always smiling. I remember when you were a baby. I swear you always had a smile on your face."

She would continue gushing about little Theo and me as a baby if I encouraged her, but the last thing I want to hear about is how fucking happy I always was. Those days are gone. I have nothing to be happy about anymore.

I turn away to face the window, and Eleanor gets the hint I don't want to talk. I hear the sadness in her voice when she tells me to just let her know if I need anything before closing the door behind her and leaving me alone.

She and everyone else have no idea how much I wish I was still by myself at my apartment. They won't let me go back there, though. Not after what I tried in April.

I listen to my brother and his happy family get ready like they're going on a ten-mile hike. They're walking out to the pool in the backyard, not going up Everest. Yeah, the estate is huge, but it's not like the pool isn't less than fifty yards from the back of the house. What the hell are they doing that requires them to make so much noise?

Not interested enough to go find out, I pad across

the room to get my lunch. Maybe today I'll eat standing up instead of in bed. I'm pretty tired of spending all my time there anyway.

Is that a pun? Tired of being in bed? No, probably not.

As I take the first bite of my ham and cheese sandwich I have to admit is pretty good, I question if I'm starting to lose my mind since I've taken to asking myself if I'm thinking up puns. Eight weeks here after a couple weeks in the psych ward at the hospital, and it feels like forever. No wonder I'm starting to get a little squirrely.

I'll never forget my brothers' faces when they came to see me in the hospital. Now there was a loud place. All that screaming, and that one guy who punched the wall so many times they had to restrain him. I'd never been around people like that.

But their faces. Matthias just looked worried. Then again, he always looks that way since he took over King Industries. Marius looked lost. I'd never seen him look like that. Like he didn't know what to do or what to say. He mainly stood near the door when they all came to see me. Not that I blame him. I wouldn't have wanted to visit that place either.

Kellen was the worst. Maybe it's because he's finally happy now that he has Salem, or maybe it's because we've always been best friends since we were the two youngest in the family, but whatever the reason, damn, he looked crushed seeing me there. He kept having to turn away, and when he was able to get a few words out, it sounded like he was choking on them.

I hated seeing them like that. Worst of all, no matter what their faces were saying, I know they were scared. Even when our mother died, they didn't look like that. Not when our father died either. I guess we all knew we had one another, so we'd be okay.

And then I slit my fucking arm and they couldn't think that anymore. After losing Theo, that must have freaked them out.

If only Marius hadn't found me that day when I did it. Everyone would be better off if he didn't decide to stop by and see how I was doing. He wouldn't be fucking scarred for life. Matthias and Ava wouldn't have to keep me here so they can watch over me. And Kellen could be his happy-go-lucky self again.

"Hey, Ava sent me up to ask if you want to come outside. Any chance of that?"

Just the sound of that babysitter's voice makes me want to throw something. Does this person ever fucking knock? You'd swear she was part of my family. They rarely knock either.

I spin around to see Sabrina standing over near my bedroom door in white shorts and a pink t-shirt waiting for my answer, but she's about to get a whole lot more than that. "I see Ava either didn't mention that I didn't want to be bothered, or you ignored that. Nice."

"She did, but then she asked me to come up to invite you out to lunch. You do see the dilemma, right?"

This person irritates me to no end.

"No, but that doesn't matter. Maybe you need to hear it come from my mouth, so here goes. I don't want to see you in my room. I don't care what anyone asks you to do. Go away, and don't come back. Am I clear enough now?"

"Crystal. Jeez, you really are a miserable bastard. No wonder that girl ran out of here crying. You're a real charmer."

My mouth drops open as I stand in amazement at how fucking rude this person is. Did I ask to be bothered? No. I just want to be left alone. Why doesn't anyone understand that?

And how dare she mention Kate and what happened yesterday?

She walks out of my room before I can tell her what I think of her opinion, so I follow her out into the hallway, intending on cluing her in on how I don't give a damn what she thinks. She's halfway down the stairs by the time I get out there, but that's not going to stop me.

Not today. Today, I'm going to make sure my family and whoever this babysitter person is understand don't bother me means just that.

Do. Not. Fucking. Bother. Me.

I see her marching through the house out to the backyard, so I pick up the pace and do the same. Along the way, I see that thing little Theo rolls around in. What do they call those things? I don't know, but it's in the middle of the hallway. I scoot around it and walk outside for the first time in weeks.

Jesus, it's bright out here. I lift my left hand up to shield my eyes. Damn, it's sunny.

Matthias sees me first and nearly drops his glass of iced tea he's so surprised. "Ronan, I'm so glad to see you. Come sit with us. We're having lunch before we let the boys go swimming."

Holding my hand up, I try to stop him, but it's no use. The guy is lost in this domestic bliss of a life of his.

"Not now. Ava, didn't I tell you yesterday I didn't want to have your babysitter come into my room uninvited? She literally did exactly that, and that's the only reason I'm down here right now."

Now it's not just my brother paying attention to me but Ava, Eleanor, and Sabrina, along with the two kids. Maybe now they'll realize there's a damn good reason to never ask me to join them for these family things.

Once Ava recovers from the shock of what I said, she looks over at Sabrina who's cleaning off the new baby's face of something that looks like what you'd throw up if you ate a rancid can of peas. "Oh, I sent her up only because we were hoping you might want to hang out with all of us today. She didn't mean any harm, Ronan."

"It's as if you either didn't hear what I said just one day ago or you didn't understand it. Which is it? Because either way, that person came into my room just a minute ago."

My sister-in-law looks like she's going to cry, and when I glance over at Matthias, I can see he's not feeling a whole lot of brotherly love right now. Too bad.

"Whoa, wait a minute, Ronan. Ava didn't mean to upset you. Sabrina didn't either. They were just trying to—"

I cut him off before he goes any further. "I don't

care. You said when you brought me here that I wouldn't be bothered. I'm officially fucking bothered right now."

That's all it takes. One slip up with my language in front of the kids, and my brother is out of his chair and marching toward me like some kind of man on a mission.

"Ava, I'll be back. Don't wait for me to let the boys swim. Ronan and I need to have a conversation."

He grabs me by the arm and yanks me back toward the house before I can say another word. About my size but much stronger since he hasn't spent the last few months lying in bed, he has no problem moving me exactly where he wants me to go, and in seconds, the two of us are back inside in the living room.

I've seen Matthias angry before. Most of his life he's been angry for various reasons, much of which I never understood. I've never seen him this pissed off before, though.

In no time, he's up in my face practically breathing fire. "I've had enough of your bullshit, Ronan. I get it. Life sucks for you. I'm sorry for that. You have no idea how much I wish I could change everything that happened to you. But you will not disrespect Ava or anyone who works here, no matter how fucking miserable you are, and you will not talk that way around my sons."

As angry as he is, I stand toe to toe with him, not backing down an inch. "Then make sure she understands I don't want anyone in my room."

I'm not sure which part of that upsets him enough to shove me, but he sends me flying back into the wall.

I can't help but be shocked since I don't think my oldest brother has ever done that with me. Oh, he and Theo used to have epic fights as kids, and more than once, I've seen him spar with Marius, but that brother never seemed interested in a knock-down-drag-out fight. Kellen and I never got a dose of Matthias's full wrath because we were always so much younger than him.

Seems that's changed. Okay. He wants to fight? I'm more than ready. He has no idea how much pent-up anger I have inside me.

"Talk about my wife like that again, and I swear to God, Ronan, you're going to regret it," he barks about an inch away from my face.

I shove him away with my left hand, surprising him. "Don't fuck with me, Matthias. All I want is to be left alone. Why is that so difficult for you and everyone else here to understand?"

"We brought you here because we wanted to make sure you were safe. We're your family, and we love you. I would never forgive myself if you did anything to hurt yourself again, Ronan. Why do you have to make this so difficult?"

Something inside me snaps at his asinine question, and I throw up my right arm so he has no choice but to look at it. "Because everything for me is fucking difficult, Matthias! I couldn't even put a goddamned Band-Aid on my foot yesterday and had to let your damn babysitter do it because I couldn't get the fucking wrapper off it. I'm a grown man who has nothing to look forward to when I wake up in the morning! Everything I've ever wanted in life was lost when they cut my fucking hand off! Do you understand how that feels? I doubt it. You've never had anything this terrible happen to you, so keep your opinions on how I am to yourself!"

All the anger seems to instantly drain away from him, leaving Matthias looking nothing but sad in front of me once again. "I know this is hard, Ronan. I might not have ever experienced loss like you have, but I understand. I just wish you'd see how much we want to be here for you, if you'd only let us."

He doesn't get it. Nobody does. It doesn't matter how much I try to explain what I'm going through to them. They don't get it.

Exhausted from my little trip outside and this emotional outburst with my brother, I slump against the wall. "I don't want anyone to be here for me. I didn't want to be saved that night Marius found me. I have nothing to live for. If there's any justice in this world, some meteorite will land in my bedroom and take me out of my misery. Until then, all I want is to be left alone."

My brother takes a deep breath in and lets it out slowly before saying, "Okay, Ronan. We won't bother you again."

I see the tears in his eyes before he walks away, his shoulders sagging and the rest of his body looking like I feel. As the door to the outside closes behind him, a tiny spark of regret bites at me, but I push that away as fast as it comes.

None of this is anything I asked for, so what do I have to regret? I never wanted to barge in on his happily married life with Ava and their kids.

By the time I get back to my room, my mood is worse than ever. I don't want to make Matthias as unhappy as I am. Maybe it would be better if I left here. He and Ava will fight me on that because they're worried I'll try to off myself again, but what would be the loss?

A knock at my door makes my anger come raging back, but nobody comes in. Is this their idea of leaving me alone? Looks like I needed to be a little clearer.

"Ronan, it's Ava. I'm sorry you got so upset. I never meant to make you unhappy. All I ever want is for you to get better."

She says that like I have some disease I'll eventually recover from, or there's some medicine that's going to heal me if I only give it enough time. There's no magic pill or potion to fix what happened to me. I wish there was.

I walk over to the door and open it to see her standing in the hallway staring up at me with tears in her eyes. As much as I want to mention what she's doing isn't leaving me alone, I don't. I'm surly, but I'm not a total dick.

At least not at this moment.

"I'm sorry, Ronan. Please forgive me. I just want you to be your old happy self again," she says, sniffling through her tears.

That will never happen. That Ronan King doesn't exist anymore.

When I don't say anything to that, she steps forward and wraps her arms around me. I stare down in shock, and then she rests her head on my chest, surprising me even more. Nobody has touched me since the nurses in the psych ward.

Ava continues to sob against me, so I wrap my left arm and what's left of my right arm around her. "I didn't mean to be such an asshole outside. I'm sorry."

"I get it. You don't want to see anyone. I didn't realize we all were bothering you so much," she says against my chest.

I let out a heavy sigh as I listen to her words. She and Matthias, to say nothing of Eleanor, have been nothing but kind and caring since I came here. I wish I wasn't so unhappy because they deserve much better in return, not the misery I give them.

It's just that it's all I have to offer now.

"Look at me, Ava."

She lets go of me and wipes under her eyes. It's her house, and here she is basically apologizing to me for being nice. I really am a fucking bastard.

"It's okay. I know you don't mean any harm. It's all me, and I'm sorry."

The smile I get in return lights up her face. "You take as much time as you need. We'll be happy whenever you want to come out and hang with us, okay?"

Ava really is a good person. She doesn't deserve to have someone like me bringing such misery into her life, especially with all she's handling now with two babies.

I nod but remain silent because I don't have anything to say. I can't explain why I feel so lost. I wish I could. Then maybe everyone would finally understand why I can't see any of the positive things they all claim exist for me.

# CHAPTER NINE

ate

I DRIVE UP THE LONG ROAD TO THE KING HOUSE AND can't help but remember the first time Ronan brought me here to meet his family. I was so nervous. Probably about as scared as I am right now, even though Ava was thrilled to hear from me and loved my idea of coming over to see her. She has to know I'm really hoping to see Ronan, but she's still kind to invite me to her house.

As I shut off the engine, I see the woman Ava told me about walk out the kitchen door. What was her name? Something witchy. Blair? No, that doesn't sound right. What's another name that seems like a witch would have it? Samantha? No, that's not it either.

She stares at me as I get out of the car, and I wish I

could remember her name. Whoever she is, she's pretty. Blond hair and although I can't see what color her eyes are, I'd bet a hundred bucks they're blue. She actually looks like a stereotypical babysitter Hollywood might cast.

I walk in her direction while I rack my brain to remember her name. Nothing.

"Hi! Are you looking for Ava?" she asks in a perky voice absolutely fitting for a babysitter. "She's inside with little Theo in the kitchen."

Sensing my opportunity to have her tell me her name, I extend my hand to shake hers and say, "Hi, I'm Kate."

"I'm Sabrina," she chirps.

Sabrina! That's the name Ava told me. I seriously need to work on remembering people's names better from now on.

"Hi, Sabrina. It's nice to meet you. Ava's in the kitchen? I'll just scoot on in and say hi," I say in my schoolteacher voice.

She smiles, and I can't help but notice she's really quite pretty. Even more, I was wrong about her eyes. They're deep brown, not blue, and they resemble Ronan's. Something about her reminds me of the girls I went to high school with. Not the ones I hung out with since I was a nerd, but the cheerleader type. I sort of want to ask her if she went to the same prep school Ronan and I did, but I stop myself.

Eleanor is just inside the door when I poke my head in, and she brightens up the moment she sees me. "Kate! Come in! Ava just went upstairs to put Theo down for his nap. I tell you those two boys keep us on our toes here. Thank God she hired someone, or I'm not sure we'd be able to handle it. I'm not as young as I was when Ronan and his brothers were little boys."

I point toward the kitchen door and nod. "I met Sabrina outside. She seems very nice. I hope she works out because two little boys so young are a handful."

The housekeeper rolls her eyes. "I'd forgotten how much work babies are. Between the two of us, it was like we never got to rest. Matthias has tried to help too, of course, but he's busy running King Industries again, so he has to spend much of his time with that. Would you like a soda or some iced tea?"

Pulling out one of the kitchen chairs from under the table, I smile at her offer. "Oh, I would love an iced tea. It's so hot already today, and we haven't even gotten to the heat of the afternoon."

As I sit down, I notice a plate with food and a can of soda sitting on the far end of the table. The meal looks like it might be a turkey sandwich with corn chips on the side.

"I didn't interrupt your lunch, did I, Eleanor?" I ask, immediately worried I'm bothering her.

She looks at me oddly for a moment before noticing I'm staring at the food. "Oh, no. That's not mine. It's Ronan's."

Eager to have the chance to see him again, I ask, "Would you like me to take it up to him? It would be no bother, and it would give you a chance to sit down and rest for a bit."

I watch her shake her head before she sets my glass of iced tea down in front of me. Taking a seat beside me, she leans toward me slightly and whispers, "We're not taking his food up to him anymore. Ava told me yesterday that from now on we aren't to go to his room at all, unless he asks us to. So he had to come down for breakfast this morning, and I'm assuming he'll come down for lunch at any time now. I have to say I'm having a hard time not running it right up to him, though. Old habits die hard."

Assuming Ava is trying to help Ronan by forcing him to come down to the kitchen for meals, I nod at what Eleanor says, even as I try to temper my disappointment at not having the opportunity to see him alone. Hopefully, he'll come down for his lunch while I'm here and I can try to talk to him then.

Ava walks in just as the housekeeper finishes talking and sits down across from me looking exhausted. "I have no idea how Matthias's mother did this. She had two kids close together and then had another one and then a couple years later had two more close together. I've only got two, but I swear Theo and Matty are more than I can handle. Thank God for Eleanor here and now Sabrina."

"How about a nice cold soda full of caffeine for you?" Eleanor says with a chuckle. "It's just what you need to keep yourself awake."

Relieved, Ava smiles. "Better make it a double, bartender."

Eleanor hurries away to the refrigerator to get the soda, and I say, "I met your new helper outside as I was arriving. I'm glad you have someone to assist you. My mother says having two kids back to back was the hardest thing she'd ever done. There's only a year between my sister and me, so she had it like you do now."

Taking the can of soda from the housekeeper, Ava chugs a few gulps and then lets out a huge burp. Embarrassed, she blushes and shakes her head. "Sorry. I've gotten so used to kids being able to belch that I've forgotten my manners."

I laugh, not bothered at all that she's so down-to-earth. "It's not worth mentioning. You're in your own house, so you can do as you like."

That seems to make her feel better, and she sinks back against the chair like this is the first break she's had all day. "Matthias says that all the time, but nobody cares when men walk around burping and acting like pigs. When a woman does it, she gets looks and people wonder what's wrong with her."

I wave away her worries. "I say do as you like in your own home. If anyone has an issue with it, they can leave, right?"

"Right!" she says, raising her can of soda. "But if I'm being honest, I'd love it if I was the kind of mother who always looks so put together and never burps or makes any weird noises. I don't know why I'm not like those Instagram moms. I guess I just don't have the perfect girl genes."

"Forget Instagram," Eleanor chimes in from across the room at the sink. "All of that's fake anyway. Instagram, Facebook, TikTok. All phony. None of those mothers are actually like that. And anyway, what kind of person uses their babies as props like they do?"

Ava and I look at each other, and I smile at Eleanor's on-point criticism of social media. "She's right, you know. I say you're doing great. Forget those Instagram moms."

"Thanks. That's what Matthias said when I mentioned it the other day. He's never on there, so he has no idea what I'm talking about, but as far as he's concerned, we're doing fine with the boys. We could use a little more sleep, but other than that, they're healthy and happy little boys."

Curious if my guess about where Sabrina attended high school was correct, I ask, "Sabrina reminded me of girls from where we all went to school. Did she go there too?"

Ava shakes her head and takes another gulp of soda. "I don't think so. I don't remember seeing the name on her application. I think she went to a different school further upstate. She's not from around here. I think she's from near Albany. Then again, my memory doesn't seem to be as good as it used to be, so I could be wrong. Mommy brain fog."

"That's the lack of sleep. It'll do it to you every time."

Footsteps coming down the hall make my heart skip a beat, and a few seconds later, Ronan appears in the kitchen. Dressed in black shorts and a white t-shirt, he looks like he just showered before coming down to get his food. He still has that horribly bushy beard that desperately needs a trim, but he looks much better than he did when I saw him the other day.

But I also notice he's hiding his right arm behind his back.

He glances at me before turning his attention to Ava. "I didn't know you two were friends."

An edge under his words make me worry he's angry I'm here, but Ava quickly puts me at ease when she says, "We weren't until recently. Would you like to join us? We're just sitting around talking and burping."

She throws her head back and laughs, and Eleanor and I chuckle along with her, but Ronan doesn't even smile. Maybe if he knew what she was referring to he would, so I attempt to clear it up for him.

"The soda made Ava belch really loudly. That's what she means by us talking and burping."

My explanation falls flat, and he doesn't even seem to listen as I speak. Turning his attention to the plate and soda at the other end of the table, he asks, "Is that mine?"

Eleanor can't stop herself from those old habits, so she picks up the plate and soda can and walks it over to where he's standing. "It is. I made you a turkey sandwich and put some of those corn chips you like on the side. I didn't put any mayonnaise on because I didn't want to make the bread soggy since I know you don't like that. I can put it on now since you're going to eat it soon. Would you like me to?"

He listens to her kind words that show she's trying so hard to be considerate and thoughtful and then turns on his heel to leave with his lunch. "No. It's fine."

And that's it for our time with Ronan. Not exactly a positive step in any good direction, unfortunately.

The three of us don't say a word for nearly a minute before Eleanor finally breaks the silence. "It practically tears my heart out to see him hurting like this. I miss the happy person he always was."

Ava and I look at each other, and she says, "I bet no

one misses that guy more than you. You and he were closer than anyone in this world for years."

Nodding, I want to say so much, but I simply agree and quietly answer, "He was my best friend in addition to my boyfriend. I could tell Ronan anything. I couldn't have gotten luckier than to have him as my first real boyfriend."

It sounds silly saying it like that now that I'm a grown woman in my mid-twenties, but that's what Ronan was to me. We weren't just dating. We were there for one another through thick and thin. I thought we'd be like that forever.

Reaching her hands across the table, Ava takes mine in hers and gives them a sympathetic squeeze. "I know he was crazy in love with you. Theo used to tell me how you two were together constantly."

I smile, remembering how frustrated his brothers' opinions on our closeness made Ronan. "He hated that they teased him about us. I used to tell him they just weren't used to seeing their baby brother with a girlfriend."

She takes a deep breath in and lets it out as a heavy sigh. "Theo was probably the worst at teasing him."

With a chuckle, I correct her. "Actually, it was your husband who gave him the hardest time."

"Of course!" she says, laughing. "Matthias was the world's biggest hater of anything regarding romance or love back then. Thank God he's changed, or I'd be married to a very miserable man."

That right there gives me hope that maybe things can change for Ronan too. Matthias used to be a real bastard, but now he's a wonderful husband to Ava and doting father to their two little boys. Can that change happen for Ronan?

I don't know, but I can hope. The problem is if I don't ever get the chance to talk to him, I'm not sure I'll get to be a part of that change I want to see for him.

"Even though it's none of my business, and feel free to tell me exactly that, I'm wondering what happened to break you two up," Ava says.

If she or anyone else asked me that right after I broke up with Ronan, I would have burst into tears. He had no idea how he broke my heart when he cheated on me. I couldn't even hear his name without feeling like I'd lost my entire world.

Thankfully, I can talk about it now with at least a little detachment. It still hurts to think about, but I forgave him a long time ago.

Not wanting to paint him as a son of a bitch, I choose my words carefully as I answer her question. "I think he and I grew apart because we were going to different colleges. He went far enough away that I couldn't see him as much as I used to. People drift apart, and he ended up with someone else."

It's taken me years to master the ability of saying that instead of blurting out the oh-so-painful words *he cheated on me*. That may be the truth, but he's got enough to deal with now. He doesn't need anyone looking at him and judging a mistake he made years ago.

But Ava sees right through my attempt at being diplomatic and says, "He cheated on you? Of all the people in the world, Ronan is one of the few men I'd say would never do that to someone he loved, and I know he loved you."

Well, now that it's out there for everyone to know, I guess I don't have to act like I'm working for the U.N. I don't want to bash him, though. I understand what happened. It still makes me sad, but I understand.

"We were young. He was away and on his own for the first time in his life, and he was having a good time. I guess that good time went a little too far one night."

I stop, unsure I should mention who he cheated with, even though her name is practically tattooed on my mind. It doesn't really matter now, but since Ava and I attended the same school and she was just two years ahead of Ronan and me, she might be curious to know.

"It was Amanda Isaacson," I quietly add.

A look of instant recognition fills Ava's expression as she stares at me like she can't believe I just said that very name. "Amanda Isaacson? The girl who got the nose job and who bragged about it constantly? As if having an operation was anything to brag about. That girl?"

I nod as all those feelings from back then come rushing back. "Yep. Do you know when Ronan and I first started dating she told me she'd wanted him for a while? Who says that to someone?"

"A petty bitch. I wish my friend Eden was here. She could tell you chapter and verse about Miss Amanda Isaacson. They had a habit of liking the same guys in school, and it irritated Eden to no end that some underclassman always thought she had a chance with guys our age." Ava stops for a moment and smiles.

"Actually, it's good she isn't here because she'd have nothing nice to say about her."

"Well, I forgave Ronan. He was young, away at school, and it never surprised me that other girls liked him. He was Ronan King. All the things that made me crazy about him were obvious to everyone, so why shouldn't they want him?"

That sounds far more secure than I've ever been, but it's true. I knew how good I had it when he was mine. Maybe somewhere deep in my mind I knew he'd eventually end up going with other girls. I was just little old me, Kate Abbott. Other than making great grades, I wasn't anyone special.

He made me feel like I was, though.

"You guys have talked since you broke up, right?"

"Yeah, a few times. I made sure to call him when his father and Theo passed. We fell out of touch, though, after that. I can't tell you how many times I've thought about what if I'd been around and called him that night of his accident. Maybe he wouldn't have been on that particular stretch of the Taconic. Maybe we would have been hanging out at that coffee shop we loved catching up on old times instead of him driving that night."

Again, Ava reaches over and touches my hand to give it a squeeze. "You can't think like that. It was an accident that should have never happened, but you didn't do anything to make it happen. Nobody did but that damn drunk driver, who of course, walked away from the accident with barely a scratch."

Across the room, Eleanor says, "Matthias told me

the lawsuit against him is going well. I hope they get the bastard. Pardon my French."

Ava agrees with her but adds that getting money from the guy isn't going to change things. The Kings have billions. A few million more isn't going to make Ronan's hand reappear. It's just money, and when all you want is something money can't buy, winning some lawsuit doesn't really matter much.

I wish so much I could do something to help him get back what he lost.

# CHAPTER TEN

onan

I KNOW WHAT AVA'S UP TO. SHE THINKS SHE'S BEING clever or sly, but I see right through her plan. She thinks inviting my ex-girlfriend over here is going to make me want to leave my room more often. She's probably hoping I'll want to talk to her. I can see her actually telling Kate how good it would be for me to see her.

Well, she's wrong. It's not fucking good. It's torture. There she is looking as beautiful as ever sitting downstairs, just like she did when we were together. Even seeing her brings back a million memories of all the good times we had. I've never loved anyone like I loved her.

Except those days are long gone.

Then I was a high school kid with big dreams and a

belief I could have anything I wanted. She was completely out of my league, but I didn't think twice about asking her out. Kate Abbott got great grades, was gorgeous, and was as sweet as any guy could ask for. I was just a jock who came from a family with a lot of money. Still, I never doubted myself when I asked her out that first time.

Why would I? I had the world by the tail.

I push away the half of my turkey sandwich left, disgusted by how dry it tastes without mayonnaise. But I couldn't hang out down there even long enough for Eleanor to slap some on the sandwich because then Kate would see once again how fucking broken I am. It's only a matter of time before she realizes the truth and doesn't want to be anywhere near me.

Better for me to save us both the time and stay away.

My mind drifts back to seeing her downstairs, no matter how much I try not to think about that. She wasn't wearing a wedding ring. I wonder if she's still single. If so, then the entire population of males in this area have lost their minds.

I look down at my own left hand and think about how I imagined I'd marry her. She was my first girlfriend, but I didn't want anyone else. I'd found the one for me. My brothers could do all the comparison shopping for women they wanted. I didn't need to do that once Kate and I were together.

All that went away that New Year's Eve. Even if I wanted to try again with her, I can't think about that. She's the whole package. Smart, sexy, beautiful, and kind. And what am I? A guy with no right hand and no future because the only thing I ever wanted to do is now an impossibility.

She deserves better than a life with someone like me. All I can offer her is money, and why would she give a damn about that when she has so much more to offer a man?

I walk into the bathroom and catch a glimpse of my face in the mirror. I've definitely let myself go. Fuck, I look like some goddamned mountain man. Not that I can do anything about that. I haven't gone looking for a razor, but I doubt my brother, Ava, or Eleanor left one in here.

What's it matter anyway? Who the fuck am I shaving for?

Just as I suspected, when I open the medicine cabinet, I see nothing sharp. There's not much at all, other than those pills they gave me that I won't take. The doctor claims they'll make me feel better. All they ever did was make me feel like my damn head was three feet above my body.

Frustrated, I slam the cabinet door and storm out into my room. I'm not a fucking child. It's not like I'm planning to slice myself up right here in my childhood bedroom with my brother, Ava, and my nephews in the same house. It would probably be Eleanor who found me anyway, and I wouldn't do that to her. She's been like a mother to me, for fuck's sake.

Maybe there's one in Marius or Kellen's rooms. They made Theo's room into the nursery, but I overheard Matthias say to Ava that they won't be changing my other brothers' bedrooms to the boys' rooms until they're older.

I look out into the hallway and don't see anyone, so I hurry over to Kellen's room to look for a razor. You'd swear these things are made of gold the way they've hidden them from me.

Even as I think that, I know that isn't the reason. I get it. I tried to off myself. That was a rough period for me. I swore to Matthias I wouldn't try it again, especially here. You'd think they'd believe me.

Kellen's bathroom is so spotless you could eat off the floor. Eleanor probably had one of her people scrub the place down after he stayed here for a couple days when Ava had Theo. Nothing but towels in the linen closet, and when I look in the medicine cabinet, it's empty. Not even a damn Q-Tip.

If I've ever needed Eleanor and her staff to be slackers, it would be now.

I make my way down the hall to Marius's room, but it's the same story. Nothing but a perfectly clean floor and surfaces with nothing left behind anywhere.

My last chance is Matthias's old room. Actually, there are probably a few razors in the room he and Ava share that used to be our parents' bedroom, but I'd rather not try there and have to answer for what I'm doing if Ava walks in.

Matthias left nothing in his bedroom when he moved down the hall. Damn. You'd think in a house that once had five young men living here that I'd be able to find a single razor.

So much for trying to shave. Not that I know if I can even do it since I've never shaved with my left hand. Ava helped me with that right after I came here, but since then, I've let it grow until now I look like I've been lost in the outback for weeks.

Feeling defeated, I start back to my room but run into Sabrina. She intentionally avoids making eye contact with me, probably because of what I said yesterday out on the patio. She might know where I can find a razor, though.

"Hey."

Not exactly my best conversation starter, but I'm a little out of practice.

She stops and looks at me like I've grown another head next to mine but doesn't say anything. Terrific. One day, she's all about giving me her opinion, and the next she's acting like someone's cut out her tongue.

"So what is your job here exactly?" I ask, not really knowing why I said that but trying to get a conversation going.

Sabrina takes a moment to respond, but finally says, "I'm here to help Ava with the boys. That's all. By the way, I'm sorry for yesterday. She talked to me, and I get it now. No bothering the guy who never leaves his room."

Right after she says that, she looks down the hallway toward my bedroom and then back at me. "Except for today, it seems."

"I'm looking for a razor, but I can't find one. Any chance you've seen one in your travels around here?"

She narrows her eyes as if to let me know she thinks I'm an idiot. "I work with babies. There's not really much of a call for razors with them."

Super.

I don't bother continuing talking to her since

there's no point, so I walk back to my room and shut the door behind me. So much for shaving today. Or any other day, for that matter, it seems.

Then again, I could ask Ava to help me, but that will only encourage her to think she should bring Kate around more. I want to see her, but why bother? Even with a decent shave, I'll still be the guy I am with this mess of a beard.

On that happy thought, I climb into bed and wish I had room darkening curtains so I wouldn't have to struggle to fall asleep.

~

I SKIPPED BREAKFAST TODAY TO SEE IF ELEANOR would bring it up to me, but she seems to be made of stronger stuff than I gave her credit for. I guess I could explain to everyone when I said I didn't want to be bothered by people that I wasn't saying I didn't want to eat.

It's nearly one, which I'm thinking means I'm on my own for lunch, so I walk out of my room and nearly run into the babysitter. Why she's standing in front of my door I have no idea, but she's lucky I didn't flatten her.

Before I can ask just what the hell she thinks she's doing, she holds up her hand to show me a blue disposable razor like the kind I started on when I first learned to shave. I haven't used one of those since I was fifteen, but beggars can't be choosers, I guess.

"You said you needed a razor, so ta-da!" she announces proudly with a huge smile.

When I reach for it, she snatches it away. Is she playing some game? If so, I'm not in the mood.

"One rule. You don't give me a hard time ever again when I appear in the same place you do. Deal?"

"You didn't just appear in the same place I was. You walked into my room uninvited."

That gets me a disinterested shrug. "Same difference. So do you agree to my deal?"

"Fine. Give me the razor."

Shaking her head, she smiles again. "Nope. That's not the way people get what they want. What's the magic word?"

"Give it to me or else?" I say, already tired of whatever this thing is she's doing.

A look of disgust comes over her, and she juts out her right hip completing the vibe. "Why don't you try please? Weren't you ever taught manners? Sheesh."

"Please give me the razor," I say through gritted teeth.

That satisfies her, and she hands it to me with a huge grin. "Very nice. I hope you aren't planning to shave your head. You have nice hair, so it would be a shame to see it go. Plus, you might have one of those lumpy skulls that never look good bald."

Seriously, who the hell is this person, and what gives her the idea she should talk to me or anyone like this?

"What's it matter what I'm shaving?" I say before walking back into my room, happy to be away from her.

I honestly think Ava must have advertised for the most annoying person to help her with my nephews.

No matter. She did bring me a razor, so maybe she's not all bad.

Just aggravating. And rude.

Since there are no razors in my bathroom, there's no shaving cream either, so I'm stuck with soap. Not exactly the best way to shave off all this hair, but it'll have to do.

A bigger problem presents itself as soon as I lather up my beard and start to use the razor. The hair's too long to just shave. It needs to be trimmed first, and there's no way in hell Matthias, Ava, or Eleanor left me a pair of scissors.

Why is nothing fucking easy?

I slam my fist into the mirror, but it doesn't break probably because my left arm and hand are much weaker than my right. All that outburst does is hurt my knuckles. Christ, I can't win today.

From outside the bathroom, I hear Sabrina say, "Everything okay in there? You aren't really shaving your entire head, are you?"

Walking out to my bedroom, I see her standing in the doorway to the hall. "I'm fine, and what is your obsession with my hair? As you can see by the soap in my beard, I'm trying to shave my face. I just didn't think about how I'd have to trim it first, so I'm shit out of luck."

She stands there staring at me for a few moments before holding up her hand. "Wait here! I think I can help."

And then she disappears, helping more than she could possibly know.

I don't bother waiting since I doubt she can

actually do anything for me now, but a minute later, she walks into my room, uninvited as usual, and holds up a pair of small scissors. They look like they might be to cut something on babies, although I can't imagine what they need trimmed since they have next to no hair anywhere.

"You can say thank you right now," she says as she walks toward where I stand.

"Maybe after I use them for my beard you can go trim the hedges with them. You might be done by Thanksgiving."

My attempt at a joke misses entirely, and she points toward the bathroom. "Let's go. The babies are only going to be napping for a little while longer."

"Go where?" I ask, confused where she means or what she's doing right now.

Like yesterday when I asked about a razor, she gives me a look like I'm the world's biggest moron. Her eyes squinted and a disgusted expression on her face, she says, "Into the bathroom. You're going to need help with this, I'm assuming."

"Well, you assumed wrong. You can leave now," I say as I push past her to walk into the bathroom, grabbing the scissors from her hold as I walk by.

Why the hell would I need her help? I've been shaving since I was in tenth grade, for God's sake.

Not twenty seconds later, it becomes obvious that not using my left hand since I lost my right one hasn't been smart. I can't grip the tiny scissors properly, and each time I try to cut the hair short enough so I can shave, the damn things fall out of my hand and into the sink.

"Fuck!"

"Ready for my help yet?" she calls from outside the bathroom.

I'm ready for her to get the hell away from me. That I'd be on board with. Helping me shave is another story entirely.

"I don't need your help."

She appears in the doorway and shakes her head. "Yeah, you're doing a hell of a job there. You might be done by Thanksgiving."

Smartass.

Without waiting for me to invite her in, she marches into the bathroom and takes the scissors from my hand. Pointing at the toilet, she says, "Sit. You're too tall for me to do this with you standing up."

"It'll get all over the floor."

"Then you can clean it up."

Damn, she's bossy, but since I want to shave and I can't seem to handle it by myself, what choice do I have but to let her help? Reluctantly, I do as she orders and sit on the toilet seat lid.

"Good! Now sit still or I'll stab you, and you don't want that, I'm sure," she says as she takes a step toward me and stops.

Just before she starts cutting my beard, I mumble, "Nothing like a threat to go with a shave."

Sabrina gets to work with the scissors, trimming the course hair as I sit watching her. I've had fantasies that involved this kind of thing. They just all involved Kate and not some pushy babysitter who's done little more than get on my last nerve since the moment I met her.

"So what made you want to shave? Not that I think you're making a mistake or anything. I mean, beards are hot, but yours looked like birds might be nesting in it."

When she moves the scissors away from the area around my mouth, I look up at her and ask, "Have you ever had a thought that didn't drop straight from your brain to your mouth like a slot machine?"

Stopping for a moment, she smiles and answers, "No, I haven't. By the way, what's going on with that hand of yours? Not the one you don't have but the area right above that."

I lift my right arm and see the scar from what I did in April. "I tried to kill myself."

She makes a huffing noise. "Well, that's stupid."

Stunned and a little hurt by her answer, although I don't know why since she's nobody to me, I snap, "Nice. Just leave. I don't need your help."

I reach for the scissors, but she backs away, refusing to give them to me. "Okay, that might have been a touch rude, but seriously? Someone like you wanting to kill yourself is so wrong. I can't imagine why you'd even think of that."

Without saying a word, I give her my answer by raising my right arm. She stares at it for a long moment and then points at my left hand.

"What about that one?"

"I'm right-handed. Or at least I was," I answer.

Without missing a beat, she chops off more of my beard and casually says, "And now you're left-handed."

Jesus, I think I might hate this person. If I didn't

need her help to get this beard gone, I'd tell her to get the fuck away from me in a heartbeat.

"Nice bedside manner you have," I grumble, disgusted that yet another person is acting like it's just fine that I lost my right hand because I have another.

Sabrina returns to trimming my beard and says, "I'm not a nurse. I'm here to help Ava with chores and the babies, and I think she mentioned something about driving you to doctor's appointments, although I don't see how that's going to work since you basically never leave this house. But no matter. You don't need a nurse. You look as healthy as a horse, and once we get all this awful hair gone, you'll be back to new."

The conversation, or what there is of it, falls away, leaving us in silence. All the better. She has a way of making me feel like I want to lash out at something every time she opens her mouth.

As she continues to prune away at my very shaggy beard, she asks, "Have you gotten a pair of left-handed scissors yet? I bet that's cool having special scissors."

For a moment, I can't tell if she's serious, but since she stares down at me waiting for an answer, I say, "I think those are only for little kids."

"Too bad. I bet that would be cool to have some for adults. Okay, the first part is done. Now it's time to shave. Hand me the razor."

I consider telling her I can shave my own face, but I don't feel like failing at that too, so I point to the blue plastic razor sitting on the vanity. She grabs it but then puts it down again.

"Need some soap. This would work better with shaving cream, but soap can work too."

She seems to have the need to talk, but I'm not interested, so I close my eyes. She lathers my face and then starts shaving along my jaw. As she takes care of one side and then the other before moving to around my mouth, I let myself enjoy this. It's not as good as that time I went to that barber with Kellen in high school, but this comes in a nice second place.

When she finally finishes, she wipes off my face with a warm washcloth sort of like that barber did and says, "There you go! Good as new. You know, you have a really nice face."

I open my eyes and stand up to look in the mirror to check out how she did. Running my hand over my newly smooth skin, I have to admit she did a decent job.

Smiling at how good I look, I turn toward her and say, "Not bad. I'm guessing this isn't your first time doing that."

That makes her chuckle, and as she rinses out the razor, she says, "I'm twenty-one, Ronan. My first time for most things is long gone."

Surprisingly, she leaves without another word, and as I sit alone on my bed, I realize I'm smiling. I haven't been like this for so long I forgot how it felt.

I think I sort of like feeling happy again.

Then I look down at my right am, and I feel my smile fade. Nothing's changed.

# CHAPTER ELEVEN

onan

I OVERHEARD AVA TELL ELEANOR THAT KATE IS coming over today when I walked down to the kitchen to grab my dinner last night. I can't explain it, but I've felt like I've been walking on air ever since.

That's stupid. Nothing is different from the other day. Well, other than I got a decent shave and don't look like the damn Unabomber anymore.

As much as I want to be happy I might see her today, a dark voice inside me keeps reminding me that I'm still a messed up man who lost his hand. Why would she even think about being with someone like me now?

Every time I hear that in my head, I try to push it away, but it keeps returning. That darkness in my very soul is stronger than I am. I don't know how to change that.

I smooth my hair back off my face and like what I see for the first time in weeks. That Sabrina might be as irritating as nails on a chalkboard, but she did a good job.

"Yoo-hoo!" Eleanor calls from the hallway. "May I come in? It's sheet changing day, and you're the lucky contestant this hour."

"Come in."

The door opens, and in she walks with the laundry basket. She sets it on the floor and gets to work on my bed like she does every Thursday. Then she looks over at me standing in the doorway to the bathroom and her mouth drops open.

"Ronan, you shaved! You look like your old self again," Eleanor says with a bigger smile than I've seen on her in a long time.

"Thanks," I say, stroking my hairless chin. "I thought it might be time yesterday."

Then she realizes I needed a razor to get my face to look like this, and her smiles quickly disappears. "I didn't think we left anything…I mean something you could use…"

"Ava's helper hooked me up. It's okay. I just wanted to clean up a little. Nothing else."

When she doesn't return to smiling, I put my left hand up and add, "Swear to God, Eleanor. I promised Matthias I wouldn't try anything like that again, and I won't."

Relief washes over her, and she sits down on my bed. "Please don't. I wouldn't be able to handle it if…"

Once more, she can't finish her sentence. "You've been the closest thing to a mother that I've had since mine died. I wouldn't do that to you. I promise, Eleanor."

That makes her smile return, but now it's accompanied by tears in her eyes. "Oh, honey. I know things have been hard for you. I only want you to find all the happiness you deserve."

"Well, I figured I needed to start with my face. I was looking pretty rough there for a while."

Eleanor returns to stripping the sheets off my bed but shakes her head at my attempt to be self-effacing. "You always looked like yourself. Just with a little more hair. I like this version better, though. It's more you."

"Thanks. I'm going to head downstairs for breakfast now."

As she tosses the dirty sheets into the basket and makes her way to the linen closet to get a new set, she says, "I think Matthias is down there with Theo. The baby had a doctor's appointment early this morning, so Ava and Sabrina took Matty and he offered to lighten the load by hanging out here with him."

I'm not sure if she's warning me so I don't go down to the kitchen yet or just trying to be helpful like usual. I haven't exactly been uncle of the year to either of my nephews. In fact, I've spent very little time with either of them since I came to stay here, so she might think I want to avoid that today.

I feel so good this morning that maybe it's time to change how I've been with little Theo and Matty. Before I leave, I walk over to Eleanor and hug her. I feel her sigh against me and wonder if I've underestimated how bad things have been for everyone these past few months.

"Thank you for always being here for me, Eleanor."

She covers my cheeks with her hands and smiles, her eyes full of tears again. "Oh, honey. We're all here for you. I'm so happy to see you feeling better. I know things have been so hard for you, but I think you're turning a corner. You watch. Life is going to be much better from now on."

I don't say it, but I hope she's right. I'd like to be happy again. It's been a long time since I've truly felt that way, but I remember being happy, and I miss it.

MATTHIAS AND HIS OLDER SON SIT AT THE KITCHEN table, my brother in the seat he's always sat in and Theo in his high chair with the tray filled with Cheerios. They both look up when I walk into the room like they're surprised to see me. I guess that's warranted since until this week I've taken every meal up in my room.

"Ronan? You look like yourself again," Matthias says, clearly happy by my effort to look human once more.

Then, just as Eleanor did a few minutes ago upstairs, he realizes what I must have gotten my hands on to be clean shaven. His expression morphs from happy to worried like always, but I quickly explain so he isn't stressed.

"It's okay. Sabrina helped me, and she took the scissors and razor with her when she was done. You don't have to worry. I promised I'd never do anything like that again, and I won't. You can trust me."

For the second time this morning, I watch as relief washes over someone I love when they realize I might be getting better finally. My brother smiles again and points to the chair across from him.

"Sit down and enjoy some breakfast. Eleanor made waffles a little while ago." He stops and looks at Theo. "Obviously, my son decided today was a Cheerios day. He doesn't seem to understand they're for eating, though."

I haven't spent much time with this nephew this year, and he looks up at me like he doesn't even know who I am. Sitting down, I look over at him and give him a guy nod.

"What's up, little man? How are those Cheerios?"

I'm not sure he understands me, especially when he starts babbling and then dropping the cereal on the table just beyond his high chair tray. I look back at Matthias for some translation, but he seems as confused as I am.

"Ava would say he's showing you his Cheerios, but I don't know. All I do know is that this kid loves playing with those little rings. How much he likes eating them is another story."

Then Theo smiles and in a tiny voice says, "Da-da."

That's it. Just one nonsensical word, but my brother's eyes light up.

"That's his first word. Oh, when Ava hears he said da-da before ma-ma, she's going to be so jealous," Matthias says, beaming a smile.

I watch as he leans over to kiss Theo, which makes

the baby excited so he throws some of his cereal in his father's face. It's a scene I never thought I'd see in my entire life, and I can't help but laugh.

"Funny, huh?" he says as he picks those little oat circles out of his hair. "Just wait until you have one. Then you'll see."

"To be honest, I can't believe you have not one but two already. You and Ava seem to be on track to have as many as Mom and Dad had and in the same amount of time."

He smiles and shakes his head. "I'm not thinking five. She'd like a girl, so we'll keep going until we have one of those. Then we'll be done. I can only hope it doesn't take until we're up to five because I'm not sure I can do that. I had no idea until I had kids of my own how much Mom and Dad had to do. Even with Eleanor, the staff, and Sabrina helping, I feel like I'm constantly running on a sleep deficiency. I'm like a damn zombie most of the time. Seriously, I'm so tired I'm thinking I might have to ask Kellen to step in as head of King Industries temporarily again."

"That'll make him happy," I say, knowing my older brother would be over the moon to once again be in the job he always hoped to have.

Little Theo starts to nod off, so Matthias lifts him out of his high chair and holds him in his arms. It's a picture I still can't believe, but it's a great thing to see. Matthias spent so long being so unhappy that getting to be around him happy and content is a nice change.

"Sometimes I think maybe I should just walk away from the company," he says, sitting back against the chair as his older son falls fast asleep against his chest.

"I don't need the money. I could just hang out in my studio and work on my art. I know Ava would be happy for me whatever I choose."

"Then why don't you?" I ask as I make my way over to where a stack of waffles sit on the island.

I grab three and put them into the oven before turning on the heat to warm them up while Matthias answers my question. "This is going to sound crazy, but I like going to work. Dad must be laughing his ass off in heaven, right? The son who never wanted to work at the family business now doesn't want to leave it."

"Dad would definitely love knowing that, but I bet Mom would want you to spend more time on your art. You know how she always loved it when you'd draw things for her."

Matthias nods and then stands up from the table. "I hate to leave, but this little guy likely needs a diaper change before he goes down for a nap. I'll never hear the end of it if he turns up with a rash because I didn't change him, especially once Ava finds out he said his first word. She told me before she left that he'll probably fall asleep at the table, but I absolutely can't put him down with a dirty diaper."

I can't help but smile at how lost in domestic bliss my oldest brother has become. After all he's gone through, it's the least he deserves.

Alone, I let my waffles heat up before sitting down at the table to enjoy them with lots of butter and maple syrup, just like I did when I was little. I'm getting better using my left hand to do things, thankfully.

My mind drifts back in time, and I remember my

mother sitting with me after my brothers all left one day. She did that whenever she saw me all alone.

*I stuff one last forkful of waffle in my mouth and wash it down with milk. My mother sits beside me watching silently as I chew and then hold my glass with two hands so I don't drop it.*

*"What are you planning on doing today, honey?" she asks. "It's a beautiful, sunny day. Would you like to go to the playground? We can get Kellen to come, and the two of you can have a nice time. What do you think?"*

*Eight-year-old me smiles as I finish the last of my breakfast. "I want to, but Kellen went with Marius and Theo. They're playing outside and told me I couldn't come."*

*Concern fills her expression. "Why did they say that?"*

*"Because I can't run as fast as they can. They get mad at me, especially Theo. He says when I'm older I can go with them. But I want to go now."*

*She stands up from the table and walks over to the sink before returning with a dishcloth she dampened. Handing it to me, she says, "Wipe your face, and then we'll see what we can do outside, okay?"*

*I nod and rub the white dishcloth with pink flowers all over my mouth and cheeks before handing it back to her. "I'm really now! Can we go?" I say excitedly.*

*My mother spots a part of my face I missed and rubs near my eyebrow with the cloth. When she finishes, she smiles. "We're ready. Are your sneakers tied?"*

*Happy to show off I'm completely ready to go outside and play, I point down at my feet and grin like I've just climbed the highest mountain. "Both. Just like I'm supposed to. Can we go now?"*

*With a smile, she takes my hand, and I hop off the chair,*

eager to go outside and play with my brothers. She'll tell them they have to play with me, so they won't have a choice.

I hold on to her warm hand as we walk out the kitchen door. Marius, Theo, and Kellen are playing catch, although Kellen isn't doing much of anything but running after the ball when either of my older brothers throw it past the other one.

"Boys, come here!" she announces, and all three of them stop everything.

They run toward her, Marius slower than everyone else because he doesn't like to be told what to do. Theo might be the one who says I can't play, but it's Marius who will fight against our mother's order to include me.

When they all reach the two of us, I stand next to her and look up at her as she talks to them. "Why aren't you letting Ronan play with you?"

Kellen doesn't speak, but Theo gives me a dirty look and says, "Tattletale."

"I didn't tattle! Why won't you let me play?"

"Because you're too small and too slow," Theo answers.

My mother holds her hand up like she always does when she's done listening to us fight. "No more. Now boys, your brother can play with you. There's no reason he should be stuck inside on a beautiful day like this."

Mumbling, Marius lowers his head and says, "Okay. He's too small, though."

I open my mouth to say he just turned twelve, so he's not much bigger than me, but my mother stops me with a stern look before turning her attention back to my older brother. "Honey, he'll never learn if you don't include him."

That doesn't make him any happier, and she turns to look down at me. "You listen to your brothers so you know the rules of the game, okay?"

*"I will," I say, thrilled to be included for once.*

*She bends down to kiss me on the cheek and lets go of my hand. "Now go have a good time!"*

As the memory of that day fades away to the back of my mind, I sigh, wishing my mother was here right now. I don't know if anything would be different if she was still living, but I miss having her around to watch out for me.

One final memory comes back to me as I walk my plate and fork to the sink. I ran off to play with my brothers, who reluctantly agreed to involve me in their fun that day, and when I looked back at my mother, she was slowly walking into the house watching all of us.

She always had time for her children, and even though sometimes it meant having to do things we didn't want to do, we never doubted she loved us. Being back here in the house where I grew up makes it easy to remember how happy we were.

I can only hope someday that will be possible for me again.

# CHAPTER TWELVE

ate

*My hand's so sweaty I can barely hold onto Ronan's as we walk down the hallway to our hotel room. Still dressed in our clothes from the prom, I have to hold my dress up so I don't trip over it, but he looks so handsome in his black tux.*

*"What room number is it?" I ask as we turn a corner and begin walking down another long hallway.*

*He turns his head to look at me and smiles. "Six twenty-four. Almost there, I think."*

*My parents looked so proud when we stood in the living room at the house for pictures before the prom. We never told them about coming here to hang out after, but I had a feeling they suspected we would since it's practically a tradition at the school we attend.*

*We finally reach the hotel room, and it's even nicer than I imagined when Ronan suggested we get a room for tonight. I* look around at the coffee maker on the counter above the mini fridge and then at the air conditioner on the far wall under the windows. The bedspreads on each full size bed are navy blue with splashes of grey like someone took a barely wet paintbrush and randomly flicked it over the material.

"This is really nice."

Ronan tosses his tux jacket on the bed closest to where I stand and undoes his tie so both ends hang loose around his neck. "My brother said it was a nice place when he came here after prom. That was a while back, though, so I'm glad it's still okay."

I can only imagine which brother of his he's talking about. Probably Kellen. Maybe Marius. I bet he's seen the inside of a lot of hotels.

A little nervous, I sit down on the bed and run my fingertips over his black jacket. "Did you hear if anyone else was coming here?" I ask, suddenly unsure what to say.

It's not like I don't know why he suggested we come here tonight after the prom ended. Ever since we started dating, we've had a hard time finding ways to be alone. His house is so busy with his brothers and his father always around, and while my parents are often out of our house, we never know when they're going to return.

To say we've struggled to find a way to be together would be an understatement. Most of the time, we've had to settle for his car, but that's nothing less than truly uncomfortable.

Ronan shrugs as he thinks about my question. "I heard Amanda Isaacson was having a party at her house. I didn't mention it since I didn't think you'd be interested. You didn't want to go to that, did you?"

The last place I want to be with Ronan looking as good as he does in that tux is anywhere near her. She made it perfectly clear when he and I started dating that she'd had her eye on him for a long time, and a drunken Amanda hitting on my boyfriend isn't how I wanted to end prom night.

I shake my head and hope my expression doesn't make it too obvious I don't like her. I've never told him what she said to me about wanting him, so he probably wouldn't understand my feeling about her.

"Are you hungry?" he asks as he opens the mini fridge. "Not that there's anything in here, but I can run for something if you are."

Again, I shake my head. "No, not really."

God, I wish I had something else to say. We've been dating for a year, but suddenly, I have nothing clever in my head.

I used to get like this a lot when we first started going out. Ronan was so cute and so popular, and back then, I often felt like I didn't belong with him. I'm not hideous, but I'm not like the other girls at school. They all seem to know exactly how to do their makeup and hair the best way to make them as beautiful as they can be. My hair rarely does much of anything but hang straight down from my scalp. And when it comes to makeup, I'm almost completely ignorant on how I should use it. On most days, I slap a little mascara and blush on before breaking out my favorite lip gloss, and I'm ready for school.

Thankfully, my sister Kelly knows all about makeup so she did mine tonight. If not, I would have looked like my usual self in this pink prom dress.

Ronan stands in front of me, so I look up at him. He really is the most gorgeous guy I've ever seen. If he knows that, he doesn't seem to care, though.

"Is something wrong, Kate? I didn't want to go to that party either. If you want to go somewhere else, we can. Just tell me, and I'll get us there."

*God, is there another girl who has a better boyfriend in the world?*

"No, I'm okay here. Unless you aren't. Do you want to go somewhere else?" I ask, suddenly unsure he even wants to be here alone with me.

He smiles, and it's like the sun coming out from behind the clouds. "No. I'm right where I want to be."

When he's like this—sweet and so caring about everything I want—I want to tell him I think I'm the luckiest girl in the world. All my friends tell me never to do that because then he'll get complacent and not be so great once he knows how crazy I am about him, but it's not like I haven't told Ronan how much I love him before. Anyway, he's not like other guys at school. How many of them would sit next to me at my dining room table watching me study and helping me get ready for finals?

Ronan, my Ronan, is one of a kind.

When he leans down to kiss me, the ends of his silk bow tie brush against the sides of my face. I push them out of the way, but I can't help but giggle at how cool they feel on my skin.

He realizes what's happening and slides the black tie from around his neck, tossing it on top of his jacket. I reach up and unbutton his top shirt button, and for a long moment, I can't help but stare at how good he looks.

In truth, he could wear a ratty t-shirt and a pair of his oldest basketball shorts, and he'd still look incredible. I don't know how, but for him, it seems almost effortless.

Ronan returns to kissing me, but now he cradles my face in his strong hands. I feel like I'm in heaven when he touches me like this. Like I'm something so important he wants to cherish me.

When he slowly pulls away, I miss the feel of his lips on mine. He's probably wondering why I'm not doing anything to *reciprocate. I want to, but it's like I get lost in how he makes me feel when we're alone like this and I forget he'd probably like to know I care too.*

*"I'm sorry. I got a little into my head there for a few seconds," I say, avoiding his gaze.*

*He crouches down in front of me and smiles, making my insides do a flip. "It's okay, Kate. I like how you're someone who spends time thinking. It keeps me on my toes and makes me have to figure out what to do."*

*Hearing that makes me sad. Ronan doesn't deserve to wonder if I care about him as much as he cares about me.*

*I reach out and cradle his face like he did with me a minute ago. "Don't ever think I'm not absolutely, positively crazy in love with you, Ronan King. Because I am. I just don't show it all the time because I'm too busy thinking stupid stuff."*

*"Nothing you could think would be stupid, Kate."*

*Tonight was supposed to be about us having a place to have sex without worrying someone would walk in on us, but it's quickly turning into my ruining our time together because I'm insecure. I don't want to be. It's just that I sometimes worry one day Ronan will figure out he wants to be with someone who knows how to do her hair and makeup expertly.*

*Maybe someone who's a cheerleader since he's a star athlete.*

*I shouldn't say anything about that, but it's like I can't stop myself.*

*"Sometimes I wonder why you want to be with me at all. I'm not like the girls all your friends hang out with. They probably ask you why you'd want to date a girl like me whose head is always in her books."*

*Oddly enough, after I say those words, I don't feel better. I should have just kept my worries to myself.*

Ronan shakes his head and sighs. "You have no idea how perfect you are, do you? I look at you sometimes and think there's no way you want to be with me. I'm just a guy who hopes to someday be a professional baseball player. You're smart, and when you go to college, it's going to be because you belong there. I love you because you're not like other girls, Kate. When are you going to understand that?"

Other guys might try to make me feel better, but they'd never be as sweet and understanding as Ronan. That's the biggest reason why I love him.

"I guess tonight?" I say with a smile, trying not to giggle but I'm so happy after hearing him say all of that.

"Good. Stop doubting yourself. If anyone should doubt themselves, it should be me. I'm just some jock who probably makes you question why we're going out at all."

I hate when he talks like that. Ronan has so many good things going for him, but all he ever focuses on is his playing sports.

"You're not just a dumb jock. You never give yourself enough credit. I think you're smart, and since you've already said I'm intelligent, you should believe me."

That gets me a big smile I could stare at for the rest of time. "Well, I guess I better believe it since the smartest person I know said it."

I lean forward and kiss him softly on the lips. "I love you, Ronan. Just the way you are."

"And I love you just the way you are."

He stands up and eases me back onto the bed, his dark brown eyes looking down at me in that intense way that never fails to excite me. I've never been with anyone else but him. All my friends have had two or three guys they've slept with, but I've only been with Ronan. I know he's been with other girls, *but as unsure of myself as I am, that fact doesn't bother me. Those girls were before he and I found one another. Plus, I sort of like that he has a past since I don't. One of us has to have some experience.*

*"You were the most beautiful girl there tonight," he whispers before brushing his soft lips against my neck.*

*My eyes flutter closed as the most exquisite sensations fill every inch of me. "And you were the most handsome guy at the prom," I say as I slide my hand over the back of his head.*

*His dark hair is soft against my fingers, and when he nuzzles my ear, I can't stop myself from tugging on his hair. It's like whenever he's this close, I can't control how I feel.*

*I slide my other hand under his shirt collar and feel his soft skin. He's hot, like he's burning up. His muscles tense as I slowly run my fingers over his shoulder.*

*He moves his right hand down my body to burrow under my prom dress, and a second later, he stands up, leaving me alone and wanting so much more. I stare up at him in confusion, wondering if he finally figured out he'd rather be at that party tonight than here alone with me.*

*"As nice as these clothes are, they have to go."*

*I smile at his complete lack of subtlety as I watch him unbutton his white dress shirt and shrug out of it. His body is perfect beneath it. Tanned and muscular, he looks like my own personal Adonis meant only for me.*

*At least I like to fantasize that's the truth.*

*I've never been able to see Ronan without a shirt and not stare like some horny schoolgirl. He's simply the most perfect thing I've ever seen. All that working out for baseball has benefits long after he leaves the field.*

*And I get to enjoy every bit of them.*

*He doesn't get to his pants before he turns his attention to* my dress. In no time at all, he pulls me up off the bed and pushes my spaghetti straps off my shoulders. Then it's just a matter of unzipping the back of my gown. Seconds later, I'm sitting in front of him in just my underwear since I couldn't wear a bra with the straps.

"It's no fair that I'm practically naked and you still have pants on," I say with a giggle before reaching out to remedy that.

He lifts his hands away from his pants so I can do what I want, and after unbuttoning and unzipping them, I push them down his legs, leaving only black boxer briefs covering him.

Not that they're concealing much. He's rock hard, and the thin fabric barely hides that fact.

I palm his cock and watch as his eyes roll back. I love seeing him like this. He's so raw and open with how my touch makes him feel.

Ronan leans over me and stares into my eyes like he's looking into my soul. "I've been waiting all week to be with you. Tonight's been perfect. Hasn't it?"

Nodding, I wriggle my hips to help him when he slides my panties down my legs and tosses them on the other bed with his jacket and bow tie. "It has."

I don't say what else I'm thinking. That it's because of him that this night has been so wonderful. From the blush rose wrist corsage he bought me to how he danced every dance with me to how he fed me my dessert of those adorable cupcakes in our school colors of royal blue and gold, he's made my senior prom one I'll never forget.

Naked on the bed, I try not to feel self-conscious as he stands watching me while he pushes his underwear down his legs. So often, I wish I had bigger breasts or longer legs like the popular girls at school all seem to have. I don't want to feel that way because if I let them, my insecurities will ruin my time with Ronan, and that's the last thing I want to do.

He leans over me again and sets his hands on either side of my head before slowly lowering his body to cover mine. He's so much bigger than I am, but I'm not worried. He always makes sure not to crush me.

"You got quiet there. Everything okay?" he asks in a low voice tinged with need.

I know he's afraid something's wrong because I seem to be somewhere else at the moment, so I quickly work to make sure he knows there's nowhere else in the world I'd rather be right now. "Everything is perfect, especially you."

He smiles and then lowers his mouth to mine in a kiss that takes my breath away. I run my hands down his back and feel the corded muscles as he holds himself back from laying all his weight on me. He's strength and power all in one, but I know he'll protect me.

With his knee, he gently nudges my thighs open, and there's a sudden chill that rushes over me. I shiver involuntarily, and he lifts his head to look down at me.

"Are you okay?" he asks with such sweet concern in his voice.

I nod, feeling silly even though I couldn't help myself from being cold. "I'm fine. Just got a little chilly for a second."

"Then I better warm you up," he says with a smile.

The combination of how wonderful he is and how sexy he looks on top of me makes my belly feel like it's molten lava. He slowly tilts his hips forward, and I feel him press his cock between my legs.

I set my hands on his waist and open my legs as wide as they can go. Ronan gently pushes into me, filling me so completely it takes my breath away. I've heard some of the girls in school talk about how fast or hard their boyfriends are during sex, but he's too big to go fast or hard with me.

Fully inside me, he falls still, except for kissing me. His hands once more cradle my face, and it's like he's everywhere all at once. The sensation is overwhelming, but I love it like I love him.

Our lovemaking is slow and probably wouldn't be something any of those girls in school would like, but I adore how gentle he is with me. I sometimes think about surprising him with something seductive, which would be completely out of my nature and would probably thrill him, but the best I've been able to do so far is get on top. He's just too big for anything else.

"Are you sure you're okay?" he asks, probably sensing I'm a million miles away.

Well, not that far, but I'm definitely not focusing on us like I should at the moment.

"I'm fine. Actually, I was just thinking of how I know you like me on top sometimes."

His eyes get a twinkle to them now, and he grins in that way that's so sexy to me. "If you want to change places, I'm all in."

Giggling, I say, "I think you're all in anyway."

Ronan's eyes grow wide with surprise. "My Kate, making a sex joke. This is why you're the perfect girlfriend."

Before I can respond, he flips us over so he's on his back and I'm on top. Still inside me, he inches his hips up off the bed, sending waves of need rushing through me.

My legs are spread so wide as I sit on top of him that the muscles in my thighs ache, but what's a little pain when the man of my dreams is looking up at me and waiting for me to *begin riding him? I may not be as experienced as other girls, but I've read enough to know what I should do.*

*I ease myself up just a little and then slowly sit back down on him. He smiles and sets his hands on my hips, his thing to control the pace. I don't fight him, and when he wants to go a little faster, I take a deep breath in and go with the flow.*

*Ronan knows my body as well as I do, so he slides his right hand down in front of me to stroke my clit. That's all it takes for me to find my groove, and a moment later, I'm riding him with all I have.*

*Like always, it doesn't take me very long before every inch of my body is practically screaming in ecstasy. I come hard and nearly collapse, but he's not there yet.*

*I lean forward and kiss him, and that's all it takes for him to kick things into overdrive. He's careful not to go too fast, but he picks up the pace just as my orgasm begins to taper off, making me come a second time.*

*"Oh… God…" I practically sob into his mouth as my thighs quiver from my release.*

*A few moments later, I feel him come. He holds me tightly to him, his face buried in my neck as his release rolls over him.*

*"God, you feel so good, Kate. Don't stop moving."*

*I do as he commands, happy to give him what he wants. He always makes me happy, so it's the least I can do for him.*

*When we finally fall still, I lift my upper body and look down to see him staring up at me. His dark eyes look glassy now, but I know that's how he always looks after we have sex.*

*"I love you, Ronan. Thank you."*

*He narrows his eyes and asks, "For what?"*

*"For everything. For tonight. For who you always are with me. For giving me the perfect senior prom."*

*Ronan pulls me down to him and kisses me long and deep. "You make me so happy, Kate. I'm the luckiest guy in the world, so why wouldn't I try to make this night perfect? You deserve it."*

*We lay there in each other's arms until I break the silence. "I didn't want to go to Amanda Isaacson's party because when we first started going out, she said she'd wanted you for her own for a while."*

*I don't like to hide anything from Ronan, but I've kept that to myself for nearly a year. Now that it's out in the open, I feel better. But I don't know if it was a mistake to tell him that.*

*He leans back away from me and stares at me for a long moment. "I didn't want to go to her party because I only wanted to be with you. I've never been interested in her, even though I know she's been into me for a while. I only want you, Kate."*

*I smile and let out a heavy sigh of relief. Ronan really is the most incredible guy in the world.*

As I turn off the road onto the long driveway to the King estate, I smile as I think about how utterly happy I was that night. It really was the perfect prom, and that was all because I was with the only person I've ever truly loved.

Is there any chance at all we can ever get back to who we were then?

# CHAPTER THIRTEEN

ate

NOBODY'S AROUND THIS TIME WHEN I DRIVE UP TO the King house. I don't see Ava's car either. Did I misunderstand when she said to come over around lunchtime?

I check my watch and see it's quarter after twelve. Maybe she's running errands and will be back soon.

For a moment or two, I hesitate to go into the house because the person I'm supposed to be coming to see isn't here. I'd love to see Ronan, but I don't want to be too obvious about it. Ava told me that he's started to come out of his room in the past day or so, but she's worried something might upset him, and he'll go back to holing up in there.

I'd hate to set his progress back any, so I hang out around the kitchen door to wait for her. It's a gorgeous summer day like we get in the northeast. Not very humid with a ton of sunshine, it reminds me of every great summer day I enjoyed growing up.

"You don't have to wait outside, if you don't want. You can go in."

I instantly recognize that voice as Ronan's, and turn around to see him walking from the side of the house. He's shaved and looks like the man I used to know instead of that angry, scraggly person from the other day.

"Oh, hi. I didn't want to intrude. Ava said to come over around lunchtime, but I guess I'm early," I say as I study his face, happy to see the Ronan I knew and loved.

He stops in front of me, and I watch as he slowly hides his right arm behind him. "She and Sabrina took Matty shopping, I think. I'm sure they'll be back soon."

I wait for him to ask me to come in the house or ask me if I want to do something, but that's just wishful thinking because he makes no move toward involving me in his day before walking toward the door. I hate that I don't know what to say to make him stay, but I've never been very good with that kind of thing. We introverts prefer to have people bring us along with them instead of inviting ourselves.

Disappointed, I stand there as he walks inside the house. There was a time that whenever Ronan and I were in each other's presence, we had a ton of things to talk about and loved being near one another. I had hoped that maybe seeing me again would make him remember those days.

After I check my phone and find I don't have any

messages from Ava, I reconsider coming here. I like Ava and enjoy getting to know her, but I can't deny seeing Ronan is my true reason for visiting. If he's not going to even want to spend a few minutes with me, should I just give up?

Just as I think that, my phone vibrates with a call from Jessie, so I answer it, knowing I sound like someone just ran over my dog. It takes her exactly a nanosecond to recognize I'm unhappy.

"What happened?"

"Nothing," I answer honestly.

"Then why do you sound so awful? Where are you?" she asks in that demanding tone of hers.

I look around the beautiful grounds of the King estate and say, "I'm here visiting Ava. She's not back yet, so I'm waiting for her. It's a nice day, so I don't mind staying outside and catching a few rays."

My lame attempt at being chipper falls flat, but that's not surprising. I wouldn't have believed me either.

"What kind of people make a woman stay outside while she waits for someone?"

Taking a deep breath in, I exhale and try to explain. "They aren't making me wait outside. I could knock on the door, and I'm sure they'd let me in. I just don't want to."

"Why?" Jessie asks, sounding utterly confused.

Yeah, I'm not sure why I'm acting like this either.

"I don't know. Maybe I can't handle it."

"Handle what? What the hell is going on there, Kate?"

Sure I don't want anyone to hear me when I

explain things to her, I start walking toward my car and say, "I saw Ronan. He barely said ten words to me and then went inside. It's clear he doesn't want to see me. So I decided to stay outside. See? Nothing major."

"It sounds ridiculous. Are you sure he didn't have a head injury from that accident he had?"

Her defense of me makes me laugh. "A man doesn't have to suffer from a head injury to make it logical he doesn't want to talk to me. I'm not that irresistible."

"Awww, don't say that," Jessie says in a sad voice that makes me wince.

"It's not that big a deal. I just hoped when he saw me that he'd want to hang out. No biggie. I'll just visit with Ava today, and then I'll figure out if I want to keep coming around. I'm sure she'll understand. It's not like we're that close."

"Well, I met this guy yesterday who I think you'd love. He's tall, dark hair, and yummy!" she says in a singsong voice. "What do you say I tell him about you and we get together with him this week?"

As an introvert, this is how I meet most of the people in my life. I'm okay with that. It's just that I had such high hopes about Ronan that are now pretty much dashed to pieces that I don't think I can give anyone else a chance. Not yet, anyway.

"I don't know, Jess. I'm probably not going to be a lot of fun, so maybe not. Did you like him? Maybe you could go out with him. It sounds like you're into what he's got going on."

But she's not having any of my excuses.

"First of all, you're always fun, so stop talking about yourself that way. Second of all, you need to get out there so you can meet the guy for you. So this Ronan guy isn't working out? So what? He's one fish, Kate. Grab your pole and get back out there because there are lots of fish in the sea."

She doesn't bother addressing my suggestion that she go out with him, which tells me he's a decent guy. Not that Jessie doesn't deserve a nice guy, but she's never attracted to them. If she likes a man, he's no good. She knows that as well as I do, but somehow, it doesn't bother her.

"I'm not a fisherman. Or fisherwoman. Whatever the word is, I don't fish."

Jessie sighs in my ear, telling me she's come to the end of her patience with me on this issue. "Fine. It's okay. If he's the one, he'll come back. Just tell me you aren't going to hang around waiting for this guy who clearly can't see greatness right in front of him."

My friend can be a lot to deal with, but she's as loyal as they come and my biggest cheerleader. I appreciate that, even as I can't tell her the truth that I want to try a few more times before giving up on Ronan.

"Thank you for saying I'm great, but I don't think that's the problem. I think it's that he just doesn't care about me like that anymore. It's been a long time. I guess he's just moved on."

My heart hurts just from saying those words.

I hear footsteps on the pavement behind me, so I turn around and see the man himself walking toward where I'm standing at my car. Quickly, I say to Jessie, "Hey, let me call you back."

Stuffing my phone into my purse, I spin around to

face him and smile. "I hope you're okay with me waiting for Ava out here."

It's a ridiculous statement, but that's all my brain could think of on the fly. Of course, he's okay with me standing outside here. What the hell does he care where I wait?

Suddenly, it's like I'm back in high school and don't know how to act, except now Ronan's not taking the lead to make me want him. Now it's the other way around, and I doubt I'm doing anything to make him realize he should want to be with me again.

He stares at me for a long moment, his dark eyes trained on mine like he can see straight into my soul, before giving me a little smile. "I never moved on, Kate."

I look at him in stunned amazement. He heard what I said, and he just told me he still cares about me like he used to? I can't believe my ears! What do I say now?

As all those thoughts run through my head, Ava pulls up the driveway and parks the car. I desperately try to think of something to say so he knows I still care too, but before I can utter another word, she and Sabrina walk up to us with the baby.

"I hope you weren't waiting long. Come in and once I get the baby settled, we can have some lunch."

Hoping that will involve Ronan, I turn to look at him, but Sabrina stops him from saying anything when she tells him, "Hey, I had an idea for something you can do. Come in and I'll tell you all about it."

He doesn't seem terribly eager to follow her, but he does, only looking back once before walking inside the house. Damn! Who is this Sabrina person, and why did she just do the female version of cock blocking me?

Discouraged and disappointed for the second time since I got here, I force a smile for Ava and say, "Sounds great! How was shopping?"

She begins describing in minute detail how Matty not only spit up on one of the salespeople who asked to hold him but also pooped so stinky that she was embarrassed, and they had to leave the store immediately. I try to pay attention, although hearing about baby poop isn't top on my list of topics, but all I can think is Ronan just told me he's never moved on from me.

From us.

Maybe there is a chance after all.

Once she gets the baby down for a much-needed nap, Ava sits down with me at the kitchen table. We aren't there for more than a few seconds before she says, "It's so gorgeous out today. Would you like to sit outside? It'll give me a chance to get a little sun, and I want to get Theo some fresh air. I think it'll help him sleep better. At least I hope so."

"Okay. Lead the way!"

After informing Eleanor of our plans, she and I walk outside with our glasses of iced tea to sit out on the patio in the backyard. That word makes it sound like anyone else's yard behind their house, but at the King estate, the backyard goes for hundreds of yards beyond the patio and pool area.

"Ronan used to tell me about how when he and his brothers were young they'd play outside all day," I say as she gets Theo into his baby swing that's attached to a tree near the corner of the patio.

"They did, and I was always tagging along, once I got big enough."

"That's right. You lived in the house down the road on the estate. I bet you have stories from when those boys were kids," I joke.

She sits down looking worn out, and it's not even one o'clock in the afternoon. Taking a sip of iced tea, she sighs. "Mostly Theo. He was my best friend, so we did everything together. I rarely played with Matthias when we were kids since he never seemed interested in hanging out with us, but the other brothers were always around."

We settle into an awkward silence after her mention of Theo. I wonder if I should say how sorry I am that he passed. I came over after the funeral, but I never spoke to Ava that day since I she wasn't around. I heard she didn't handle it well, so maybe I shouldn't.

Thankfully, she interrupts my thoughts with something else entirely.

"Did you see Ronan shaved? I wasn't feeling too good about him getting his hands on a razor, but Sabrina told me he wanted to clean himself up yesterday but couldn't do it, so she helped. I think he looks a million times better without that mess he had on his face, don't you?"

I smile and nod, saying he looks much better, but all I can think of is Sabrina shaving Ronan's face. I didn't realize they were that close. Is that why he went with her as soon as she mentioned wanting to tell him something?

Jealousy fills me as Ava talks about being relieved that he may have turned the corner from the months of being so unhappy since his accident. All I can think of is this Sabrina person is the reason he's coming around, not me. I should be happy for him, but all I feel is ugly envy.

"So, Matthias told me last night he thought you'd become a schoolteacher. Is that true? What grade do you teach?" Ava asks, tearing me from my misery of thinking I've lost my chance with Ronan because of Sabrina.

"I did. I start teaching third grade at the Rosemont School in midtown this fall. I was working part-time for the past few years, but then I got hired there. That's why I took the opportunity to go on a trip to Europe with my friend this year. I'd always wanted to, so we figured this might be my last chance before I start my job."

Ava nods and says, "Not a fan of Europe in the summer? I mean, teachers usually get the summers off."

As I watch Theo bounce in his seat to let his mother know he needs another push, I say, "To be honest, I'm not a fan of summer anywhere but around here. Everywhere else is too hot and humid. My father swears we have the nicest summer weather in the world right here in New York."

She gets up to give the swing a little push and sits back down again. "I think he's right. My brother lives in Florida, and I swear I don't know how he does it. Hurricanes and rain every day? No thanks. I'll take what we have over that any day."

I start to mention about how my parents are thinking about moving to Florida if they ever finally retire when Sabrina walks out of the house wearing a teeny-tiny black bikini and a beach towel slung over her left shoulder. All I can think is she looks fantastic and has an incredible body.

"Are you going in for a dip?" Ava asks, seemingly perfectly fine with her babysitter enjoying a swim.

"Yeah, it's nice out, so I figured I'd get a swim in while Matty is sleeping."

Ava looks over at me with an embarrassed expression. "I should have told you to bring your bathing suit so you could swim too. Matthias occasionally swims and Ronan never does, so it's just Sabrina and me and the babies, but they don't really swim. They just sort of splash around."

I wave off her suggestion, still fixated on Sabrina who at the moment is parading around the pool deck like some model at a trade show. I know it shouldn't bother me, but does she have to look so damn good? Meanwhile, I'm sitting here in my pink sundress looking like I just auditioned for some lame off-off-Broadway production of Mary Poppins.

"I have a great idea!" Ava says as she jumps up from her chair, nearly knocking over our glasses of iced tea. "I've got a few bathing suits, and I bet you'd fit in one. Let me go see if I can find them so we can go swimming too! I'll be right back. Just give Theo a little push if he stops swinging or starts crying."

Before I can stop her, she runs off, leaving me staring at Sabrina as she makes her way toward where

I'm sitting. With a smile, she gives Theo a tiny push before turning to talk to me.

"So you knew Ronan back in the day?" she says, instantly annoying me.

Back in the day? I'm twenty-four. How back in the day could it have been when we dated between the ages of seventeen and twenty?

I nervously chuckle and answer, "He and I dated, so yes."

She looks me up and down and smiles. "Yeah, I can see that. You look very much like the type of girl he would have gone for in high school."

Unsure how to take that but having a sneaking suspicion what she said wasn't a compliment, I smile and wonder if holding her under the water would be rude of me as Ava's guest. Probably. Then she'd have to find another person to help her out with the babies, and I'd hate to do that to her.

"How long have you been working for Matthias and Ava?" I ask, curious that she should feel so comfortable since I think she's only been living here for a couple weeks, at most.

She takes a gulp of Ava's drink and answers, "Oh, just a week. They've made me feel right at home, though."

"I can see that."

I want to say other things, but none of them seem appropriate. Sabrina gives Theo a kiss on the nose and then turns back to face me.

"It's been great. If they'll have me, I'd love to stay here forever. Between Ava, Matthias, and Ronan, I've felt so welcome."

In my mind, I mentally correct her grammar. Among, not between, since she listed more than two people.

With a smile, I nod, not wanting to continue this conversation. Between my failure to get to talk to Ronan earlier because of her and now my jealousy as I sit here staring at her great body in that bikini, I'm not really in the mood for a chat with Sabrina.

"Yeah, I plan on sticking around. The King family is definitely the best place I could land, and I want to keep that going for as long as possible."

Something in the way she says that rubs me the wrong way. Does she mean as the nanny for Theo and Matty or something else entirely that has more to do with Ronan?

I watch her walk away back toward the pool as I try to dissuade myself from believing the worst about her. So what if she's young and gorgeous? That's not a crime. And so what if she's become friends with the man I still care for? Ronan can use all the friends he can get now after going through such a terrible trauma. Ava seems to love her, and she does help with the kids, so it works for everyone.

A few minutes later, Ava returns with two bathing suits, and since I won't be able to get out of swimming, it seems, I take the purple and blue one-piece, leaving her with the white one-piece.

"We'll be right back," she calls to Sabrina standing on the pool deck.

I follow her into the house, but on my way, I see Ronan watching out the window.

And he's not looking at me or Ava.

## CHAPTER FOURTEEN

onan

Now would be my chance to talk to Kate. Ava's convinced her stay and take a swim with her and Sabrina, so it's perfect.

Except I don't swim. Not anymore.

I can't help but think it's strange that Sabrina didn't mention she was going to go swimming when she pulled me aside to talk to me. She couldn't wait to tell me about some dream she had about me and then give me a rundown of everything she planned to do today, but she never said a thing about spending time in the pool this afternoon.

Then again, what does it matter? What she does with her days has nothing to do with me.

"See anything interesting out there?" Matthias asks behind me.

I slowly turn around to see him smiling. I'm not sure what he's thinking, but he's way off base.

"No. Why?"

He shrugs as if he meant nothing by his question, but I know what he and his wife are up to. They think having Kate here will make me happy. They aren't wrong, but it's not as simple as they think it is. It's not like I'm the same old Ronan I used to be. That guy would have no problem chatting her up and asking her out on a date. I know Kate as well as I know myself, so old me would be sure to say exactly the right thing.

This version of me isn't that guy.

"You going swimming? I'd love to, but I have a meeting in fifteen minutes I can't avoid."

My brother has no idea how much I wish I could just throw on swimming trunks and dive into the pool. It's not that easy, though.

"I don't think so," I say as I turn back toward the window and see Kate walk onto the pool deck.

"Why not? It's hot out, and I'm sure you're sick of sitting in the house doing nothing. Aren't you?"

Now I shrug, not because I actually like hiding out here like some kind of freak who can't go out in public, but because no matter what I say to explain what I'm feeling, he won't understand. I'm not like him. I never was, but now it's different.

I'm not like anyone else either.

"You should," he says, continuing to push like he always has. "You and Ava get along, and I know you like Kate. You seem to have formed some kind of friendship with Sabrina too, so why not join them?"

Spinning around, I snap, "Because I don't want to!

Stop bothering me about this. I'm not like you. I'm fine with being alone inside the house here."

Matthias steps back in surprise at my outburst but doesn't stop his pushing. "I'm just trying to help, Ronan. I don't want to see you wither away here when you have your whole life ahead of you."

I lift my right arm up in front of him. "My whole fucking life? I have nothing ahead of me. Everything there was for me to look forward to is gone. So don't give me your bullshit about having my whole life ahead of me."

As usual, pity fills his eyes, something I hate more than anything else. I can handle anything but pity.

But then my oldest brother surprises me with a little anger of his own.

Taking a step toward me, he stops just inches away. "Nobody's trying to make you do anything. We all just want to help you. You do have your whole life ahead of you, whether you want to believe it or not. Ava and I wanted you to stay here with us because we were afraid you might try to hurt yourself again if you stayed in your apartment. We're not asking for a medal or anything, but could you try to remember we fucking care?"

He doesn't give me a chance to reply, even though I'm not sure what I'd say, and spins on his heel to march toward the hallway on his way to his office for that meeting. I get I'm not exactly the best houseguest, but what the fuck? He acts like I want to be stuck inside here watching the only woman I ever loved outside having fun when all I wish I could do is talk to her.

I take one last look at Kate as she dangles her feet in the shallow end of the pool. She always was timid about swimming. Any time she and I would spend the day at the pool here when we were together, it would take her forever to finally get her whole body in the water.

She's like that with everything, though. Cautious to extremes, she prefers to stand on the sidelines as other people blaze a trail ahead of her. She hates that she's like that too, and I can see by her tiny frown that hasn't changed, but I never had a problem with her being so timid. I was brash enough for both of us.

*I hold Kate's hand and feel it getting sweatier by the second. She has no reason to be nervous. I'd never let anything hurt her.*

*"Ronan, please. It's okay. We don't have to do this. We can just go back to the lodge. I actually could really use a hot chocolate right about now," she says, her teeth chattering with every syllable.*

*Looking around at the top of the slope, I watch as everyone passes us and eagerly attacks the hill. "You have to get down to the lodge anyway, so why not try to enjoy yourself?" I ask with a smile.*

*Her blue eyes grow big, and for the fifth time, she looks down the hill with nothing but pure terror in them. Shaking her head, she tightens her hold on my hand.*

*"I can't. I told you I didn't know how to ski. Why couldn't you just let me be my non-skiing self?"*

*I hear tears in her voice, so I lean over and kiss her softly. "It's okay. I promise you're going to have a good time. Just stick with me, and you'll be fine."*

*"No, I'll be dead."*

*"You won't be dead. So you fall? No big deal. I promise if I see you fall, I'll fall too. Then the two of us can slide down the hill on our asses. Come on. Take a deep breath, tell yourself you're going to be fine, and stay with me, okay?"*

*Once again she turns to look at the hill we need to ski down and shakes her head. "What if I break my leg? Are you going to take care of me day and night if I can't walk? See, that's what I'm afraid of. I'll break my leg, and then I'll be stuck at home until spring comes."*

*I love every part of her, including her wild imagination. "I promise that if you break your leg, which you won't, but if you do, I'll wait on you hand and foot the entire time you can't walk."*

*Kate levels her suspicious gaze on me. "You know, if I get hurt, we won't have sex for God only knows how long. Ever think of that?"*

*I'm an eighteen-year-old guy. All I think of is sex. I can barely be near Kate without wanting to get her alone.*

*"You have no idea what even being around you makes me want to do, so yes, I think of sex with you. You're not going to get hurt."*

*She still isn't convinced, and we're never going to get down this hill at this rate. Time for me to break out the big guns.*

*I set my hands on her shoulders and stare into her eyes. "Do you trust me?"*

*"Of course, I do," she answers with an eyeroll.*

*"No, I mean really trust me. Like you believe in your heart I'd never let anything hurt you level of trust."*

*"Ronan, I do trust you. I would never have come on this skiing trip if I didn't."*

*"Then I'm going to let go of you, and you're going to ski*

down this hill. It's just a medium size hill. You made it down the baby slope fine. You can do this."

That gets me a pretty pout I secretly love. "The baby slope was for babies, Ronan. This is for people who know how to ski, which isn't me."

We've been standing here for ten minutes already. If we keep talking about skiing instead of actually skiing, she'll never conquer her fears.

The time has come for us to get down this hill.

I slip my gloves back on and set my poles in the snow. "We need to get to that lodge for some hot chocolate. Get ready."

She tries to fight me even more, but as soon as she gets her gloves on, I know we can go. I give her a tiny push, and she screams like I just set her on fire.

"Ronan! Nooooooo!"

There's no turning back now, so I follow her, catching up pretty quickly. Side-by-side, we ski down the mountain slower than I've ever moved on skis in my life. She doesn't fall, surprisingly, and even though she looks completely petrified every time I look over at her, she makes it down like a champ.

We reach the bottom, and now that we've conquered what I imagine will be the only adult hill we'll tackle today, I stop next to her and give her a kiss. "You did great! You didn't fall once, and you made it down in one piece. You want to go again?"

Instantly, I see by the look of horror on her face that I'm pushing my luck, so I smile and say, "Then hot chocolate it is."

"If you want to go again or hang out with your brothers, I'll be fine. I just can't do this."

I kiss her again. "You already did, but it's okay. I don't want to be with them today. I'm fine curling up with you and some hot chocolate in the hotel room."

*She gives me a knowing look and starts removing her skis. "You just want to get to the room to have sex. I'll be lucky if I get a sip of hot chocolate before you make a move. I know you, Ronan King."*

*There's no doubt if I'm not skiing that I'd like to be in bed with her. I'm a red-blooded American male with the only girl I want in the entire world.*

*"I promise you can drink a whole hot chocolate before I make any moves. Deal?"*

*Kate looks at me with her typical sweetness and kisses me, her cold nose touching mine. "Deal."*

I lie back on my bed as the memory of our one and only ski trip together slowly fades away. We did get hot chocolate, but Theo sidetracked us with whatever girl he was with that weekend so we didn't get back to our hotel room for a couple hours.

And just as Kate suspected, I couldn't wait to be with her as soon as we were alone.

More than once, Kellen and Marius asked me why I didn't want to find girls who were more like me. They thought I needed someone more adventurous who would be a good time, but I told them the same thing every time they said that.

I don't need someone like me. All I need is Kate.

Never once did I regret that choice. When I was with her, I felt like I was in the only place in the world I belonged. She accepted me for who I was, and I loved her for who she was.

When I was with Kate, I was home in every sense of the word.

Regret fills me for what I did to ruin what we had. Why did I go with that girl who meant nothing to me when I had the one for me already? Every time I've asked myself that question, I've lied and told myself I was lonely and it wasn't a big deal. So I went with someone else one time? We could have gotten past that if she just realized I'd never do it again.

That answer worked for a long time, but now it rings hollow. It was wrong to think cheating on her wasn't important. She trusted me, and I blew it. I took that trust and threw it away for one lousy night with someone who was available and meant nothing to me.

God, I was stupid.

When I had my whole life to look forward to, as Matthias likes to say, I could lie to myself and think I didn't miss Kate and all we had together. She went on with her life, and I went on with mine.

Even though I never really moved on.

But now that I have nothing to look forward to, I understand. I had everything once. I had someone who loved me not for what I could do or how much money I had but for me.

And I threw it all away for nothing.

# CHAPTER FIFTEEN

ate

AFTER AN HOUR OF SWIMMING, I CLIMB OUT OF THE pool and head for the table to get a drink and dry off while Ava and Sabrina play with Theo. Out of the corner of my eye, I see the living room door open, but it's Matthias, not Ronan.

I check my cell and see Jessie sent me a message after we got off the phone earlier. She wants to go out tonight, but her client is running late, so she isn't sure she'll be able to get off in time for us to keep our plans for dinner.

What a disappointment this day has been. First, Ronan barely talks to me and disappears while we're all outside having a good time, and now my plans for the night are in jeopardy. Just wonderful.

"Where did you come from?" a deep voice asks.

I look up expecting to see Matthias since he was just walking out of the house, but to my surprise, it's Marius, Ronan's other older brother. I stare at him for a long moment, shocked I've never noticed that he and Matthias could pass for twins they look so similar.

"Katie Abbott as I live and breathe. You're a blast from the past."

The only person in the entire world who has ever called me Katie, Marius King has never liked me. At least that's the way it seemed when I was dating his brother. If he wasn't scowling and surly toward me, he said nothing and seemed to be silently judging me. No matter how many times I asked Ronan why this brother didn't like me, he'd never admit Marius hated me, though.

I give him a tepid smile, unsure what to say since we've never been close. "Hi, Marius. I didn't realize you were here too."

He grins and strips his black t-shirt off to reveal a stunning muscular body. This King has always been more artistic than athletic, so I didn't expect to see him look that good under his clothes.

"I came to see my brothers, but I had no idea you were around again. Are you and Ronan back together?"

His question sounds innocent enough, but I struggle to answer it. I've never considered him to be an advocate for Ronan and me together, so I don't think letting him in on my desire to get back with his brother is a good idea.

So I go with a vague statement that says nothing about what he asked me.

"Ava invited me to come visit her."

That only makes him more curious, and he says, "I didn't know you two knew each other. Who's the new girl?"

I follow his gaze to Sabrina walking along the edge of the pool to pick up Theo's orange pool noodle. "The babysitter. Her name is Sabrina. That's about all I know of her."

That's not true. I suspect she has her sights set on the same man I do. I'm not going to tell Marius that, though.

"Interesting. So where is that youngest brother of mine? Still avoiding the sun like a vampire?" he asks before waving to Ava and calling out, "He's a natural. Just like the brother he's named for!"

From the pool, she yells, "Marius! I didn't know you were coming. Are you here for long?"

He stands up and walks over to the edge of the water. "As long as you'll have me. I'm on a break from work."

Giggling, she splashes him and says, "You need a break from taking pictures of beautiful women on gorgeous beaches? In my next life, I want to come back as you, Marius King."

I watch as Sabrina can't take her eyes off this King brother. Good. Keep eyeballing him, and stay away from Ronan.

Marius spreads his arms out and laughs. "It's not bad work, if you can get it. Where's the new little guy?"

"We were just going to get him up from his nap. Marius, this is Sabrina. She's living here now and helping me," Ava says as she hands Theo up to the babysitter.

Or maybe I should be calling her the nanny. Whatever she is, she's entirely too hot in that black bikini, and I have a feeling Marius is thinking the same thing.

But as soon as Ava explains who she is, I notice a change in his body language. Suddenly, he doesn't seem as interested and walks back to join me at the table.

"So, Katie, what's new?" he asks before taking a drink of his sister-in-law's iced tea.

"Not much. Just returned from a trip to Europe last week. Oh, I start my new job teaching at Rosemont School in the city starting this August."

My answer seems to be funny to him because he gives me a big grin. "Let me guess. Kindergarten. I can't think of a more perfect person for that job than you."

Now I know he's making fun of me. He never did like me, so I guess it's good to see nothing's changed. If only the same could be said for his younger brother.

"Actually, it's third grade," I say as I stand up to leave.

I don't give him a chance to comment on my correction of his mistake and take my towel with me to get changed back into the clothes I wore here today. This visit has been unsuccessful on so many levels, so maybe it's time for me to go home.

"Kate, are you going inside? Can you tell Matthias I'd like to see him?" Ava calls after me.

"Sure."

Just as I'm walking into the living room, I look back and see Sabrina strike up a conversation with Marius. I can't think of a more perfect couple. He's annoying, and she's irritating.

A match made in heaven.

Disgusted, although I'm not sure why, I take a detour upstairs and knock on Ronan's door. I should just leave and never come back here, but I guess I need to find out a few things before I give up.

He opens the door and seems confused to see me. How nice. One brother can't think of anything but busting my ass about being a nice person, and another can't figure out why I'd be standing in front of him at all.

I open my mouth to speak, but I can't help but notice he moves his right arm behind him again. I hate that he thinks he needs to do that in front of me.

"Why does your brother hate me?" I ask, figuring I'll just dive in head first and not bother with manners. Not exactly my style, but when I get flustered, all the nice in me goes out the window.

"Matthias? I don't think he hates you. In fact, if you're not Ava, Theo, or Matty, he barely knows anyone else is alive." He stops and then in a low voice adds, "Well, except for me lately."

"No, not Matthias. Marius. He's never liked me, and today just proved it. What is his problem with me, Ronan? Tell me before I never come to this house again."

When I say that, he winces, like just hearing I'm going away forever hurts him. "Marius is here?"

"Please answer the question. I'd like to know."

Ronan shrugs and shakes his head. "I don't know, Kate. He used to tease me about how nice you were, but I think that was probably more against me than you."

"Fine. I guess I'll have to settle for that answer."

I turn to leave, but he says, "He won't be here forever. Maybe you can come back when he's gone."

Without turning around, I throw my hands up in the air, nearly tossing the towel down the steps. "Why bother? The only person who seems to genuinely want me here is Ava."

He doesn't say anything more, so I hurry downstairs to the guest bathroom where my clothes are hanging on the back of the door. I quickly get dressed, but then I remember I forgot to tell Matthias that Ava wants to see him. Sorry I got sidetracked by Marius and his bullshit, I rush down the hall and knock on the office door.

The oldest King looks up from some papers on his desk and gives me an awkward smile. "Oh, hi, Kate. What's up?"

As he stands to come toward me, I answer, "Ava wanted me to tell you she wants to see you. She's outside with Marius, Sabrina, and Theo. I have to go."

"Wait," he says before catching up to me not two steps down the hallway.

I turn around and see a far more serious expression staring back at me. Maybe this brother hates me too.

He lowers his voice and says, "I'd like to talk to you. Can you come into my office? I'd prefer to have some privacy for this conversation."

Since I don't believe I've spoken more than ten

words on any occasion to this King, I'm intrigued and a little uncomfortable, but I nod and walk back to his office. When he closes the door, I'm really feeling strange. What could he possibly want to speak to me about?

Pointing at the black leather couch just inside the door, he asks, "Would you like to sit down?"

"No, I'm okay. Is something wrong?"

His expression is downright somber, so I naturally assume either I've done something to offend him or there's some other problem that relates to me. He probably wants to say that it would be better if I didn't come over anymore. Ronan probably told him to say that.

He finally smiles again and walks over to his desk to lean against it. Dressed in gray suit pants, a blue dress shirt, and a dark gray tie, he looks every bit the CEO of a company. "No, nothing's wrong. I was just wondering if you're coming over here to visit with my wife or to see Ronan."

I look down toward the hardwood floor that's so polished I can almost see myself in it. Embarrassed because my true intentions must have been more obvious than I thought, I try to find a polite way to explain my behavior.

Finally, I look up and meet his gaze. "It's not that I don't like hanging out with Ava. We have a nice time talking, and those babies are just the cutest things ever. I never meant to make it seem like I was using her to get to see Ronan. I was just hoping that maybe he and I could…"

I can't find the words to explain that part of my

thinking, so I don't bother. Better for me to just let things drift off to silence than to dig the hole deeper.

He surprises me by not appearing angry, though. "It's okay. I know she likes talking to you, but she was hoping that by having you over that maybe you and Ronan would start talking again. My wife has a good heart and good intentions, but she was trying to play cupid. I hope you understand."

I'm relieved he isn't upset by my confession, but nothing he says makes me any happier. "It's no use, I'm sorry to say. He barely acknowledges I'm here. If she wants to play cupid, I think I'd suggest the nanny instead of me. Ronan at least talks to her."

"Sabrina? No, he doesn't care about her. She helped him clean himself up, but I think he did that because he wanted to look good for you."

What an emotional rollercoaster today has been. First, Ronan basically blows me off and chooses to chat up Sabrina, and then Marius shows up and picks up on his mocking me where he left off when I was nineteen.

And now it seems like Matthias is telling me that Ronan actually wants to spend time with me.

"Maybe I'm not the person he needs now. Marius was just teasing me about being so nice that, of course, I teach elementary school. Maybe nice isn't what Ronan wants."

Matthias doesn't say anything for a long time. Finally, he sighs and says, "I'm breaking some code we brothers have by doing this, I think, but here goes. Ronan is having a hard time. He isn't accepting his life the way the doctors and those of us who care about him had hoped he would by now. Nobody is saying we want you to fix him, but I know he's liked seeing you these last couple times you were here. As for Marius, ignore him. He's a ball buster from way back. He's probably giving Ronan a hard time as we speak. Nobody escapes his teasing. It's just who he is."

For a moment, it seems like Matthias is overcome by emotion. He looks down toward his black dress shoes and clears his throat before lifting his head to meet my gaze again.

"I don't know what might happen between you and Ronan. I don't think he has any interest in Sabrina, but you might know better than I do. Ava tells me I don't read women the way she does, so it's possible I'm not seeing things right."

My heart sinks at the thought that Ronan actually does like the nanny. But why wouldn't he? She gorgeous with a great body, especially in that bikini. Even more, she's found a way to get him to talk to her. Meanwhile, I've had very little luck at all getting any words out of him.

"What I do know is Ronan cares about you. He always has. Maybe things can't be the way they used to be between you two, but if you can find it in your heart to give him a few more chances to talk to you when you come over, I hope you two can at least be friends. He needs people like you now, Kate."

Touched by how much Matthias cares about Ronan, I nod my head and smile at his suggestions. "Okay. I do like coming here. I have such wonderful memories of my time here with him when we were together."

With a big smile, Matthias walks over to the door

and opens it for us to leave. "Excellent. Thank you, Kate. I guess I better go find out what Ava wants, or I'm going to be in the doghouse."

As we walk down the hallway toward the living room, I see Ronan standing at the door looking out. My heart aches at the thought he can't even go outside to spend time with his brother or his nephews.

Matthias gives me a knowing look at then walks out to the pool area, leaving me wondering if I should say something to Ronan. Maybe we can't be together again because too much has changed, but I'd like it if we could at least be friends.

Swallowing hard, I try to find the right words to say, but nothing seems to be in my brain at the moment. A fine time to suddenly become empty-headed. What I wouldn't give all those nights when I lie down to sleep and can't stop thinking about all that happened during the day to have an empty mind.

"You used to like to swim," I say, instantly wishing I had said something more interesting.

He turns around and nods. "I did."

"I wish you would have been out there with us before."

Ronan takes a few steps toward me and stops. "Why?"

He really doesn't know, does he?

"Because I would have liked to spend some time with you."

"Maybe next time," he says quietly, as if he doesn't want to announce it too loudly and be held to that like a promise.

"I'd like that."

God, if only I was better at letting people know I like them. It's just not my style to be that forward, though. If he could remember that, he'd realize how much I'm trying right now.

"Will you be coming back anytime soon?"

I swallow hard again because I know this is my chance to say something that shows I'm hoping to spend time with him. "I'd like to. Would you like to have lunch or something sometime?"

Not exactly the most impressive effort, but for someone shy like me, that's about as obvious as I get. God, I wish he'd remember what I'm like. If he did, he'd know my tepid words have so much more meaning behind them.

That question finally makes him smile. "I'd like that. What about tomorrow?"

Just like that first time he asked me out at my locker in junior year in between classes, he doesn't play any games. It's what I always loved about him. Other guys would make it seem like they're busy or have other things going on, but never Ronan. He always made me feel like I was the only person in the world he wanted to be around.

"Tomorrow's good! Do you want to go somewhere or stay here?"

Darkness washes over his expression, and he moves his body so I can't see any of his right arm. "We'll stay here."

"Okay. What time?"

He doesn't think for more than a second or two before he says, "One. Be here for one and come with your appetite because you know how Eleanor likes to make a big deal out of things."

I can barely contain my excitement at the thought that Ronan and I will be having lunch together tomorrow. It's a small step, but it's progress, nonetheless.

"Okay, one o'clock. I'll see you then."

"See you then, Kate."

I hurry toward the front door but realize halfway through the house I didn't say goodbye to Ava. Turning back, I see Ronan walking up the stairs to the second floor. As much as I hope he isn't going to spend the rest of the day in his room, I like that he's not going back to get another look at Sabrina in that teeny bikini.

Ava is hurrying toward the guest bathroom off the living room with little Theo when I finally find her to tell her I'll be back tomorrow. The baby's got something yellow all down the front of him, and I think it's something gross.

"Do you need help?" I ask as I follow behind them.

She waves me off, laughing. "No. It looks worse than it is. His uncle gave him a sip of lemonade, and Theo here spit it all down the front of his shirt. Are you going?"

I stop in the bathroom doorway as she sits him in the sink to get washed off. "I am. Thank you for letting me take a swim. I'll be back tomorrow, though."

Ava looks over as Theo plays with the water, and I say, "Ronan asked me if I'd like to have lunch. Well, actually, I guess I asked about lunch, but he said he wants to. That's okay, isn't it?"

A look of pure joy comes over her. "It's fantastic!

He hasn't wanted to do anything with anyone before this. I'm so happy! I'll see you tomorrow, but I promise I won't stick around."

She really is so thoughtful.

"See you tomorrow! See you later, Theo," I say, smiling at the adorable baby who's decided to take a full bath in the sink.

I walk out to my car practically floating on air. Ronan and I are having lunch together tomorrow. I need to find the perfect outfit and make sure I look my best. Or maybe I should go shopping and buy something new.

It's only lunch, but it's a start.

# CHAPTER SIXTEEN

onan

"ELEANOR, I NEED YOUR HELP. KATE'S COMING OVER for lunch tomorrow, and I'd like to have all her favorites," I say as I walk into the kitchen.

She spins around at the sink, and I swear she looks like she's going to burst from happiness. "Of course! Just tell me what she likes, and I'll be sure to make it."

I sit down at the table and think about what I know she loves to eat. Assuming her tastes haven't drastically changed, I remember she enjoyed lobster, shrimp, chicken salad, and anything with chocolate. How those will figure into a lunch menu I have no idea.

"Maybe something with shrimp? I know she loves anything with that. Or chicken salad, but that doesn't feel like it will be good enough. Whatever we go with, I want to make sure she has a dessert with chocolate as the main ingredient."

Eleanor wipes her hands on the dish cloth hanging next to the sink and walks over to the table to sit down across from me. She seems upset with tears in her eyes.

"Did I say something wrong?" I ask, trying out my new effort to be nice like I used to be.

Shaking her head, she sniffles and gives me a big smile. "No, not at all. I'm just so happy to see you excited about something."

"It's only lunch."

"I know. I know. It's just that you haven't been like the old you in a long time. It's good to see this Ronan again. I missed him."

The last thing I want is to make her cry for real, so I merely shrug and say, "So what do you think we should have tomorrow?"

Nothing gets Eleanor more excited than planning out a great meal, so she shakes off all her emotion and sets her jaw. "Hmmm. Let me think. We could do shrimp kabobs with rice and a salad. Oh, I can make a wonderful chocolate cake for dessert. I saw a recipe the other day that sounded delicious! How does that sound?"

I have to admit it sounds great. Leave it to Eleanor to make a simple lunch sound like a grand meal.

A playful sparkle fills her eyes, and she asks, "So will it be just you and Kate? Where are you planning to have lunch? If it's just going to be the two of you, then you're going to want it to be somewhere other than right here or out near the pool. There's no peace and quiet in either of those spots."

She's right. Ava and the boys spend every day outside, and when they aren't out there, they're right where I'm sitting. Not exactly the kind of vibe I'm going for with this lunch.

"What about asking Matthias if you can use the carriage house? I know he's changed it to his studio, but there's still a kitchen there and the backyard of that house has that adorable little patio. I know it's been spruced up recently because the gardener was complaining that we shouldn't let it go so long between cleanings. That might be a perfect spot, and it will ensure you aren't bothered by any of us."

The way she says that makes me feel like I've been mistreating everyone in this house. "You guys don't bother me."

She tilts her head and stares at me for a long moment, like she can see right through me. I did just blow up on my entire family the other day about leaving me alone.

"I know what you're trying to do, Ronan, and having me or Ava and the boys or Sabrina march through your lunch isn't your goal. And now that Marius is here, there's another chance you'll be interrupted. What do you say? Ask Matthias this afternoon. I'm sure he'll say yes."

After our last few interactions, I'll be surprised if my brother doesn't tell me to go fuck myself and my lunch plans. He'd have every right to tell me to go stick one of those shrimp kabobs straight up my ass.

I smile like I'm going to do exactly as she's suggesting, but I see by her expression she knows I'm not. "Ronan, I know you and Matthias haven't been the best of friends lately, but he loves you. You're his baby brother. He would do anything to help you find happiness. So ask him. Go right now. I know he's in his office."

"Then he's probably busy with work," I say, not budging.

Eleanor screws her face into a grimace and stands up from the table. Pointing in the direction of my brother's office, she says in her sternest voice, "Ronan, go talk to your brother. You don't want this lunch to go badly, do you?"

She always knows exactly what to say to make me do as she thinks I should.

"Okay. I'm going. Wish me luck," I mumble as I stand from the table.

"You won't need luck. Now go."

I can only hope she's right. She hasn't been around when we've had our disagreements lately. Love me or not, if he decided to kick me out of his house, nobody would blame him.

By the time I reach his office, I've convinced myself he won't even be interested in the idea to use the carriage house's patio for my lunch with Kate. I stop just outside the door and reconsider whether I should even bother. I'm sure Ava and the kids will be outside, and I can just tell Marius to stay out of sight for a while.

As I think that, Matthias calls out, "Ronan, is something wrong? Why are you standing out there? Come in!"

So much for reconsidering.

I step in and can't believe how much this room

reminds me of when our father used it as a home office. He spent much less time here working than Matthias does, but I can't see a single thing my brother's changed since he began calling it his own. The walls are that same light beige color. The black leather sofa is still here and in the same spot just inside the door. Even the big cherry wood desk is the same sitting near the windows that look out at the front of the estate.

All those years Matthias spent telling anyone who'd listen he had no interest in ever running King Industries or being anything like Maximilian King, and here he is like his doppelganger sitting behind the very desk our father used to sit at.

"I guess you've decided to stick with the way Dad used to keep the place?" I ask as I look around.

The Thanksgiving picture I drew in kindergarten with my hand as the turkey is still hanging on the wall to the left of the desk in that wood frame my mother let me pick out. The sun has faded the yellow and oranges where my fingers made the feathers, but the brown for my thumb and the turkey's head is still going strong.

Pointing at it, I laugh. "You know, you can take that down. Pretty soon your own kids will be drawing you ugly Thanksgiving turkey pictures."

He turns to look at the picture and nods before looking back at me. "I don't think I never noticed that was there until now. Dad must have really liked that turkey you made for him."

As the youngest, I always got the best treatment out of the five of us kids. I don't think my parents loved me any more than any of my brothers. I just think by the time I came along, they had smoothed out all the rough spots and kinks in how to raise kids, so I simply seemed easier than the four who came before me.

"That's the best drawing I've ever made in my life, you know. Things just went downhill from there," I joke. "I didn't get the artistic gene, sadly."

Until recently, if I said that, anyone who knew me would say that I more than made up for it with the athletic gene. Nobody, including Matthias, says that anymore.

For a few seconds, that ugliness that always springs up in me whenever I think about all my dreams coming true and then losing everything that night on the Taconic threatens to ruin my mood. I fight it, though, because I don't want to feel that way anymore.

I'm tired of being unhappy.

"So what's going on? Why were you lurking outside in the hallway?" Matthias asks, and I hear the fear and worry under his words come through loud and clear.

He has every reason to feel that way. For the past six months, nothing about me has put a smile on his face. I'd like to change that today, although I don't know if he'll feel anywhere as pleased as I do that I'm having lunch with Kate tomorrow.

"I wasn't lurking, per se. Just taking my time deciding if I wanted to bother you. I know you're busy with work, and I didn't want to interrupt anything important."

My brother listens as I hedge, nodding as a slow smile lifts the corners of his mouth. "Okay, well, I'm not doing anything that can't be interrupted. What's up?"

I guess I can't stall anymore. Well, here's to hoping Eleanor was right.

"I'd like to use the carriage house's patio for lunch tomorrow."

He looks confused for a few seconds and then shrugs. "Okay. Can I ask why?"

"Because Kate and I are having lunch together, and I'd like it to be just the two of us."

That sounds like this lunch we're having is far more important than it actually is. It's not really a big deal, but his eyes immediately get huge, and he stands up like he's going to run around the house to tell everyone else who lives here what's happening tomorrow.

"Really? Well, yes, of course. Use the carriage house. I can go down there tonight after work and straighten it up for you so you don't have to stay outside. I've got brushes and pencils all over the place, to say nothing of my easels, but I can put them all away."

I hold up my hand to stop him before he gets too carried away. "No, it's okay. That's your place. Keep it just like you want. I only want to use the patio. Eleanor was the one who suggested it. She thought it would be more private than the kitchen here or out by the pool."

"Okay. Just let me know if you change your mind. I can have it all straightened up in no time. In fact, Ava would probably love that since every time she comes down to see me when I'm there she mentions how much of a mess it is. So lunch with Kate? That's good! That's really good."

He stops and then asks, "It's good, right? I'm not seeing a ton of excitement in you right now, but it seems like it's a good thing you two are having lunch together."

"It is," I say, tempering my emotions about what may happen with her tomorrow.

I'm out of practice and don't know how to act around people much anymore. That comes from hiding out first in my apartment after getting out of the hospital before hiding out in my childhood bedroom since I got here two months ago.

"Well, I'm glad. You've put a smile on this very tired father's face today, Ronan. Thank you for that."

Happy to change the subject from my plans tomorrow, I smile and ask, "Is Matty still having a hard time sleeping through the night?"

My brother lets out the heaviest sigh I've heard in a while and sits back down in his office chair. "Not only him but now Theo. They seem to be feeding off one another's sleeplessness at night now. I told Ava maybe we should try not putting them down for naps during the day and see if that helps, but she doesn't think that's a good idea."

"Probably because that's the only time she gets to rest, Matthias. She's with those kids all the time, and I know Sabrina is helping, but it's still a lot. Give her a break."

He looks at me oddly for a moment and then sighs again. "You know, I hadn't thought of it that way. Probably because my brain is only half working these days. You're right. Still, we need to do something, or one or both of us is going to go crazy without enough sleep."

I don't think a Benadryl joke would be good at this moment since my brother's ability to judge humor is likely not what it needs to be for him to get a laugh from that, so I smile and say, "I'm sure you guys will figure it out. Mom and Dad did."

"God, I have no idea how they did it. Maybe Theo and I slept through the night from the moment they brought us home from the hospital?"

That gets him a laugh from me. "I highly doubt it. Didn't Mom used to say he was colicky until he was like two or something?"

Pinching the bridge of his nose, Matthias shakes his head. "God, don't let that happen with Matty. I don't think I'll make it. I really don't."

"You'll get through this, and then you guys will have another one when you forget how rough having two within two years was. That's how it works with parents, I think. At least it must have worked that way in our family."

The look of horror that settles into his expression tells me he's not ready for a third. Since Ava wants a girl, he better get ready, though.

"Well, I'll let you get back to work. Or maybe you should head over to that sofa of yours and take a nap for an hour or so," I say as I turn to leave. Looking back at him, I add, "Thanks, Matthias. For the patio down at the carriage house. It means a lot to me."

"My pleasure."

Just as Matthias says that, Marius walks into his

office wearing a big grin. "Whose pleasure are we talking about? Ronan, I got to chat up that ex of yours today. She's still as pure as snow, isn't she?"

This brother never misses a chance to bust balls. I wish he would when it comes to Kate, though.

"She thinks you hate her, you know. She asked me why does Marius hate me, and I told her I didn't think you do. Now I'm not so sure."

He throws his head back and laughs. "Hate her? Clearly I need to work on my flirting skills. Or maybe she needs to work on hers because I was giving off some very clear signs I liked what I saw. I mean, who doesn't like a girl who still looks like a virgin in her mid-twenties? I'll have some of that, for sure."

I feel my protectiveness rise up inside me and step close to him to get in his face. "Don't talk about Kate that way. Whether or not she's a virgin is none of your business."

But Marius doesn't care how angry I am. "Of course, she's not a virgin. She was with you for more than two years. You're the nice King boy, but even you weren't hanging out for two years without getting some of that pretty thing."

I want to lay him out, but Matthias stops me before I see if I can hit as well with my left hand as I used to be able to with my right. "Marius, lay off. Kate's a nice person, and Ronan has always cared about her. Step back with that bullshit you're giving off today."

Marius raises his hands like he's surrendering, but I can tell by the smirk on his face he isn't sorry for a single thing he said about her. "My bad. I was just saying she looks great. I meant no offense. Honest."

I pass by him, shoulder checking him as I head toward the hall. "Thanks, Matthias! Get some sleep."

Behind me, I hear Marius ask him, "What's his problem? He knows how I am."

My oldest brother sounds far less pleasant now when he answers him. "You don't have to bust balls all the time, you know? Let it go sometimes. Ronan is finally feeling better. Don't fuck it up by riding him."

I don't hear what my other brother says, but knowing him, it's something smart ass. No matter. My day's been made. First, Kate agreed to hang out tomorrow, and now I know we can have some peace and quiet when we have lunch down at the carriage house.

Tomorrow's going to be a good day.

# CHAPTER SEVENTEEN

onan

THRILLED I'LL GET TO HAVE LUNCH WITH KATE tomorrow, I don't want to stay hidden away in my room today. I'm sure Ava and Matthias would be happy to see me show up out near the pool, but I feel like I have so much energy to burn that I can't just sit around in the sun all day.

I head outside and look up at the crystal blue sky. Maybe I could go for a quick run. I haven't done much of anything physical since the accident. My legs still work, though, so they should be fine.

After thinking about it for a minute or so, I break into a jog and instantly feel incredible. I used to love to run. It gave me a chance to think about things without being interrupted by anyone, especially one of my brothers. It's good to know I still have it in me.

By the time I reach the carriage house, my thigh muscles are sending signals to my brain that they can't be expected to just be their old, reliable selves after half a year of doing nothing but sitting around. I push through and keep going, though, feeling stronger than I've felt in so long.

It's good to be doing something active. Before my accident, I kept myself in good shape. Not that I've gotten all out of shape this year. Surprisingly, I'm still pretty cut looking. It's just the muscles underneath the surface that have atrophied a bit.

Those days are over now. I've got Kate back in my life again, and I feel like I have something to live for.

A hundred yards past the carriage house I start to lose steam. I guess I can't expect my body to do nothing for months on end and then launch into a full-on run. Like everything else, I'll have to build up to that.

But for the first time since my accident, I believe in myself enough to try. That's something new for me, and as much as I want to think I deserve the credit, I know that's not entirely true.

Like before when she was mine, it's Kate's influence on me that lets me even consider trying to live a normal life again.

"Ronan!" a voice calls to me, and I look around to see Sabrina trotting down the road toward me.

When she reaches me, she nudges my left arm and chuckles. "I didn't know you were a runner. I would have suggested we go for a run if I knew."

Doubled over, I shake my head. "I'm not really a

runner anymore. I used to be, though. Just felt like trying the old legs out again."

Her gaze moves down my body and then up to my face again. With a smile, she says, "I don't think they're that old. What are you? Twenty-five?"

I stand up to my full height and take a deep breath into my lungs. Letting it out slowly, I answer, "Twenty-four, but I haven't done much in the past six months. Muscles get old when you don't use them."

She purses her lips and looks me up and down again. "Then you should make sure you use those muscles."

"Why aren't you up at the house with the kids? I thought that was your job," I say as I start walking toward the back of the estate.

Sabrina pushes her fingertips into my bicep and laughs. "I get a few minutes off each day, you know. In fact, when the boys are down for their naps, I can do whatever I want. If you'd like, we can go for a run every day from now on. I bet you'll get back in shape in no time."

I glance over at her to see if she meant for that to be insulting, but since she's all smiles, I assume it was her usual clumsy way of talking. This woman sure does like giving her opinion on things.

"Well, thanks."

Even though she doesn't seem to have the ability to censor herself, she does appear to understand when she's offended someone. As I keep walking, she says, "I wasn't trying to make it seem like you aren't in good shape already. I just heard you were a baseball player at some point, so I thought maybe you wanted to get back to that level. That's all."

That she mentions baseball surprises me since nobody in my family has dared uttered a word about that subject since I came to stay here. I stop and look at her, unsure if I should be furious or happy there's at least one person here who doesn't insist on handling me with kid gloves.

I hold my right arm up in front of her. "No more baseball for me, obviously."

Sabrina stops in front of me and reaches out to poke me in the abs. Smiling, she looks up at me and says, "Still seems pretty tight to me."

Everything about this person confuses me. One minute she's insulting me, and then the next she seems to be flirting with me. Then again, maybe I'm not understanding the signals she's putting out. I have gotten a little rusty after avoiding nearly all of humanity for months on end.

"What are you two doing out here?"

I turn around to see Marius walking toward us. Christ, I'm not sure I'm up for his ball busting today.

"I could ask you the same question," I say as he stops next to me.

"You guys aren't misbehaving, are you?" he asks with a smirk that instantly gets under my skin.

Sabrina doesn't seem bothered by my older brother, though. "Define misbehaving," she says with a chuckle.

Marius looks at her and then me, raising his eyebrows like he's surprised by her comment. "She's got the right idea. Your idea of misbehaving is probably not what I'd call misbehaving."

"I imagine most people's idea of misbehaving isn't yours, Marius. You have a pretty loose version of morals."

My brother smiles and turns his attention to Sabrina. "I like to think of them as situational ethics."

"What exactly are situational ethics?" she asks, clearly intrigued by Marius and his willingness to entertain anything as long as it's enjoyable.

"Basically, every situation you encounter in life has its own version of what's right and wrong. For example, what might be wrong for you as an employee of my brother's wouldn't be wrong for me as his brother."

Sabrina nods like she understands, but since Marius pretty much makes up that bullshit as he goes along, I'm not sure there's much to really grasp. To me, his situational ethics always felt pretty much like his willingness to do whatever he wanted and claim he was in the right.

I prefer a higher standard.

"What do you think of your brother's situational ethics?" Sabrina asks me, touching my left forearm for a brief moment as if to punctuate her question.

Without missing a beat, I answer, "I think he uses that idea as a way to justify doing things he should feel bad about."

Marius throws his head back in laughter before sliding his arm around my shoulders. "Sabrina, let me introduce you to the most moral and upright of all us King brothers. If there's a right thing to do, Ronan will do it."

I push him off me and say, "There's always a right

thing to do in every situation. That's where Marius and I differ."

Sabrina touches my left arm again and smiles. "I think it's admirable that you're a moral man, Ronan. More people should be like you."

As I open my mouth to thank her for the compliment, Marius laughs. "If I followed this brother's example, I'd be perpetually trying to do the right thing. I prefer our brother Theo's way. Whatever you're doing, make sure you're having the time of your life doing it."

"Oh, so Matthias and Ava's son is named after another brother? Will he be coming to stay too?" Sabrina asks.

I shake my head as Marius simply smiles. "No, Theo's dead. He was killed in a car accident a couple years ago."

"I'm sorry."

As I silently thank her for that, Marius says, "He lived his life at top speed. We should all follow his example. Squeeze every drop of life there is and lap it up because there may be no tomorrow."

Already tired of this brother and how easily he can preach a life of no morals or ethics, I look at Sabrina and say, "I'm going to head back to the house. Maybe Marius will want to go for a run with you."

"That's what you two were doing?" he asks like the very idea of a run sounds horrible. "No thanks. I already worked out today."

"Do you work out at a gym somewhere close?" Sabrina asks.

I get the sense she's just being polite, but he

answers, "Right here at the house. I'm not surprised nobody told you about it. Matthias and Ava are always too exhausted to even think about the gym, and this guy here hasn't been a gym rat in ages. Come with me. I'll show you where it is."

He starts to walk back toward the house and grabs Sabrina's hand to take her too, thankfully, but just as I'm sure I'll be left alone, she grabs my left hand and begins to tug me along with them. I have no interest in checking out the gym, but as much as I try to pry my hand from her hold, she won't let me go.

"Come on, Ronan!" she says, as if we're about to do something fun.

No one seems to remember the reason why I wouldn't be spending much time in the gym. I only have one hand, so unless I want to be lopsided, lifting isn't in the cards for me anymore. It seems since neither one of them have to deal with that problem that they don't recognize it's an issue.

Unfortunately, I don't have the luxury of not knowing all too well what I'm lacking.

Marius looks back and winks at me. "Come on, baby brother. It'll be fun."

What the hell could be fun about showing someone where the gym is here at the house I don't know. He's up to something, I'm sure. Marius is always up to something. Most of the time it involves busting someone's ass, and I'm not interested in that today.

"I think I'd like to just grab a drink," I say, but neither one of them is listening.

In fact, they seem to be having a grand old time talking about what they like to do at the gym as

Sabrina continues to pull me along with them. I don't want to hurt her feelings because she's important to Ava and Matthias, but I have no doubt she and Marius would have a better time without me.

Just as we reach the kitchen door, Sabrina stops and turns to me. "You've been really nice to me ever since I got here, Ronan. I just wanted to give you that in return. You aren't angry, are you?"

I shake my head as our first introduction to one another runs through my mind. It wasn't exactly a friends from the very beginning situation. That's part of the reason why I don't want to tell her I have no interest in going to the gym with her and Marius. That day I met Sabrina wasn't my finest moment.

"Good! It'll be fun! Come on!" she says as her worry fades away and she tugs on my hand once more.

We walk past Eleanor on our way through the house, and the look she gives me when she sees me holding hands with Sabrina is nothing short of pure shock. I guess since I've spent the last two months working very hard on being as standoffish as possible to everyone in this house it's a little surprising to see me happily spending time with Sabrina.

"Marius wants to show her the gym," I explain as we pass through the kitchen.

There's no time for her to respond since we're halfway down the hallway only a second later, but I bet she's thinking I'm being a third wheel with Sabrina and Marius. My gut says I am too, though Sabrina does seem very interested in having me come with them.

Then it dawns on me. She's probably uncomfortable being alone with him. I get it. Marius comes off like a complete horndog. Sabrina is likely thinking he's going to make a move on her if I'm not around.

Little does she know that won't stop him. I've seen Marius hit on women who were in the middle of embracing other men. If he's got his mind set on someone, my brother is like a man on a mission. Nothing short of being told to go away stops him.

The two of them talk about his gym routine, thankfully leaving me out of that discussion. When we finally reach the basement, she's impressed by the home gym Matthias and Ava have set up here.

"Wow! At least I know I won't ever get out of shape."

Marius says something about how he doubts she's going to suddenly get out of shape, and the two of them laugh. I just stand there listening and wondering when he's going to give me the sign to get lost. If he's into her, the last thing he wants is me hanging around.

After a few minutes, I say, "I think I'm going to go. You two have fun."

Surprisingly, that bothers Sabrina, who comes rushing over to stop me. "No, don't go. We didn't mean to ignore you. Why don't you come over and hang out? Marius is just talking about his favorite machine."

I want to tell her I can't imagine anything less interesting than that conversation, but since I'm trying to be nicer to everyone here, I swallow that snide remark. "I've got some things to do before tomorrow when Kate comes over again. Don't worry about me. You and Marius will be fine without me."

Her eyes grow big and she frowns. "Are you sure?

I'm fine if you want to leave and go back for another walk. I'll come with you. It'll be fun!"

"No, that's okay. Enjoy a workout, and I'll see you later."

As I turn to leave, Marius says, "Let him go. He's got to get ready for his big date."

I throw him a nasty look and leave, not interested in discussing my plans with Kate for tomorrow. Marius always poked fun at my being with Kate before, and it seems he's picked up where he left off years ago.

# CHAPTER EIGHTEEN

ate

J ESSIE STARES BACK AT ME FROM MY PHONE AS I wait to hear her opinion on my new dress. As soon as I left the King estate yesterday, I went shopping and found the cutest yellow and blue sundress. Not usually a huge fan of the color yellow, I fell in love with it as soon as I saw it hanging on the rack.

"Well? What am I missing?" I ask before twirling one more time to show her the whole look.

She hums like she's considering what would make my outfit outstanding and then claps her hands. "Lip gloss!"

I stare at her in disbelief. "Lip gloss? Seriously? I'm desperate here, Jess! I need to make the best impression possible. Lip gloss is not going to help me."

"Why? You want your lips to be kissable, don't you? Then you need to draw attention to them."

"First of all, I haven't worn lip gloss in like five years. Probably more. Why would having sticky lips make them appealing? Now come on. I need to know if I should do anything else. Take another look, okay?"

She nods, and I watch her eyes move from my face down the full length of my body. She stops at my white sandals I've had for years and then looks me in the eyes.

"I don't see anything, Kate. You look fantastic. If he doesn't agree, then he's a damn fool. I can't understand men's reactions to us anyway, so I might not be the right person to ask."

"I'll take the fantastic, and we can leave the discussion of what men might think of women for a later date. I need to be there by one, and I want to be a few minutes early, so I need to get going. Wish me luck!"

She smiles, and her entire face lights up. "You don't need luck! Now go get 'em, tiger, and remember I want to hear every juicy detail when we talk later, so no trying to give me that same old 'it was okay' bullshit. Got it?"

I love Jessie like a sister, but she really has no idea of privacy. She's an open book with every part of her life, so she assumes everyone else is. Since I tend to prefer keeping things to myself, especially when it comes to my love life, I find her demand for details awkward.

Then again, I haven't had many details to share

with her in the past year or two, so she might just want me to remember it's normal to be with a guy. I don't need to be reminded of that. I simply didn't have any interest in any.

Until I saw Ronan again.

"Yeah, yeah. Details. I want to remind you we aren't girls here. Maybe it's time for us to not share all the details of every encounter we have with men?" I suggest, knowing what her answer will be.

"Not share details? Are you kidding me? I'm living vicariously through you right now, Kate. All I have are the usual nights with guys, but you have a second chance with the love of your life. Since that will never happen for me, I need to enjoy this through you, so don't go getting stingy with the details, lady. Now go have a wonderful time. Oh, and remember, don't forget the lip gloss!"

Shaking my head, I end the call as I try to understand what her fascination with lip gloss suddenly is. I don't even own a tube of that stuff. I haven't for years. She hasn't either, so what's with this constant drumbeat for lip gloss? She probably read some article in a magazine that said it's the must-have beauty product for the summer.

I take a deep breath and check out my look one last time in the mirror. I love how this dress hangs on me. Never someone who could say she has nice breasts, I have to say this dress highlights what I do have quite nicely.

Then again, Ronan never seemed to care about that part of me not being like any of the models, so maybe it's not important. I just want to look as good as possible today.

"Okay, it's show time," I say to my reflection before heading out.

AFTER A SHORT DRIVE FROM MY APARTMENT TO THE King estate, I park just outside the kitchen and begin to walk toward the house when Ava comes rushing out and stops me. Instantly, I wonder if something's happened.

"Hi, Ava! I'm supposed to have lunch with Ronan today," I explain, my disappointment preemptively building in case she's about to tell me it's not going to happen.

But thankfully, she gives me a big smile and says, "He asked me to tell you he's down at the carriage house waiting for you. He's around back on the patio there."

Confused, I look down the road toward the smaller white house on the estate grounds and then back at Ava. "Oh, okay. I guess I'll head down there now then."

"Great! Have a wonderful time!"

As I walk slowly down the driveway to get to the road, I silently curse my choice of shoes for this lunch. Then again, I didn't know I'd be walking what looks to be about half a mile in sandals that have three inch heels. I could have worn flip flops, but I don't own actual nice shoes that aren't heels since I always feel like dresses look best when my legs look longer.

And I'm so short at just over five and a half feet compared to Ronan's six foot four height.

Even as I'm eager to reach the carriage house to see why he chose that spot for our lunch together, I walk slowly because my feet are already hurting less than halfway there. He appears on the front porch and waits for me, but I make one wrong step on a rock, and a second later, I tumble to the ground.

Embarrassment fills me as Ronan rushes up the road, and he reaches me just as I get back up on my feet. I look down and see a tiny trickle of blood near my right ankle courtesy of that same rock cutting me.

"Are you okay?"

I brush myself off and try to pretend that I'm not mortified that I just tripped over a tiny rock. "I'm fine. Just a little busted up. Should we go back up to the house, or are there Band-Aids down at the carriage house?"

Ronan thinks for a moment and then places his left hand on my lower back to guide me. "I don't know, so let's go up to the house to get one, and then we'll head back down the carriage house for lunch. I had Eleanor make a meal I think you're going to love."

The way he beams when he says that makes me wish I hadn't fallen like an idiot so I could see what this lunch she made is right now. He and I walk up to the house, and when we walk in, Ava and Eleanor turn to look at us with nothing but worry on their faces.

I quickly move to explain why we're there. Pointing at my shin, I sheepishly say, "I fell, and we weren't sure there were any Band-Aids down at the other house, so we're here to steal one."

Eleanor hurries to where I stand, takes a brief look for a second at my leg like she wants to judge the size bandage I need, and rushes out of the kitchen. "Don't move! I'll be right back."

Ava too studies the cut that's dripping blood down over my ankle. "Let me guess. You stepped in the grass on the side of the road. I've always hated how it dips just enough to make you fall. I can't tell you how many times I went feet over head because of that."

I look at Ronan and see his attention is fixed on my very minor injury. "Actually, I stepped on a rock. Leave it to me. I should have worn flip flops. At least in those, I know I can walk right."

My attempt at being self-effacing succeeds, and Ava directs our attention at her feet in black flip flops. "I wear them as long as I can during the year, and then when my feet get too cold, I move to slippers. I can't wear heels anymore."

Eleanor returns with the Band-Aid and seems to be intent on putting it on me, which only serves to make me feel like a bigger fool. She rips the paper off, but Ronan takes it from her and pulls one of the chairs out from the table for me.

"Here, let me get that."

I sit and watch in awe as he manipulates the plastic coverings on each end by using his teeth. Then he crouches down and sweetly lifts my leg to place the bandage on my skin. When he puts the first half of it on, I press my finger to it so he can easily affix the second half.

Looking up at me when he finishes, he smiles. "All better now? Ready for lunch?"

Ava and Eleanor watch with utter pride at the scene in front of them, and I stand, eager to get down to the carriage house. "I'm ready!"

We don't make it more than a couple steps toward the door before Sabrina appears from the hallway. "What's all the excitement?" she asks with a chuckle.

Eleanor answers before Ava can, and in a voice full of joy, she says, "Kate tripped outside and got cut, so she and Ronan came in for a Band-Aid, which he put on her."

She sounds like a proud mama bragging about a child doing something for the first time, and although I sense Ronan feels uncomfortable with her comment, I think it's charming. Sabrina, however, doesn't seem to care much for what the housekeeper has to say and ignores her in favor of paying attention to Ronan.

"You must be better at that whole Band-Aid thing than you were the other day," she says to him, smiling like it's a private joke between the two of them.

Turning to the three of us who don't understand the reference, she explains, "Ronan cut himself on glass the other day, so I had to help him with the Band-Aid. Then I shaved all that terrible beard off so he looks like he does today."

Every fiber of my being senses red flags with this woman. Why did she bring up that story other than to take credit for helping him when he couldn't do something himself?

Ronan doesn't say anything and quickly escorts me out of the kitchen toward the door. "Thanks, Eleanor. Time for us to head down to lunch."

I notice Sabrina's expression falls when she hears

we're leaving to have our meal in private somewhere else and not here in the kitchen. What is this person's interest in where Ronan and I spend our time together?

Even as I wonder that as we walk outside, I suspect I know the answer. She likes him. And to her, I'm an inconvenience she'd rather would disappear, the sooner the better.

Once we're alone and walking down to the carriage house, I say, "That was really nice of her to help you with shaving."

Jealousy hangs off each word, and even though I can't control how I feel, I do hope he can't hear it. I don't want to be petty about this Sabrina thing. It's just that she seems to be incredibly interested in the man I care for, and I need to know how he feels about her before I let myself get my hopes up about us.

He shrugs, like it meant next to nothing for her to do that for him, and says, "It was. I would have gotten the hang of it after a while. It's just a matter of getting used to working with only my left hand. To be honest, I could have shaved on my own. I needed her help with the scissors to trim my beard first, though."

Everything in the way he says that tells me he doesn't think anything of her. Relieved, I sigh and say, "Well, you look great."

"Thanks," he says with a smile.

We walk the rest of the way down to the carriage house in silence, but I notice right before we reach the front gate that he isn't attempting to hide his right arm today. That's something new and a great improvement.

I wonder if I should mention it, but I think twice about that and decide not to.

Whatever the reason he feels more comfortable around me today, I don't want to ruin it by drawing attention to anything that might make him feel awkward. If he wants to tell me about why he feels better about that, he will.

Like the gentleman he's always been, he opens the gate for me, and I walk through. In all the times I've been to the estate, I've never been down here to the carriage house. It's so much cuter up close.

"This is a really sweet looking house," I say as we climb the stairs to the front porch. "I was just thinking that in as many times as I've been here at the house with you, I've never come down here."

"That's probably because when we were together, Ava, her brother, and her father lived here," he says as he opens the front door. "Now Matthias uses it as an art studio since she lives up at the main house and her father moved down to one of the Carolinas, I think."

I walk inside and see Matthias definitely has set the place up as a studio. "She mentioned her brother lives in Florida, I think," I say as Ronan guides me through the house toward the back where the kitchen is located.

"Yeah, I think so. She said something about hurricanes one day. Okay, now out the back door. Sorry, about the half-assed tour of the house. I can show you the rest of it after we eat, if you want. I just don't want the food to get cold."

I nod and walk out onto the back porch before

seeing what he's done to the patio below. A round table with a white tablecloth sits waiting for us, complete with food in covered containers, a pitcher of iced tea, plates, and silverware. I'm touched he went to such an effort just for lunch with me.

"This is lovely!" I step off the last step and look at him behind me smiling. "You didn't have to go to all of this trouble. Thank you, though."

He always did know how to show someone he cares. I love that he hasn't lost that with everything that's happened to him.

"No need for thanks. I wanted us to enjoy ourselves. It was Eleanor who suggested I ask my brother to use this house for today."

Pulling out one of the chairs, he waits for me to sit and leans down next to my ear. "I'm glad you're here, Kate."

I'm charmed and lightheaded at the same time. It's been so long since Ronan and I have been together in any way that I want to believe this is the beginning of our second chance.

He sits down across from me and proudly lifts the cover off the platter in the center of the table to reveal shrimp kabobs with green peppers, onions, and mushrooms surrounded by white rice. It looks delicious and smells divine.

"Is that something sweet drizzled over the kabobs?" I say after I inhale a deep breath of that incredible scent coming off them.

Ronan leans forward and breathes it in. A smile lights up his entire face when he answers, "Yeah, I think Eleanor must have made that sauce I said I liked a while back."

"This looks so good. I can't wait to eat it." I look at the white container next to that one and ask, "What's in there?"

"It's a surprise, but we can't have it until after these. Let's dig in so we don't have to wait long to see what it is!" he says with such sweetness that I want to climb over this table and kiss him like I've been dying to since I first saw him again after so many years.

The two of us take a shrimp kabob and begin to eat, and the meal tastes even better than it looks and smells. The sweetness we recognized has to be honey, but there's something else mixed in too. I don't know what it is, but shrimp has never tasted so good.

Ronan lifts the pitcher to pour me some iced tea, but as he begins to fill the glass, it wobbles. I quickly reach over to steady it as a frown settles into his expression.

"I got it. No worries."

He looks across the table at me and smiles. "Thanks. I thought I was going to ruin our entire lunch there for a second."

"It wouldn't have ruined it. This food is too good to stop for a little iced tea spill. You'd just be giving the ants a little treat, and what's an outdoor lunch without ants?"

In his eyes, I see how thankful he is that I don't care if he spills iced tea. He doesn't have to worry. I don't mind a little mess in life if I can have him too.

"So what have you been up to? I think you

mentioned that you were traveling around Europe. Or maybe Ava told me?" he asks as we continue to eat.

"I was. It was so much fun. My friend Jessie and I went together, and I had the greatest time."

He listens like I'm saying the most important words he's ever heard and then asks, "Did you spend any time in Italy?"

"Yes!" I know I'm probably overly excited about my trip, but Italy was one of my favorite parts of it. "We went to Venice, which I loved, and then travelled to Rome and toured the Colosseum, the Forum, and all of the city. Then we went down to Pompeii to see the ruins. I bet we could have spent another two weeks in Italy."

The whole time I'm gushing about how wonderful the trip was, Ronan gives me his undivided attention. It's been so long since any man listened to my stories like this, but he always cared about everything I wanted to talk about.

I got spoiled with him as my first real boyfriend. I didn't realize until after I started dating other men that most of them aren't like him.

"A few years ago, I had to go to Italy to see the house my father left me when he died. It's in Rome, so if you ever want to go back, you have somewhere to stay instead of a hotel. It's a nice place. I haven't been there in a while, but I think you'd like it."

"Oh, that would be great!" I want to ask if he'd like to ever go there with me sometime, but travelling to Rome isn't like asking someone if they ever want to grab lunch together.

As we finish the meal, he reaches over and lifts the

cover off the container to show me a chocolate cake for dessert. I feel my eyes grow big at how wonderful it looks.

Ronan remembered my favorite foods and asked Eleanor to make them for our lunch together. He's the same thoughtful person he's always been.

Tears fill my eyes, but I'm embarrassed, so I turn away to look at a honeysuckle bush nearby. "I love honeysuckle. It's such a pretty plant with the soft yellow flowers, and I love how it smells so sweet all around it."

He doesn't answer, but I can't turn back to face him yet because I can't stop my eyes from filling with tears. Nobody has ever been so sweet to me, and I'm not even sure he knows how much I appreciate all he's done for our lunch today.

"Kate, what's wrong? Don't you like the cake? You don't have to eat it. I just thought you loved chocolate," he says, his words full of confusion.

I shake my head and finally turn to look at him. "Nothing's wrong. This is wonderful. All of it. You asked her to make my favorite foods. I can't believe you even remembered, but no, that's not true. I know you, Ronan. Of course, you remembered. That's just the kind of person you are."

"So you're happy?"

Sniffling, I dry under my eyes and smile. "I am. I'd forgotten how incredible it feels to be with someone so thoughtful."

That makes him smile like he's the happiest man on earth, and he cuts a slice of chocolate cake for me. "Eleanor said it had something special in it, but I can't for the life of me remember what it is. It's good, I'm sure, though."

I take the plate from him and cut a tiny piece of the cake with my fork. It melts in my mouth like the best chocolate should.

"Oh, my God. This is straight from heaven."

Then I remember Ronan doesn't like chocolate. Never did the entire time we were together. Ever since Theo and Marius let him eat too much Halloween candy when he was very young and he spent the entire night throwing up, he's avoided chocolate like the plague.

"What are you going to have? Unless you've overcome your hatred for chocolate?" I ask, suddenly unsure I know that fact about him anymore.

He shakes his head and puts back the lid on the cake container. "Nope. Still hate it. But I never failed to enjoy watching you eat chocolate because you love it so much. Go ahead. Enjoy! Have a second piece. Eleanor will be heartbroken if I bring back this entire cake with only one slice gone."

I take another bite of her wonderful creation and the second one is even better than the first. "Well, I don't want her to feel bad, so I guess I'll have to take another piece."

Ronan watches me eat, and I swear he may be enjoying this cake as much as I am. "That's one thing I always loved about you, Kate. You were never the kind of girl who worried about eating too much cake or anything like that."

I see his expression change as soon as he finishes

talking. He switches from being happy to looking uncomfortable, but why?

"Do I have chocolate all over my face? Is that why you look like that?" I ask as I look for my napkin to wipe my mouth.

He shakes his head. "No. You look perfect. Just like always."

But even as he says that, he doesn't look like he's happy. Why?

# CHAPTER NINETEEN

onan

I WATCH AS KATE EATS THE CAKE I ASKED ELEANOR to specially make for her and can't stop wishing I didn't fuck things up between us. Even something as small as her love of chocolate I miss. I threw away the best thing in my life for nothing that night, and I've regretted it ever since.

She hasn't flinched once when she's around me, unlike most people do when they see my missing hand. I get it. It's a shock when they first encounter it. My family has gotten used to it, but Kate doesn't even seem to notice.

Maybe it doesn't matter to her.

That's stupid. Of course, it matters to her. It matters because I'm missing a fucking hand. You only get two, and I don't have both anymore. That doctor I see wants me to believe it's not a big deal. That it bothers me more than it does anyone else, but how could someone like Kate ever accept a man who isn't whole?

"Now I'm sure there's something on my face or chocolate in my teeth," she says, hiding behind her napkin.

"Nope. Still nothing."

I wouldn't care if she had it all over her face. I'd still love just sitting here watching her enjoy it.

We don't begin talking again, so as she finishes that first piece and I serve her a second, I try to remember a time recently that I felt like I do now. Happy. Content. I don't have the love of life I used to have back yet, although that doctor claims it will return sometime, but I haven't felt this good since the accident.

It's not that I don't want to feel good. Fuck, who wants to be miserable all the time? Anyone who thinks I like hating myself and my life is sadly mistaken. It's not something I choose. It's just what happens when I wake up in the morning and look down to see it's not all simply a nightmare and my hand is still gone.

This morning I woke up feeling something different, though. Today, I saw my hand was missing when my eyes opened, but I didn't immediately want to pull the covers over my head and hide away from the world. I was excited to see Kate and have lunch with her. I could barely contain my anticipation all day until she arrived.

I remember feeling this way when she and I were dating in high school. When she said yes to going out with me that first day I stopped at her locker and asked her out, I was so happy I couldn't focus on anything but where we'd go that Friday. I don't recall anything about the rest of that school day or the rest of the week, for that matter. All I could think about was my date with Kate.

My brothers took great pleasure making fun of me, but I didn't care. Nothing ever mattered because she was mine.

And then I blew it, and here we are nearly five years later, and I'd give anything to have her feel for me what I feel for her. Things have changed, though. I'm no longer the high school athlete with all the confidence in the world. Now I'm this person who spends all his time here at my brother's because my family doesn't trust me to be alone.

If they only knew how much having Kate around made me want to live like a normal person again.

"You're quiet. I wish you had something you like for dessert."

I smile and shake my head. I don't need anything else right now. Just being here with her is enough to make my day.

But I can't say that to her. I have no idea how she feels about me. She seems to have forgiven me for what I did, but that doesn't necessarily translate into her wanting to be with me again. Even if I had two hands, I don't know if that's what she'd want.

"I'm good. I'm just glad you like the cake."

When she finishes, she sets her fork down on the plate and sighs. "I know you liked that I never cared about calories, but two pieces of cake might mean I need to do an extra workout today."

"Would you like to take a walk?"

She's excited by that suggestion, but then says, "Do you mean at the park down along the river? It's warm out today, but it would be nice to see it again. I haven't been down there in ages."

"No, I meant around here. It's a big estate. We could go for a long walk, if you want."

I hate disappointing her, but I can't leave here. Not yet.

Still, she seems happy with my idea and nods before standing up. "Okay! I'll have to go barefoot because there's no way I can walk in those shoes. They couldn't even get me down the road without failing me."

As I stand to join her, I say, "Then we'll keep to the grass. It'll feel cool on your feet."

We take everything from our lunch inside and leave it on the kitchen counter before walking across the road to start our walk. When Kate takes off her shoes, she loses at least three inches of height, and I remember how small she always seemed next to me.

"Why do you wear them if they're so hard to walk in?" I ask as we head toward the back of the estate.

Kate swings the shoes in front of her and shrugs. "I hate that I'm not as tall as I want to be, so to fix that, I wear heels. In my defense, I had no idea you had such a wonderful lunch planned at the carriage house. I thought we'd just sit in the kitchen at the house."

"Well, I wanted to do something special for our first time together."

As soon as the words leave my mouth, I realize what I meant didn't come out right. She notices it too, and I swear she blushes, just like on our first date when I slipped up and told her I'd been thinking about her for a while before I asked her out.

But before I can clarify I wasn't talking about us running up to my bedroom and getting naked, I feel her hand touch my left hand. Looking down, I see her holding it as we walk.

Maybe she does care, after all.

"Tell me about this house in Rome," she says, stepping over a tiny patch of clover. "Did you ever live there or just visit?"

I give her the best description of the place as far as I remember it, and she listens with rapt attention. Then she asks a question about its location, but it's been so long since I've been there that I don't know the exact address.

"That's okay. I was wondering if maybe I had seen it when I was there." Very quietly, she continues, "Maybe one day we can go there, and you can show me it in person."

She has no idea how much that thrills me even thinking about that. If only I could tell her that might happen, but I don't know if I'll ever be able to go all the way to Rome again. Even the thought of all those people in the city seeing me like I am now makes me think that can never be.

I don't want to make her think I'm a complete mess, so I force a smile and nod. "That would be nice."

We're quiet for a long time as we walk holding hands toward the rear of the estate. I never come out this far anymore, and I don't know what it even looks like these days. Matthias has a beautiful place here, and I'm happy to see the people he's got landscaping it are keeping it like it was when my parents had the property.

"I've always loved this place," Kate says in a dreamy voice.

Surprised, I look over at her and see her expression is pure bliss. "I loved growing up here. It was like we had our own private place to get lost in. My brothers and I weren't supposed to go past where my mother couldn't see us, but we always did. Then she'd come out to find us, and she always looked the same when she finally did. She'd have her hands on her hips, and she would shake her head. She didn't even have to yell at us. We just knew when we saw that we were in trouble."

Kate listens to my story and the next one I tell about the day Theo fell out of a tree at the edge of the estate. I talk about how angry my mother was when she had to walk all the way out there to find my older brother had broken his leg and how we all were grounded for a week after that, forced to stay inside.

"Not that hanging out in the game room was really any sort of punishment," I say with a laugh. "I know Marius didn't think it was since he spent the whole time shooting pool."

My mention of the one King brother she's sure hates her gets Kate's attention, and after a few long moments of silence, she quietly asks, "Why is he back here? I'm sure he has a house of his own somewhere, right?"

"He likes to check up on me. He pretends like he isn't here for that reason, but I think that's it."

"Oh."

I don't know why, but before I can stop myself, I add, "He was the one who found me. After I tried to…"

My sentence remains hanging in the air, unfinished because I instantly regret bringing up trying to kill myself. We were having a wonderful time, and now it's all gone to hell because I couldn't keep that to myself.

But Kate doesn't shy away from that conversation. "You mean when you tried to commit suicide?" she asks in a voice full of emotion.

I nod, still regretting I brought it up. "Yeah. I'm sorry. That just sort of came out. I didn't mean to bring down our good time."

She stops walking and slips her hand out of mine. In a flash, that regret I felt a second ago mushrooms until all I want to do is go back to my room. Maybe tomorrow will be better. I just have to not fuck it up.

Kate steps in front of me and stares up into my eyes. "I hate thinking you were so unhappy you tried to do that. I know why you would. I get it. But if you ever feel anything even close to that, promise me you'll call me, Ronan. I don't care where I am or what I'm doing, I'll come over, and we can talk it out. Or if you don't want to talk, that's fine too. We can just sit in silence. All that matters is you don't go through with it."

No one outside my family has ever said anything like that to me. Her kindness makes my breath catch in my chest.

"I don't want to do that. Not anymore. I was in a really dark place after the accident. I got strung out on the painkillers they gave me, and when I had to stop them, things got bad. I hid it from everyone, but that one day I couldn't imagine going on. So I tried, but Marius found me, thank God."

With a smile, she takes my left hand and gives it a squeeze. "Then maybe I had him all wrong. Maybe he's a good guy after all."

"He is. He's just a pain in the ass sometimes. Don't take anything he says seriously. He just likes to bust ass."

"Well, even if he hates me, I can't hate him now because he made it possible for us to be here on this beautiful day in this beautiful place."

I silently finish her sentence as we start off walking again. With a beautiful woman.

When she takes my hand this time, I feel like the entire world is lifted off my shoulders. That day when I wanted to leave this world, I couldn't imagine ever feeling this good again. Now I can't imagine even considering taking my own life.

Kate begins talking about her job she starts later this summer, and I listen to every word, happier than I remember feeling since my accident. I can tell she's nervous about finally having a full-time teaching position, but I can't think of a better person to work with third graders.

"You're going to be great at it. I know it."

Fear fills her expression. Blowing the air out of her lungs, she says, "I hope so. I don't want to screw up some poor little kid's mind. All I've ever wanted to be was a teacher. You know that. I'm sure you're bored of me talking about it since I've been obsessed with being a teacher from when I was fifteen and I got to be junior counselor at summer camp."

The way she says that makes it seem like we've been together all that time, and I like that. I regret nothing more in my life than what I did to break us up. It was stupid, and I swore to myself so many times if I ever had the chance to make it up to her, I would.

Now I have that chance, but can I do it as the man I am now?

"So I start in August, but I've already been gathering ideas and supplies. I guess I'm a little excited about it."

The way she says that makes me think she feels like she should be ashamed of feeling that way. I don't like that. Kate has never been as confident as she should be. She has so much going for her, the best thing being that she cares about people. She's the perfect example of who should be a teacher.

"Hey, I want you to think positively. You're going to be great."

She sighs and looks down toward her feet as we keep walking toward the edge of the estate. "You know me. I don't have the confidence I wish I had. I know I can do it. I guess I just don't act like it."

"I know, but you've got this."

Kate turns to look at me and shakes her head. "I wish I could be like you."

"Like me?" I ask, not understanding why she'd want to be anything like the person I am now.

"You're always so confident. I remember thinking when we dated that you were always so sure you could do things, and then you'd do them like they were so easy. I wish I had that kind of confidence."

I don't say it, but I wish I had it now too. Those days are gone, though. Now I spend all my time hiding out here on this estate wishing I could go back in time and never get into my car on New Year's Eve.

Not every moment of my time here, though. The past week seeing Kate has made me feel better.

"You aren't like me. You have your own type of confidence, and I think that's just what a teacher should have. I was cocky. You've got the goods and can deliver on your abilities. Never forget that."

Like she did when I mentioned my suicide attempt, she stops walking and moves in front of me just as we reach a huge oak tree. Standing in its shade, she keeps holding my hand and looks up at me.

"Hey, you had the goods and could deliver on your ability too. Don't forget that."

Even thinking about playing ball makes my chest hurt, and this moment is no different. I lower my head to avoid showing her how low I feel compared to the person I used to be.

"That was a different time and place. I can't think about that now."

Kate steps toward me and lets go of my hand. I look at her, wondering if what I said turned her off, but then she wraps her arms around me in a hug I never expected.

"Then don't think about it, but don't forget you're the same person you've always been, Ronan King."

I put my arms around her as she tilts her head back

and looks up at me sternly. "You don't want me to have to put on my teacher face, now do you?"

She always could make me smile when the world felt like it was coming down around me. I shake my head at her silly threat and chuckle.

"I definitely don't want to get the teacher face."

"Then no more forgetting who you are. No matter what you look like or what you do, you're the same person you've always been. Remember that, okay?"

"Okay."

I expect her to step back away from me and release me from the hug, but she tightens her hold and rests her head on my chest. Looking down, I can't believe she's standing here in my arms again. I doubted I'd ever get this chance another time, even though it's all I wanted for so long.

Then that was pushed out by how full of misery I was after my accident. I don't want to feel that way now, though. I want to feel this, the happiness coursing through me as I stand here with the one girl I've always loved hugging me.

I want to feel love and show her love again.

Touching the top of her head, I run my hand over her silky brown hair. I always loved how soft Kate's hair felt. Like something expensive and luxurious only few people in the world have the pleasure of possessing.

That's what she's like. Something rare and beautiful only a great man can possess.

But can that man be me again?

# CHAPTER TWENTY

onan

As I hang out in my room after Kate leaves, I realize I don't want to be cooped up in here anymore. Our lunch and the walk we took together made me see I hate hiding out now.

I make my way downstairs to find Eleanor alone in the kitchen. After grabbing a glass of soda, I sit down at the table and wait for her to finish at the stove.

She's a few minutes, but when she turns around to see me, she's happy. "Ronan! I didn't know anyone had come in. How was the lunch? I saw you brought back much of the cake. Didn't Kate like it?"

Quickly, I move to assure her everything was great. "No, she loved it. She had both pieces. She loved the shrimp kabobs too. Thank you for helping me with the whole thing."

Eleanor's round face lights up at my compliments. "Oh, I'm so happy. Why didn't she take any home with her?"

Sheepishly, I answer, "Because I forgot to offer. I'm a little rusty with the ins and outs of dates."

Waving that away like it's an impossibility she refuses to consider, Eleanor washes her hands and then joins me at the table. Sitting across from me, she sighs and then wipes away a stray crumb from next to her.

"You know, Ronan, I think you've made a lot of progress recently. I'd say Kate has a lot to do with that, but it's mostly you. I get the sense you've decided you've had enough of hanging out in your bedroom."

I nod and gently correct her. "Hiding out, you mean."

She smiles at how I accurately put what I've been up to for nearly two months since I came here. "Well, hiding out works too. I'm just glad to see you happy. I've been waiting for that for so long."

"I think everyone has."

"You know, I've watched you grow into a good man, Ronan. I always knew you would be. Your mother and I used to sit down here at this very table when you were a baby in her arms and talk about what your future would be like. Your father was sure you'd be great at business, of course, but she believed you had a different future. She didn't know what, though, and that bothered her because with all four of your brothers, she could sense what theirs would be."

Eleanor stops and sighs again. "Well, not Theo, although she was sure he was going to make a big splash in the world, no matter what he did. But she knew Matthias would be an artist, even though she also understood your father was going to make sure he took over the company someday. She hoped it would be later than sooner. And with Kellen, she sensed from when he was small that he'd be a titan of industry. That's what she called him."

I have to smile at the idea that my mother knew that about my Kellen. He's always been the bossiest of all of us.

"And Marius. Well, she had a feeling he had the artistic gene in him too, and she was right. But with you, she wasn't sure what you'd turn out to be, but I know she always believed you'd be someone people would look up to. Not in a business or artistic way, but I remember her telling me she had a feeling her last child would be someone who touched people."

Hearing my mother believed I'd be someone special makes me happy, but I can't help but wonder what she'd think of me now. Whatever incredible things I was going to do can't happen anymore. I doubt anyone is looking up to me after all that's happened.

"I hope she's not looking down right now with disappointment," I say in a low voice, avoiding Eleanor's gaze.

She reaches across the table and gently touches my left hand. "Oh, no. Ronan, your mother adored you. Your father too. You have no idea how happy she was when you were born."

"Kellen used to always tell me they should have stopped with him," I say with a laugh, remembering how he'd throw that in my face when he was angry as a kid.

"She and your father didn't know if she could have another baby after Kellen since she had such a hard time with him. When she found out she was pregnant again, the doctors warned her that it could be a difficult pregnancy that may risk you or her or both of you, but she never wavered. And oh, did she have morning sickness with you! We went through more saltines in those nine months than this house has seen in thirty years! But then you were born, and I swear I never saw her happier. Of course, she then told your father they were done having kids."

"Well, you know what they say. Stop when you finally get it right."

"She believed in you, honey. Your mother never doubted for a second that you were someone special. I know she's looking down from heaven and seeing how hard things have been for you and wishing she could help."

I know Eleanor is simply trying to be nice, but I can't deny hearing how much my mother thought I'd do in this world depresses me. She was gone before she saw me do anything with my life, and now that's all I can look back on with pride since nothing I'm doing now is worth much.

Standing from the table, I smile and say, "Thanks, Eleanor. For everything."

As I step into the hallway, I nearly run into Sabrina standing just outside the kitchen. "Hey! I didn't want to interrupt you and Eleanor since I heard you two were talking. Are you going somewhere?"

I almost answer the same place I'm always at, but I

stop myself. I don't want to spend the rest of the day in my room.

"Not sure. Maybe for a walk."

That seems to thrill her, for some reason. "Great! I'll come too! We can talk."

Unsure what she wants to discuss, I shrug and start walking back toward the door in the kitchen. Maybe I'll take a walk around the estate again. It'll remind me of Kate.

Sabrina hurries to keep up with me as we walk across the front grass. As we pass the gardener named Leo tending to the flowers planted around the front of the house, I give him a casual nod and he returns the gesture.

"Hey, have you ever gotten a message from your mother?"

I turn to look at her and shake my head. "My mother died when I was only ten. I don't think she left me any message, though."

Pushing on my left arm, she laughs. "Not that kind of message, silly. No, I mean a message like you know she's trying to tell you something but not with words."

Leave it to the babysitter to believe in new age bullshit. Where did Ava find this person?

I continue walking, already wondering why I let her come with me. "I don't believe in stuff like that."

"Well, that explains why you've never gotten one. She's probably been trying this whole time, but you're not listening."

Not really one who rolls his eyes, I make an exception for her now. "That's ridiculous. She can't tell me anything. She's dead."

Bizarrely, that seems ridiculous to Sabrina, and she twists her face into a grimace. "Not speaking. Seriously, open your mind, Ronan. There are ways people who've left us can still send us messages they want us to hear. You just have to keep an open mind and keep your eyes open. A sign can be anything, so pay attention."

"Uh-huh."

She stops and nudges my left arm again, forcing me to stop walking. "Fine. You don't have to believe me, but I bet your mother is trying to send you a message right now. Probably wants to tell you to stop being so narrow-minded."

"I highly doubt it."

Even though Sabrina can't know it since she knows next to nothing about me, I'd love to get a message from my mother or my father. I'd love to know if they see something better for me than what I'm dealing with now.

But that doesn't happen, no matter how much this hippy-dippy woman wants to believe it does.

"Do me a favor, okay? Think about your mother and try to find one thing that reminds you of her. That's all I ask. And if you happen to see something in the next few days that is the same as that thing you thought of, then that's your mother trying to send you a message."

Still not buying any of this, I ask, "And what exactly would she be trying to tell me?"

Sabrina smiles and pokes her finger into my abs. "That's for you to figure out. Time for me to go get Theo for some play time!"

With that, she spins on her heel and walks away back toward the house. I really need to ask my brother where they found this person.

What nonsense.

As I continue walking, my mind goes back to a sunny summer day much like this one when my mother and I walked out to the grove of trees on the far right side of the estate. My brothers and I were given strict instructions never to go there alone, but this time my mother took me with her. I don't remember what she needed to go out there for. I don't remember much of what we talked about on our way there, although I know we talked since my mother believed talking to children was one of the most important things a parent could do.

What I do remember is a rabbit sitting under one of the trees. I wanted to touch it, but my mother told me only to look. As we stood there holding hands, the rabbit nibbled on something and then hopped away.

Maybe that's what I'm supposed to be looking for. But that rabbit's long gone by now.

Jesus, now Sabrina has me buying into her nonsense.

MATTHIAS CALLS FOR ME FROM HIS OFFICE, SO I walk down the hall and stop in the doorway. "What's up?"

"Just wondering how things went down at the carriage house."

With a smile, I nod and answer, "Great! Thanks for

letting me use it for a little while. We had lunch and then went for a walk. It was nice. I was thinking maybe of doing that again next week."

My brother seems excited by my idea. "Feel free to use it whenever you need to. I won't be able to spend much time down there this week or next because of work, so at least someone will get to enjoy the space."

"Thanks!"

I turn to leave and what Sabrina said earlier pops into my head. Spinning back around, I say, "Hey, I know this is going to sound stupid, but have you ever seen any rabbits around the estate?"

He thinks for a long moment and nods. "I saw one a few years ago. I was sitting out under the big tree on the west lawn drawing, and I swear one posed for me so I could sketch it. I was surprised it was willing to sit that long for me. I got nearly everything sketched out on him but his fur."

"Interesting. Thanks! I'll let you get back to work."

Matthias cocks an eyebrow and asks, "Any reason you're asking me about rabbits?"

"Just something Sabrina said to me earlier. By the way, where did you guys find her?"

My brother smiles. "She's Ava's friend Eden's cousin. Or something like that. All I know is she's related to Eden in some way and was able to start immediately."

His mention of Eden brings me back to last year when Marius, Kellen, and I were hanging out at that party Matthias and Ava had. "Eden, the one that Marius is always denying he has any interest in but is always checking out? That Eden?"

"The very one," Matthias answers with a laugh.

That's also interesting, although I'm not sure why. Perhaps someone should mention to my brother that the girl he was hitting on out at the pool is related to the one he likes. Then again, knowing Marius, he'd be fine with that.

"Where is he anyway? He blew in like the wind, and I haven't seen him much since."

"He went into the city to see Kellen and Salem. I think he's coming back tomorrow? I'm not sure. You know him. He comes. He goes. He's pretty much like that wind you mentioned."

That's the best description of Marius King I've ever heard.

"All right. I'm going to handle a few things. I'll see you later, Matthias."

As I begin to walk away, he says, "I'm glad to see you out more. I hope that means you're feeling better."

I look back and shrug. "A little. Some days more than others."

With the thought that maybe Sabrina isn't completely out of her mind with that woo-woo stuff she was talking about, I walk back outside and head for the big tree that Matthias mentioned. I know that rabbit he saw is long gone, but who knows? Maybe one of his descendants is around.

After ten minutes of waiting and not seeing any rabbits at the tree, I start walking. A half hour later, I've seen nothing close to a rabbit and I'm at the far edge of the estate. I look around for a few minutes, but nothing.

God, I really am an idiot for listening to Sabrina.

It's just that the thought of my mother sending me a message made me hopeful.

So much for that.

I walk back to the house and see her sitting in the kitchen with little Theo in his high chair. Plopping down in a seat across from her, I say, "I looked and saw nothing that could mean any message. I think you're full of it."

She doesn't seem fazed by my irritation at her silly ideas, though. "Did you let your mother know you were listening?"

God, this person is tiring.

"First of all, you never mentioned anything about having to tell her I was listening. And second of all, how the hell am I supposed to do that? Talk to the air?" I ask, not even trying a little to hide my disgust.

"Then how would she know you wanted to hear from her?" she asks in all seriousness.

Disgusted I'm even having this conversation, I look over at Theo as he once again makes a mess with his Cheerios. "If it was really her, she'd know without me having to say a word," I grumble.

Theo smiles at me, so I take one of his little oat rings and pop it into my mouth. He's got the idea. Don't listen to the idiocy this woman serves up and instead simply focus on playing with your food.

I stand to leave, tired of talking to Sabrina, but as I walk out of the kitchen, she calls out, "You have to at least give her a head's up. Tell her you want a sign!"

Without bothering to respond, I walk back outside. The truth is I'd love to get a message from my mother. I may think Sabrina is full of shit, but I wish she wasn't. Even knowing my mother sees me would make me happy.

I walk back toward the big tree as I try to talk myself into actually talking to my mother. When I'm sure no one is around and no one can see me, I look up and say, "Mom, are you there? If you're there, give me a sign. Send a rabbit like the one we saw that time."

When I finish, I regret not saying something about letting me know she isn't disappointed in me, so I add, "I just want to know you still think I'm capable of doing something special and not some loser."

I look around in anticipation, but I see no rabbits. Maybe it takes time.

So I keep walking, enjoying the hot summer day. The temperature has to be close to ninety today. When all of us were small, we loved days like this. The hotter the better. My mother and Eleanor used to warn us not to wear ourselves out in the heat, but we never listened. They'd insist we take water breaks, but the last thing we wanted to do was come in the house when we were having fun.

I loved growing up here. There was space to run and play, and no matter what season it was, we enjoyed ourselves. With five of us, I always had someone to pester. I had a childhood I can look back on and know was good.

Except for the fact that my mother died. She never got to see me grow up. Never got to see me meet Kate. Never got to see me play ball.

Like every time I think about what I dreamed of doing, I glance down at where my missing right hand should be and wince. I wish she had been able to see me even once play baseball.

Looking around, I wonder if she can see me now. If she can, is she as disappointed as I am at what my life has become?

I see another large tree ahead, so I walk toward it and sit down in the shade it offers. Wiping my forehead, I close my eyes and think about how I'd be playing ball now if it weren't for my accident. I'd be out on the field, just in from the grass where I always played. I can practically smell the scent of fresh cut grass fill my nostrils.

For the first time since I was a little boy, I haven't watched even a single game on TV this year. I tried, but I could only watch a few seconds of a Yankees game before I had to turn it off. It hurt too much knowing that's all I ever wanted to do and that dream will never happen for me now.

Tears burn my eyes, so I wipe them away. When I open my eyes, I'm stunned to see a rabbit sitting not five feet away. It's just staring at me, like it thinks it knows who I am or can't figure out what I'm doing out here with him.

I wait for it to move, but it doesn't. For a second or two, I wonder if someone is pranking me and put a rabbit figurine there for me to see. That doesn't make sense, though, since I haven't told anyone what I asked my mother to send me for a sign.

Is this for real?

After a minute or so, I start talking to it. The rabbit remains still, so I say, "I hear you might be a sign. Know anything about that?"

Still, he doesn't move. He simply stares at me. So I continue.

"I asked my mother to give me a sign she can see me and isn't disappointed in me. I'd like to think that's you. To be honest, I need it to be you. I'm struggling here. I want to get back to a normal life, but I'm a mess. The girl I loved and lost is back, and all I can think is I'm going to lose her again. I want to be the person I used to be, but I can't be."

Stopping, I hold up my right arm for the silent rabbit still staring at me, and I'm surprised when it doesn't flinch at my movement. "Because of this. I don't know what to do now that I can't do what I've always dreamed of doing. I don't have to do anything, I guess. I have enough money to just lie around. I don't want to do that, though."

I take a deep breath and let it out slowly, feeling some of my sadness leave with it. "What would you do if you lost one of your paws? It would suck. Trust me. Then again, it would probably be worse for you since you walk on all four of your legs. The thing is, though, I needed the hand I lost to play ball. That's all I ever wanted to do, and I finally got my chance. And then, one night, in a flash, the chance was gone. So now I hang out here and chat up rabbits in my spare time. Nice, huh?"

He stares at me, and I feel compelled to say what I never utter out loud. Lowering my voice, I say, "If this is you, Mom, let me know I didn't let you down. Show me something that will let me think you're watching over me."

I finish talking and watch as the rabbit appears to

nod his head before hopping away. Tears fill my eyes at the thought that this was really my sign.

Tilting my head back, I look up through the green leaves above me toward the sky. "Thanks for listening, Mom. I love you. I miss you so much. It's been so hard these past few months. I wish you were here."

By the time I get back to the house, I feel like a new man. Maybe that whole rabbit thing was just one living creature watching another ramble on about his life, but maybe it was what Sabrina claimed would happen.

All I know is I want today to be a new start for my life. And for Kate and me.

# CHAPTER TWENTY-ONE

ate

MY PHONE VIBRATES ACROSS THE TABLE AS I SIT reading over my new job policies for the third time, so I reach for it and see it's Ronan. Excited to hear from him, even though it's only been a day since our lunch together, I hurriedly answer.

"Hey, what's up?"

"I was wondering if you'd like to do lunch again. How about Monday?" he asks, and I swear I hear a tiny hint of fear in his voice.

Hoping to let him know he doesn't have to worry, I quickly answer, "Sure!"

Normally, I'd ask where, but I get the sense Ronan isn't ready to leave Matthias and Ava's house yet. That's okay with me. I'm not exactly slumming it by going to lunch at the King estate.

"Okay. Say noon?"

My heart fluttering, I answer, "Okay. Noon sounds great."

"I want to tell you about something Sabrina told me about. I didn't buy into it at first, but it turned out to be true. It's going to sound completely crazy."

Just the mention of her name makes me uncomfortable. I can't put my finger on why, but I don't like her. Yes, it may be simple jealousy, but it feels like something more. Something darker. I wish I could figure it out.

"Oh?" I say, trying to sound interested when all I want to ask is, "What did she tell you, and was she wearing that black bikini at the time?"

"Yeah. I'll save it for when we have lunch because it feels like something I want to tell you in person, but it's cool."

"Oh, okay. I guess I'll see you Monday at noon," I say, wishing I didn't have to wait two days to see him again.

He remains silent for a few seconds before saying, "I'm happy you're coming over again, Kate."

And just like that, I forget about the babysitter and focus on the fact that Ronan, the only man I've ever loved, just said he's happy he's going to get to see me again. It reminds me of how he was after our first date.

"Me too. Do you want me to bring anything?"

"No. Just you is all that's needed."

I giggle, remembering the first time he said that to me. "I love that you haven't changed. You said that when we were going on our first picnic and I asked you if you needed me to bring anything. I remember it like it was yesterday. You said, 'Kate, all you need to bring is you.' Remember?"

He doesn't answer immediately, but after a second or two he says, "That's right. Then we went to that park and had a real picnic complete with checkered tablecloth I laid out on the ground."

"And ants!" I add, laughing at the memory of the two of us trying to get rid of what seemed like an entire colony of ants that decided to invade our date.

"Oh, that's right. There were a lot of ants that day. I can still feel them crawling up my legs. That was the last time I ever tried to eat on the ground. It's been tables and chairs ever since."

I love hearing him so willing to talk about our shared past. We had so many wonderful times back then. I think we can have them again too. I know I just have to be patient this time.

Unsure if I should mention how talking like this makes me feel, I take a chance that he won't be chased off by me sharing my feelings. "You know, I like talking about what we used to do. We had fun together back then."

I hear the smile in his voice when he says, "We did. I never think about those times with you without smiling."

"I'm glad. You deserve that. We both do."

God, I want to say so much more, but I'm afraid. Ava told me all he's been through, and all I want is to let him know I don't care if he ever leaves the estate or doesn't have a right hand. None of that means anything to me if I can have him in my life again.

I don't say anything, though, because she also

mentioned how withdrawn he's been. If I push too hard, he might shy away from us doing anything more together, and that would break my heart.

It's okay. I can be patient. I just hope he ends up with me and not that Sabrina girl.

"Is something wrong, Kate?" he asks, tearing me out of my thoughts.

"No. Why?"

"You just said we both deserve to smile. It sounded like you're having a hard time, so I thought I'd ask."

Ava warned me that Ronan hasn't been able to focus on anyone outside himself since his accident, so his asking me that question gives me hope that the old Ronan is somewhere inside waiting for him to let him out.

"Just my nerves about school. I was looking over its policies when you called. I hope I can do a good job. That's all."

"Kate, you're going to be the best teacher there. Nobody is sweeter than you are, and that's what little kids need. They're going to love you. I know it."

"God, I hope so. From your lips to God's ears, you know?"

He hums for a moment and says, "You got this, and you have people who care about you cheering you on. You're going to be great. I'm already thinking we need one of those signs for your desk that says teacher of the year or world's greatest teacher."

Ronan always could make me laugh even while he was being supportive. "Nothing like putting the cart before the horse, right?"

"Maybe, but I have a good feeling about this for you. Your dream is coming true. I'm happy for you."

Gone is the smile in his voice by the time he reaches the word dream, and every word after that sounds like it's being pulled from his throat. I know it has nothing to do with me finally becoming a teacher. He's happy for me. I think it just brings into focus how he was so close to achieving his dream when it all ended that night.

"Thank you, Ronan. It means so much to me that you're in my corner. I always knew I was safe when you were by my side."

My voice shakes as I say that, sure I've pushed too much. He doesn't say anything immediately after, making me sure I've gone too far.

But then he says in that sexy way I always loved, "I'll always be by your side, Kate. You don't have to worry."

Relief washes over me. I don't know if this is progress or not, but it's only been a week since I first saw him after all those years and he told me to go away, so I'm counting this as a huge step forward.

"So I'll see you Monday for lunch?"

"I'll be there. See you then!"

The call ends, and I'm so happy I can't wipe the smile from my face. Maybe on Monday we'll take the next step. Just thinking about kissing Ronan again makes every inch of me feel more alive than I've felt in a long time.

"What's that face for?" my father asks as he walks into the dining room.

"I was just talking to Ronan. We're having lunch on Monday."

My father's eyebrows slowly rise into his forehead as he sits down across the table from me. "Ronan again? I heard he had a tough time recently. How is he doing?"

"He's doing great," I answer, sort of lying.

I don't want to tell my father the absolute truth about Ronan, or he'll question whether or not I should continue seeing him. Fathers can be so protective, even about their daughters in their mid-twenties.

Pointing at his right arm, he asks, "Is what your mother told me right? Did he have to have his hand amputated because of a car accident?"

I nod, not wanting to talk about this. "He did, but he's dealing with it really well. It just takes a while to get used to, I'm sure."

My father presses his lips together, as if he wants to stop himself from saying something, but then he smiles. "It can be very hard for amputees, Kate. They have to get used to a whole new life that includes learning to do everything without the limb they lost. He wanted to be a baseball player, if I remember correctly, didn't he?"

"He got signed to the minor league team for Washington," I say proudly. "But you don't have to worry, Dad. I know what you're thinking. You're thinking he's in bad shape, but he's okay, and he's going to be even better from now on."

Again, my father's eyebrows show his surprise. Or maybe it's disbelief.

"Because you two are back together?"

Before he can start in on some lecture about how only Ronan himself can make a better life for himself and I shouldn't expect things to go smoothly just because I want them to, I stop him. "Because he has people who love him all around wanting the best for him."

I stand up because I don't want to continue this conversation, but my father continues. "Kate, I think it's great Ronan has so many people rooting for him. Just keep in mind that he's got to want to be okay for himself. Trust me. I know something about this. I may only be a plastic surgeon, but I see patients every day who think happiness comes from changing things on the outside. That isn't how things work." Tapping his chest above his heart, he adds, "Happiness comes from in here."

My father means well, but he tends to worry too much about me. I know what I'm doing. Ronan needs me now, so I plan to be there for him. He'd do the same for me if I needed it.

"I know, Dad. Remember, you and Mom didn't raise a fool."

That makes him smile even as he shakes his head. "Oh, to be young and in love again. Well, I said my piece. Take from it what you will."

"I love you, Dad. Don't worry. I'll be fine."

I will be. Just as long as Ronan and I get a second chance at what we lost before.

∼

WHY WE COME TO CHARLEY'S IS BEYOND ME, BUT I swear Jessie loves this place. It's a restaurant that wants more to be a bar, so they installed TVs everywhere throughout the building. As a result, any time any sport has something going on, every TV in the place is on and showing it while music blares.

Leaning across the table so I can hear her, my friend asks loudly, "What are you thinking of getting?"

I hate yelling what I have to say every time we come here. Maybe we should learn some sign language so we can have an actual conversation over dinner. Or I guess we could sit on our phones and text what we have to say to one another.

Instead of straining my voice, I simply shake my head. I refuse to yell in a restaurant. Even this one.

Jessie sits back and huffs her disgust. I'm not sure what she's unhappy about, but I can't imagine it's this place. She says they have the best spinach dip in the world. That's a dubious achievement, it seems, but it keeps bringing her back time after time.

I return to looking at the menu, unsure what I want to get. The decibel level in here makes thinking next to impossible. No wonder the only people who seem to come here anymore other than Jessie and me are young college guys. Clearly, they don't care about their hearing. Come find me in forty years, dude. Then you'll care.

As I decide between the turkey club and some hamburger with a kind of cheese I've never heard of, Jessie pulls my menu down so I'm looking at her. Instead of saying anything, she motions toward the door before standing up.

Okay, I guess we're leaving. That's fine with me.

I follow her out to the host desk where she tells them we decided not to stay, and a very busty redhead in a tank top nods and waves goodbye to us in the perkiest fashion I've ever seen. Thankful for the break on my ears, I'm happy when we get outside. At least the noise of the street isn't deafening.

"Seriously, Jess. I know you love that dip they have, but ever since they chose to become some sports bar and grill thing, that place is awful. I think I have ringing in my ears, and we were only there for less than a half an hour. I can only imagine how the people who work there feel after their shift."

My friend levels her gaze on me and shakes her head. "What are you? Eighty? Jeez, Kate. Did you see all those guys in the bar? It was like a hot guy smorgasbord in there!"

Now I see why she likes Charley's so much. I should have guessed.

"I didn't see them. My back was facing the bar. Anyway, I don't care about those guys."

Rolling her eyes, she sighs like I'm a hopeless cause she puts up with. "I forgot. Ronan. And what exactly is happening with that? He's where on a Saturday night?"

I start walking toward her car parked down the street. "Leave him alone. There's nothing wrong with someone who doesn't like hanging out in bars on the weekends."

Behind me, she says, "Yeah, but he doesn't go anywhere, Kate. There's a big difference between not loving the bar scene and being a shut-in."

Furious she had the nerve to say that, I spin around and snap, "Don't talk about him like that. So he doesn't feel comfortable enough leaving his house yet? Big deal. It's the twenty-first century. He can order food to be delivered from nearly every restaurant there is. He can have groceries delivered. He can buy anything he wants online and have it on his doorstep in days, if not hours. I'm not sure why anyone leaves their house at all nowadays."

She stops walking and gives me a strange look. "Hey, I wasn't being mean. What's up with you? You seem ultra-sensitive about him."

As much as I don't want to admit it, she's right. I am sensitive about Ronan. He's hurting, and I'm worried I'm not going to be able to break through that pain so we can be together. Meanwhile, he seems to have a grand old time with that babysitter or nanny or whatever she is who Ava has helping her with the kids.

And on top of all of that, my family and my best friend don't seem very enthusiastic about my being back with the only guy I've ever loved.

Looking away, I avoid her gaze and answer, "I know. I didn't mean to get bitchy there. I'm just worried about him."

Jessie steps toward me and wraps her arm around my shoulders. "I get it, but I'm more worried about you. No nastiness here, but honestly, Kate, do you think he's even capable of having a relationship in the state he's in? From what you've told me, he's having a hard time dealing with what happened to him. Maybe now's not the best time to expect anything from him."

All this talk about Ronan and how he may not be

the man I want him to be anymore makes me sad, and I hang my head while I try not to let it get to me. I know everyone is just looking out for my best interests, but I don't need to be reminded of how hard it might get for us to be back together. Why can't everyone just be supportive?

"I haven't told you everything. He's going to be fine. I know. We went for a long walk the last time I was at the house, and we talked about all sorts of things. He's trying so hard, Jess. I know you and my family weren't there, but I was, and I know he's going to be okay."

"Well, let's find ourselves a restaurant that doesn't require us to scream at the top of our lungs so every person within ten feet can hear all our business. I'm starving, and I want to know what you mean about this everything you haven't told me, okay?"

I smile and nod my agreement, even though I'm not sure I want to tell her everything. I'm not in high school anymore, but to be honest, even back then I didn't tell my friends every detail about my time with Ronan. From the first time we went out on a date, I wanted to keep him to myself. Yes, he was popular and rich and every girl around wanted him, but I didn't think of him that way.

To me, he was just the guy who liked me enough to sit around and watch me study or help quiz me for tests because he knew how important my grades were. He was all those other things in public, but in private, Ronan was a thoughtful person who never made me wonder if he cared about me. I didn't want to share that with the entire world.

I follow Jess toward a much quieter place closer to where she parked her car. The Library, an aptly named restaurant, may not have her favorite spinach dip, but at least we'll be able to talk. Plus, they have a bar, so if she wants to scope out the next love of her life, she can do that too.

Not that she'd ever call anyone that. Jessie McIntyre has no need for love, according to her. At our age, all we should want is a good time. At least that's what she likes to believe.

Personally, I've always preferred being serious about someone. I'm a one-man woman at heart, something she never fails to poke fun at because she simply can't understand it.

# CHAPTER TWENTY-TWO

ate

BY THE TIME OUR FOOD ARRIVES, I'VE TOLD JESSIE A little about my biggest concern with Ronan, and it isn't that he's struggling to deal with what happened to him in that accident six months ago. It's that Sabrina.

Shaking salt onto her baked potato smothered in cheese and green onions, she says, "Do you think he might like her? I don't like that she lives there. Too much easy access to the goods."

Just the way she says that makes me feel even worse, so she quickly adds, "Not that she's getting any of that access. Forget I said anything about that and focus on him. Do you think he's into her?"

"Truthfully, I don't know. I mean, what guy wouldn't be? She's pretty, looks great in a bikini since she's as thin as a rail but still has big boobs, and somehow she's gotten close enough to him to shave his face."

Jessie takes a forkful of baked potato into her mouth and groans. "You don't want to know what I think about that."

She asks me about it, and I tell her, and now she doesn't want to give me her opinion? Is she trying to drive me nuts?

"Just tell me so I can try to eat my salad, okay?"

Not that my stomach is in the mood for food anymore. Not with how it's twisting into a knot Alexander the Great couldn't get through.

"Shaving a man is very sexy. Remember that guy I dated in junior year? The one who turned twenty-one ahead of all of us and would buy us beer and hang out all the time? Well, I shaved him once. We had a very hot night."

I stare down at my salad as my appetite all but disappears. "You're not helping."

"Well, in my defense, I did say you didn't want to know what I thought about shaving a man."

"So it's hopeless. I might as well just jump on the next guy who shows his face in this restaurant," I say, my emotions quickly careening toward depression.

Setting her fork down, Jessie stops eating. "No, nothing is ever hopeless. We're smart women. We can figure this out. So maybe he does like Miss Young Thing paying attention to him. So what? From what you've told me, the guy deserves a little happiness after all he's had to deal with. Let him ogle the girl. I'm thinking he still cares about you."

Nowhere close to believing that now, I stab my

fork into my salad and spear a tomato covered in Russian dressing. "Oh yeah? Why's that?"

"Because he set up that whole lunch for you. He made sure that woman who works for him made your favorite foods. The man remembered that from five years ago, Kate. You told me he hates chocolate, yet he had her bake a chocolate cake just for you? He's into you."

He did do all those things. That's true.

"Her name is Eleanor, and she doesn't work for him. She's the woman who's been with his family since before he was born."

Jessie waves away my defense of Eleanor. "Whatever. Fine. What matters is he went to that effort for you. That means something."

Sighing, I stuff the tomato wedge into my mouth and chew it before saying, "He's always been very thoughtful. It's just who he is."

"So she shaved him? You should thank her. You said he looked like some wilderness guy who'd lived in a cabin for years without a shower or a razor."

The way Jessie says that makes me smile, but a second later, I see someone walk into the restaurant, and my mood instantly sours. She sees my expression fall and turns around to look for the reason.

"Sweet baby Jesus, who is the god in the gray t-shirt and jeans, and why do you look so miserable?" she says as she stares at him.

Of course, he sees the two of us looking at him and begins to walk over to talk to us. Super.

I can't answer her questions before Marius King stops next to our table, smiling like he's thrilled to see me. Since I'm convinced he's hated me for years, I have to assume that grin of his is mocking me.

"Katie Abbott, I keep seeing you in the most unexpected places. What are you doing here at The Library?" he asks like this is his spot and someone like me doesn't belong here.

Jessie mouths the word Katie, as if she's shocked anyone had the nerve to call me that, and looks up at him with nothing short of pure lust in her eyes. For his part, he seems interested in her too and turns his attention toward her, thankfully.

"I'm eating," I say, answering his question with as little effort as possible since he's clearly moved on by the time I get the words out.

"And who's this?" he asks Jessie.

She offers her hand to shake his, and with the first touch of his skin on hers, I'm convinced my best friend has finally fallen in love. I should warn her about him, but since I know her thoughts on men, I doubt he'll be more than a distraction for a short time.

"Jessie. And who are you?"

"Marius King," he answers in a voice that instantly says he thinks that means something.

My friend recognizes the last name and turns her head to face me. "King? As in Ronan King?" Looking back up at him, she asks Marius, "Any relation?"

"He's my baby brother. I'm surprised your friend here has never mentioned me. I've known her for years."

Even though neither he nor Jessie are likely interested in my response, I mumble, "I can't imagine why I'd mention you at all since you've never been anything but a bust ass every time I'm around."

I'm surprised when he turns his attention to me and says, "You always were very sensitive when it came to me, Katie. I just like to tease."

I look across the table and can almost read my friend's mind when he says that. To her, that sounds as sexy as hell. To me, it sounds like an excuse for being a jerk ever since we met.

Whatever he means, I don't say anything in the hopes that he'll go away, but then Jessie offers to have him join us, clearly not reading my mind, and he accepts, sliding into the booth next to her. How nice. She's getting to enjoy herself with this King while I sit here worrying about his brother and what he feels for the nanny.

The all-too-sexy nanny who looks unbelievably good in a bikini.

And then, it's as if Jessie suddenly can read my mind and says to Marius, "So what's the deal with the nanny your sister-in-law has?"

I watch in horror as Marius smiles at me as if he knows every worry that's filling my head about her. Throwing Jessie a nasty look, I attempt to change the topic, but of course, Marius isn't having it.

"Interesting girl, don't you think, Katie? She parades around the house like she owns the place. Not that I'm upset because the view is all right."

He and Jessie stare across the table waiting for my response, but I have no idea what to say to that. Is he goading me into something he plans to use to tease me again? Or does he genuinely not like the way Sabrina acts?

When I don't say a word, my friend says, "Well, she was nice enough to help your brother out with a shave. She can't be all bad, right?"

Every syllable gives him more ammunition to bust my ass, I'm sure, and if he doesn't use this conversation for that, he'll probably use it in some way to hurt what I'm trying to have with Ronan. God, I just want to disappear.

"That seemed a little too personal to me, but who am I?" Marius asks, clearly not interested in my opinion. "I prefer to save the shaving for women I'm closer to. My brother, on the other hand, is a nice guy, so I doubt he thought anything of it when she was shaving him."

I didn't think it was possible, but I hate Marius King even more now than I did before he sat down. Jessie looks at him like he's a god, of course, so he isn't going to leave anytime soon, unfortunately.

I'm in hell. This is what hell must be like for someone like me. The only thing that would make this experience worse is if a deranged clown walked in and joined us.

"So you don't think she's interested in him?" Jessie asks.

She's trying to help. At least I think she is. The problem is that Marius is going to go back to Ronan, and if he doesn't use everything he's heard here tonight to poison him against me, he's going to use it at some point in the future to embarrass me.

Whatever happens, nothing good will come of our little time here together.

Marius laughs at the question and shakes his head. "No way. Ronan isn't like the rest of us. Trust me. She could walk around naked in front of him, and he wouldn't bat an eyelash. I will say this, though. The opposite isn't true. She definitely has her eye on him."

My heart sinks. Oh, God. There it is. The terrible truth of the matter. Sabrina does want to be with Ronan, and there she is, twenty-four seven around him in that tiny bikini while I'm only around a few hours here and there.

And just to make things worse, Marius reaches out and touches my arm before saying, "Not to worry, Katie. Ronan never got over you. She's got nothing he wants."

I can't tell if he's making fun of me or not, and I don't care. These past few minutes with him have only served to make me miserable.

"My name is Kate, Marius. You know that. You've always known that. I've never been Katie to anyone at any time in my entire life."

The words come tumbling out of my mouth before I can stop them, and when I finish, Jessie stares at me like she's horrified and Marius simply smiles like he's enjoying himself immensely. Worse, I've probably given him the exact reason to do everything in his power to wreck my chances with his brother.

"You're Katie to me because you look like a Katie. Sweet. Innocent. Katie. Now if you'll excuse me, I'm meeting someone in the bar. See you out at the house."

With that, he gets up and walks away. Jessie

continues to stare at me in disbelief. I'm not sure what she's so surprised about. Even someone as timid as me has a breaking point.

"Um, what the hell was that?"

I shrug, not caring anymore since I imagine my shot with Ronan was just blown to smithereens. "I never liked the fact that he always insists on calling me Katie, so I told him."

"Not that. I was trying to get some details on that nanny. Why didn't you encourage him to talk? We might have found out some good stuff."

I look down at my food and stab my fork into my salad. "I didn't want to talk to Marius King about the nanny. All it does is make me realize she's got everything going for her, and I have nothing going for me."

Jessie touches my arm to show sympathy, but I doubt she understands. She's never cared about someone like I care about Ronan, and if she did, she'd just walk right up to him and tell him they were going to be together. My shyness doesn't allow that.

"If it makes you feel better, I don't think anything we said is going to hurt what you and Ronan have going."

"It doesn't."

"Then let's figure out a gameplan. So Miss Thing is young and pretty. From what his brother just said, Ronan doesn't care. That's good!"

I shake my head as despair starts to sink in. "She's there all the time, Jess. Even if she's not wearing that bikini every hour of every day, she's there. He told me on the phone before that he wants to talk to me about something she told him. They're having conversations that mean something to him. And where am I? Sitting in a restaurant being harassed by his older brother. It's hopeless."

"Nonsense!" she says a little too loud for The Library, and I look up to see diners near us glaring in our direction.

"Shhhh! Keep your voice down," I whisper. "Everyone in this entire place doesn't need to know what a mess my love life is."

Jessie leans forward, and in a low voice says, "Okay, okay. So they talk? So what? Talking doesn't mean anything."

"It does with a guy like Ronan," I say as I push the croutons in my salad around the bowl. "He's not like other guys. If I was with his brother there, then fine, conversation wouldn't mean anything. I can't imagine Marius King spends much time talking at all with women. Ronan is different. He's thoughtful, and talking to someone shows he cares."

I don't say what else I'm thinking. If he's talking to Sabrina, it's only a matter of time before he falls for her. It's who he is.

And I have no way to stop it.

"So you're just going to give up on the love of your life? Is that it?" Jessie asks sharply, like she's disappointed in me.

"What else is there to do? I can't compete with her on looks. I can't compete with the fact that she has home field advantage."

"Remember that he loved you for you!" she says too loudly again. This time she realizes her mistake and immediately lowers her voice for the rest of what she has to say. "Kate, you can't give up. If you care about him, then you have to fight for him."

Nothing she says is helping. "I love him. I always have. But what does that mean up against someone new and fun? All I am is a memory of who he used to be. She's the future. I'm the past."

That finally makes Jessie stop talking, which is for the best since I'm pretty sure I'm going to cry if we keep discussing this. I just have to accept that I can't compete against Sabrina.

"So what are you going to do? You already said you would go hang out with him again on Monday. Are you bailing on that?"

I nod, sighing as I feel everything slip away. "Yeah. What's the point of going now? And don't say at least I could check out Marius and see what he's up to for you because I'm not going to do that."

Jessie sits back against the booth and laughs. "I wouldn't ask you to do that. I have to say, though, if I had any idea Ronan came from such a good looking family, I wouldn't have given you a hard time about wanting to be with him."

"Ronan is nothing like that brother."

"So he isn't as sexy as all hell with a gorgeous body?"

I roll my eyes at her description of Marius. "Ronan is that, yes."

"So he's got money and looks like that brother, who by the way I'm absolutely sure offers a woman toe-curling good times?"

"I'm not talking about this with you anymore. Why

don't you go join Marius and whoever he's meeting? I'm sure they'd love a third."

Jessie shakes her head. "That man isn't available."

"I think you're mistaken. Marius King has always been as single as they come. I remember Ronan once saying his girlfriend back when we were dating ruined him for other women."

But my friend isn't hearing any of that. Shaking her head, she digs her heels in. "I don't care who ruined him for what. He's taken. Everything in his body language practically screams that."

I shrug, not caring if Marius is or isn't single. God help the woman who ends up with him. She better enjoy his sense of humor.

For me, there was always only one King I ever wanted.

I guess I better forget about that.

# CHAPTER TWENTY-THREE

onan

After Eleanor and I talk about what I'd like her to make for lunch on Monday, I sit alone in the kitchen wishing today was the day Kate was coming over. I should probably tell her how I feel, but every time I think about that, I dismiss it. I'm not the same person I was when we were together before. I want to be with her, but I'm just not sure she wants to be with me.

Lost in thought, I don't see Marius walk in until he sits down across from me at the kitchen table. He's smiling like some damn Cheshire cat, which can either mean he's happy or he plans to bust my balls about something.

"What's made you so happy this morning? I

thought you'd be sleeping in today since I heard you come in pretty late last night."

My comment on the time he came home surprises him. "Staying up because you're worried about me, little brother? I can take care of myself."

"Not worried. Just happened to hear you come in."

Leaning back in his chair, he chuckles. "And what were you doing up at three a.m., may I ask?"

As if I have a thrilling night life.

"I don't sleep a lot anymore, so I'm always up at that time," I answer, likely disappointing him with my boring life.

"Not hanging out with the new nanny?" he asks in that sing-song voice he uses when he's busting chops.

I shake my head, confused why he'd even ask that. "No. We aren't like that. She's usually busy with the boys."

My brother sets the chair back on the floor and leans forward toward me. "So you do know her schedule, though?"

I hate when Marius gets like this. I sense the teasing is coming soon, and although I have no idea why he insists on bringing Sabrina into it, I'm not biting.

"No, I don't know anything about her schedule. She lives here like I do and you do, for the time being. Other than that, I don't know what she does. Why the hell are you interested in if I know her schedule? Are you into her?"

That would explain his questions. And the way he was acting the other day.

Maybe I misread his mood today. Maybe he's not

eager to bust my balls about something stupid. Maybe he's just into the new nanny.

But he quickly dispels that theory when he shakes his head and answers, "She's not my type. I get a bad vibe off that one."

"Then why are you interested in if I know her schedule or not?"

Of course, he doesn't answer my question. Instead, he jumps up from his chair and walks over to the refrigerator to get a drink.

"Guess who I saw when I went to The Library last night?" he asks, again using that sing-song voice.

"No idea. The nanny?"

He pokes his head out from behind the refrigerator door and laughs. "I don't think she's old enough to get into bars, is she?"

"Fine. One of your exes? Let me guess. She threw a glass of something in your face, and then you charmed her into realizing she really wants you, and the two of you went back to her apartment and you showed her why she should miss you."

That gets me another laugh as he closes the refrigerator door and walks back to the table with a can of soda. Sitting down across from me again, he says, "I like the way you think, but no. Take another guess."

Already tired of this, I say, "I don't know. Someone you knew from high school?"

"No. Katie Abbott."

I'm surprised by his answer and blurt out, "My Kate?"

He grins like what I call her is amusing. "The very

same. She was there looking as sweet and innocent as always. Seriously, bro, you need to get going with her, or some guy is going to steal her away."

My jealousy rises with each word until I snap, "Someone like you, I presume?"

The look he gives me makes it seem like that's either the last thing he could ever imagine or the worst. Either way, I don't like it.

"Don't act like she's not beautiful and smart and everything you could ever want, Marius. I may not have both my hands anymore, but I have both of my eyes. Kate's the entire package."

My brother tips the soda can back against his lips and takes a drink before saying, "First of all, she's not my type. I like my women a bit more on the wild side. Second of all, if she's such a catch, why are you letting her be out on a Saturday night and not with you?"

As I plan on explaining to him that I don't feel the need to control Kate's every move, he adds, "And third of all, that girl you're crazy about is sure you're banging the nanny."

Thank God I'm not drinking the soda or I would have choked on it when he said that. "What? That's insane. I barely know Sabrina."

He points at my face and smirks. "You let her shave you. That's usually the prelude to fucking, man. In fact, I don't think there's ever been an occasion that a woman shaved me and then I didn't end up in bed with her. It's no wonder Katie is sure you're up to no good with the nanny."

Jesus, he needs to stop calling her that. It sounds so much worse when he doesn't use her name.

I stand up, already tired of him and this entire conversation. "I don't know what you're up to, Marius, but I'm not biting. I don't know what sick pleasure you get from busting my chops like this, but fucking drop it."

"Fine, but you're going to lose your chance with her if you keep going like this."

As much as I want to get away from him, I can't stop myself from asking, "Like what? What the hell am I doing?"

He looks around the kitchen like the answer is somewhere here and I should know it already before leveling his gaze on me. "It's what you're not doing, Ronan. She's clearly crazy about you. Always has been. Jesus, we all knew you two were madly in love, and that's before either of you likely knew what love was. The way she looks at you is the same as when you were together before. It's like the sun rises and sets with you, buddy, and meanwhile, you're planning lunches and not doing a thing to make her see you're crazy about her too."

God, I hate this brother sometimes. Everything is physical with him. He has no idea two adults can be around one another and not have sex.

"Kate likes those kinds of things. That's why I do them. I want her to see I care about her. Not everything has to be wham, bam, thank you ma'am, you know."

But he's not hearing anything I'm saying. "And all the while, there's a sweet, young thing living in this same house with you who's made it perfectly clear she'd jump you the moment she got a chance."

"I think you have a problem, Marius. Things aren't always about sex."

Sure I don't want her or Ava hearing this conversation, I look around for any sign of them. Thankfully, they don't seem to be nearby.

"Sabrina no more wants me than she wants you."

My brother leans back in his chair and sets his heels on the chair next to him. "Trust me, she'd take either of us. Hell, she'd probably take Matthias, if he ever gave her a whiff of opportunity. That one is nothing less than a gold digger there."

Even though I think he's so off the mark it's ridiculous, I can't help but be curious since it's obvious he knows something or heard something I haven't. I can't say she's ever obviously hit on me, but then again, I have no interest in her, so maybe I didn't pick up on it.

Taking a step back into the kitchen, I ask, "What makes you think that?"

He shrugs, like after bringing up the juiciest piece of gossip that's been heard in this house in ages now it's no big deal. I swear this brother lives to just get on people's nerves.

"It's the way she talks about staying around forever and loving being a part of this family. Dude, she's angling to have one of us, and my guess is she's set her sights on you because I'm too difficult to fool."

There it is. I knew this had something to do with him insulting me.

"And why would I be an easier target than you?" I ask, eager to hear what he really thinks of me. "Because you're basically a fucking horndog twenty-four seven, so from where I'm standing, you look like a much easier prize to get than me. So regale me with your expertise on why she'd think I'm easier to get."

Marius hesitates for a moment or two and then points at my right arm. "That right there, brother."

"Fuck you!"

Before I can get away from him, he continues with his nonsense. "Riddle me this, Ronan. When in the history of men and women has a woman ever offered to shave a man's face without wanting more? Seriously. It's like you're blind. I'd bet a hundred bucks she made sure to stick those pretty tits in your face while she was doing it, and all the while, you didn't even notice, did you?"

"Seriously, fuck you, Marius. To someone with a hammer, everything is a nail. To someone like you who only thinks of women as sexual playthings, of course the only reason Sabrina would want to help me is because she wants to get into my pants. Has it occurred to you that women are more than what's between their legs?"

For some reason I can't begin to fathom, that offends him. "You have no idea what I think about when it comes to women, but I for damn sure know when one wants to jump my bones. Maybe if you weren't so stuck in woe is me mode, you'd see it too."

I don't know why since Marius is always a fucking pain in the ass like this, but I lunge at him, swinging wildly with my left hand since that's all I have now. I haven't sparred with any of my brothers since my accident, so my control is next to nothing, but I land a punch or two before he starts fighting back.

He gets me good a couple times, but I shake it off because it feels so damn fantastic to take my anger out on someone other than myself. Enjoying myself far too much, I get him in a chokehold and take him down to the floor. I didn't think I could hold my own anymore since I'm missing one of the most important parts of fighting for me, but Marius isn't able to one-up me this time.

"Still got some fight in you, huh?" he says before I hit him hard in the jaw.

His eyes get big as the pain sets in, but I don't get to revel in it before he comes at me with a right hook that slams into my cheekbone. This brother has always been far more self-indulgent than the others, so I'm surprised he's still so good at landing a punch.

"What the hell is going on?" Matthias barks behind us.

I turn to look at him and let him know exactly why I'm beating the hell out of our brother, but Marius slams his fist into my right cheek, making talking next to impossible. Beneath me, he says, "Leave us alone, Matthias. We're busy."

"Doing what? Tearing up the kitchen? What the hell are you thinking, Marius?"

"He fucking jumped on me," he answers before I slam my fist into his nose.

Blood squirts everywhere, and a second later, Matthias pulls me by the back of my shirt off him. "Unless you want me to get involved in this, cut it out. Now!"

Marius jumps to his feet and marches over to the counter to get some paper towels so he can stop his nose from bleeding. I stand up and brush myself off, happy with how my first fight with only one hand went.

"You didn't do too bad, little brother," he says with a chuckle before tipping his head back and covering his face with paper towels.

I didn't do too bad?

"Who's the one who's bleeding, big brother?" I say with a laugh, taunting him.

If he wants to go for round two, I'm up for it. I haven't felt this strong since the accident. Fuck, this feels great!

Beside me, Matthias gives me a stern look. "What's wrong with you two? I come in here to get a drink to take back to my office, and I find you two brawling on the kitchen floor?"

What he means is what's wrong with me since Marius has always been a fighter. I've rarely enjoyed fighting as much as any of my brothers but especially since I lost my hand. That's all changed now, though, that I know I can still hold my own.

"He pissed me off," I answer with a smile. "So I decked him."

Matthias seems confused, like he doesn't know how to handle this new me. Turning to look across the room at Marius who's stopped the blood from pouring out of his nose, he shakes his head.

"And you? What the hell were you thinking?"

Marius lifts his hands and shows off the blood-soaked paper towel. "What? He came at me, so I defended myself. It wasn't anything big, so don't get all bunched up about it. Just two brothers working out their differences. You should know that. You and Theo used to beat the hell out of each other all the time when we were kids. You and I have gone a few rounds more than once. And you better get used to seeing this because you have two sons barely a year apart."

My oldest brother looks at me and blows the airs out of his lungs. "Well, I guess it's good to know you can still handle yourself?"

"Damn straight," I say with a big smile.

"Sure can," Marius says as he walks over to pat me on the back. "Ronan's back. It just took him getting pissed off to happen. Next time, though, could you stay away from my nose? This thing is going to be swollen all day now."

Now it's my turn to be confused. "I thought you'd be pissed."

"Nah. I meant everything I said. Your girlfriend is worried about Sabrina and you, and I think you're going to blow it if you don't get moving with her, but you're my baby brother, Ronan. I couldn't be angry with you for long."

Now I feel even better. "Even though I only have one hand and still kicked your ass?"

He rolls his eyes at that claim. "I let you get a few of those shots in, but you handled yourself."

Beside us, Matthias says, "Good. Wait, what is going on with Sabrina? Are we talking about the girl Ava has helping her with the boys?"

Marius starts dancing and undulating his body as he says, "Boom chicka wow wow, a wow wow. Better watch out, Matthias. Don't want this to become a boss and nanny thing."

My oldest brother shakes his head at him. "You watch too much porn, dude. Nobody is going to be doing anything with my kids' nanny." Then he looks at me and says, "You aren't doing anything with her, are you? I thought you and Kate were together again."

I'm starting to get a headache from my family. "No, I'm not. This one over here thinks she likes me and says that he saw Kate last night, and she all but came right out and told him she's worried about me and Sabrina. Since there isn't any me and Sabrina, Marius is full of shit."

Matthias pinches the bridge of his nose and sighs. "I don't know what's going on in my own house. I wonder if this is how Dad felt. If the two of you are done playing WWE, I'm going to get a drink and go back to work."

Marius and I nod and then look at him before saying in unison, "We're done."

Walking to the refrigerator, Matthias points at a spot on the floor. "If that's blood, you need to clean that up, Marius. Eleanor shouldn't have to deal with that."

He leaves, and I watch as my other brother grabs another handful of paper towels to clean the floor. Was he really serious about what he said about Sabrina being a gold digger?

"Hey, did you mean it when you said she wanted me?"

"Which one?"

I smile at that question. I can't remember the last time I had the possibility of two women wanting me.

"Sabrina."

Marius stands up and tosses the dirty towels in the garbage near the sink. "Yeah. Dude, you yourself said I'm a horndog. Well, listen to me then because I'm seeing something you clearly aren't. She's into you. The problem is I don't think it's because you have a sparkling personality and you're a fun guy."

Since he never lets up with busting my ass, I drop the bombshell about who Sabrina is related to. "You know, she's Eden's cousin."

His eyes grow big at that little piece of news. "Eden? Ava's friend?"

"Yep."

Shaking his head, he groans. "Oh, no. Not happening. There is no way she can be part of my family. Nope."

I laugh at his reaction to my news. "I don't plan on hooking up with her, so unless you are, I don't think we need to worry. I just thought you should know since you seem to be interested in Eden, or at least you were the last time I saw you two in the same room together at that party last year."

For some reason, this entire topic seems to upset my brother. "I'm not interested in Eden. Now she's definitely interested in me, but it isn't happening. No way. I need to go get cleaned up. I have things to do today."

He hurries out of the room, which strikes me as odd. "Okay. Nice talk and brawl. Let's do that again real soon."

While I don't really want to fight any of my brothers anytime in the near future, it feels fantastic to know I still can. When I was a kid, I could never win against them because they were so much bigger than I was. Then when I had that growth spurt in seventh grade and gained six inches in a year, suddenly I could hold my own with every one of them.

That all changed with my accident. I thought for sure I couldn't even defend myself against any of my brothers, much less win a fight. Now that I know I can, I feel like the old me again.

But as good as that feels, I need to figure out how to make Kate see I'm back to being the person she used to know.

And love.

# CHAPTER TWENTY-FOUR

ate

I STARE AT MY PHONE AS THE SECOND CALL FROM Ronan in ten minutes makes it vibrate across the table. I know I should answer it and tell him I won't be coming over tomorrow for lunch, but I don't want to say that.

If only that damn brother of his hadn't sat down to talk to us last night. If I didn't hate Marius King before, I damn sure do now.

The phone finally stops, and I push it further away from me. Everything had been going so well between us. Now all I can think is my worries about Sabrina weren't all for nothing.

Damn Marius!

Why couldn't the nanny want him instead? He's just as wealthy as Ronan, and he's as single as they come. He's also got the same good looks all the King brothers have, so why is she going after Ronan instead?

Even without thinking, I know the answer. Ronan isn't just good looking and wealthy. He's sweet, and compared to his brother, he's a much better choice for someone who wants to be happy. Still, Sabrina doesn't come across as a girl who's looking for Mr. Right. Marius could surely give her what she wants.

My phone chimes, alerting me to a new text. I pull it back toward me and see it's from Ronan. Oh, God. He probably knows I'm avoiding him and wants to know why. How am I going to tell him I can't come over anymore because of her?

For nearly five minutes, I stare at my phone, refusing to read the message. I know what it says. Ronan is nothing if not wonderfully predictable. When he cares about someone, he doesn't play games. He's straight up about how he feels, so I know that text says something about how much he can't wait to see me tomorrow.

I've dreamed of receiving a text like that again from him for nearly five years, and now that it's finally arrived, I won't even look at it. God, what is wrong with me?

My sister sits down in the chair across from me and rips open a bag of chips. Dressed in an old red t-shirt from her time at Cornell and black yoga pants with her dark hair up in a knot on the top of her head, she looks like she's decided to stay in and lounge around here at my parents' house today.

"Want any?"

I shake my head no. I couldn't eat now if I had to. My stomach is in knots over what to do about Ronan.

"What's going on? You look like something happened," Kelly says as she chomps on potato chips.

Unlike Jessie, my sister is more like me, so maybe she'll understand what's going on. "I have a problem."

She laughs and points at my face. "I already could tell that by your expression. You're like me, Kate. We'd be terrible poker players. So what's wrong?"

Blowing the air out of my lungs in a rush, I try to find the best way to explain what I'm dealing with. My sister is going through her marriage breaking up after her husband stepped out with another woman, so the last thing she needs to hear is something similar happening to me.

"It's Ronan."

That doesn't say much, so she eats another chip and says, "I could have guessed that. He's the only new thing in your life. I thought you were crazy about him."

"I am. I'm crazy, head over heels in love with him just like I always have been. All it took was just a couple times together, and I'm as in love with him as I was when we broke up."

She listens, crunching on those potato chips, and swallows a mouthful. "Ah, I get it. You're afraid he's going to cheat on you again. That makes sense. I'd probably feel that way about a guy if I started dating now too. But Ronan isn't like that. I mean, yes, he cheated on you that once, but he was crushed when you left him over that. Don't you remember how he would call and text every day after? I think if he wasn't away at school, he would have camped out on the doorstep to see you."

"That's not what I'm worried about."

At least she brought up the subject of cheating without crying. She must be feeling better. I bet if I mentioned that jerk husband of hers, she'd start bawling her eyes out, though.

Best to stay far away from that topic.

"Then what? Are you having a hard time with his disability?" she asks before grabbing another chip and popping it into her mouth.

What is she talking about?

"Ronan isn't disabled, Kelly. He's fine. He's just working through what happened to him."

That gets me an odd look, and she stops eating. Setting the bag of chips down on the table, she says, "He lost his hand in a car accident, Kate. He's disabled now. You may not want to think of him like that, but that's the way it is. I'm glad he's working through things, but that doesn't change the fact that he's disabled."

I've never thought of him as that until this very moment. Ronan has always been so much more than his physical body. I mean, of course I love how he looks. How could I not? His dark hair and dark eyes with his chiseled face and perfect mouth are nothing short of gorgeous. And that's nothing compared to the rest of him.

But I fell in love with the person who made me smile and cared about what I thought, unlike the other boys at school who always seemed interested in only one thing — getting into my pants. Ronan was sweet. Is sweet. That's what I love most about him. He's a man who's not afraid to show someone he cares about them.

He's everything I ever dreamed of in a man all wrapped up into one incredible package.

"You know, it's so typically you that you didn't think of him as disabled. This is why you're going to be a great teacher at that school. Kids need adults who see past what the outside is. You've got that in spades."

My sister and I didn't get along for a long time, but somehow through her sadness at the end of her marriage, she's become one of my biggest cheerleaders. I like that.

"Thanks. I guess I just don't care about him not having a right hand. To me, he's still Ronan, the boy I fell in love with who I thought I'd spend the rest of my life with."

Kelly returns to eating her chips and asks, "So what's the problem?"

I hesitate to say anything about Sabrina, but since my sister already broached the subject of cheating men, I guess it's okay. "There's another girl," I say quietly.

The stunned expression I see on my sister's face says I might have been mistaken about her being able to handle that, so I quickly add, "He hasn't done anything. Well, I'm not sure. Maybe he has. God, I don't know."

I'm surprised when she pushes the bag of chips away and sets her hands down on the table in front of her. "Okay, tell me everything. I have experience with this, after all, so I'll know if he's doing anything he shouldn't be."

"See that's the problem. Why shouldn't he do something? He and I aren't exclusive like we were back in the day."

She waves away that issue. "None of that matters. Now tell me what's happening."

I take a deep breath and start explaining the problem. "There's a girl working for Ava and Matthias taking care of their kids. Not really a girl, actually. I'm not sure how old she is, but the way she fills out a bikini tells me she isn't a girl at all. So let's say she's a woman. Pretty. More like beautiful. And she and Ronan spend time together. I don't know how he feels, but I think she's into him. Then I saw his brother last night, and he made things worse."

As I tear up thinking about how frustrated that brother of his makes me, she grumbles, "Let me guess. Marius. I swear he's the worst King of them all. What did he do?"

"He mentioned Sabrina like he knew something about the two of them together. I don't know what to do, Kelly. I've wanted Ronan back for so long. I know you don't understand how I could forgive him for cheating, but I did. And now that I have the chance to finally get what I want, this pretty thing with a gorgeous body who talks to him and makes him happy is getting in the way."

My sister smiles at me. "It is what it is when it comes to what he did. The only person who has to forgive him is you, and you do, so that's that. It's settled. As for this Sabrina person, first of all, can I tell you how much I hate that name? Ever since that stupid witch show, I've hated it. I hate all witchy names, but that's the worst. But I digress. She may be pretty, but she's not you, Kate. Ronan never stopped loving you. I'd bet money on it."

"But what if he sees her and thinks she's the better choice? She's not like me at all. She's always happy, laughing and having fun. I'm me. Serious. A third grade teacher. Boring."

I don't mention how much better her body is. I just can't say that out loud again. It's bad enough it's all I can think about.

"You're not boring! You are who you've always been, Kate. So you're serious? What's wrong with that? The world doesn't need any more clowns. We're goddamned inundated with them everywhere you turn. Ronan fell in love with you knowing full well how serious you were. Do you remember how he'd sit at this very table and just watch you study? I'm going to admit something to you I've never admitted before. That made me so jealous. Here you had an incredible boyfriend who loved you because you were smart. None of my boyfriends ever liked that about me. It's why I had to pretend to be bubbly or sexy all the time. Even that no good husband of mine never appreciated how smart I was. I abandoned my dreams of going to med school for him, and what did he do? The bastard cheated on me. Don't ever doubt that being intelligent is a great thing, Kate."

I know she's trying to help, but I'm just not

convinced I can make him want me like Sabrina can. "I get what you're saying, but how can I compete against some bubbly girl? She's got everything going for her. All I have is my big brain."

"Nonsense! You're fun too. You just have to make him remember the kind of fun you are."

I lower my head and stare at her in disbelief. "And what kind of fun is that?"

My sister doesn't miss a beat and answers, "The kind of fun some bimbo can't understand. Ronan isn't stupid. Unless something happened to him in that accident, he's still got a head on his shoulders. Show him you know how to have a good time."

She stops and then continues. "To be honest, though, I'm wondering if maybe you should just come clean with him. Tell him what you're worried about. He might come right out and say he has no interest in her, no matter how bubbly or sexy she is."

Looking down at the table, I mumble, "You should see her in a bikini. God, Kelly. I've never looked that good in my life, bikini or not. How can I compete with that?"

Kelly gently covers my hand with hers. "Here's the thing. If it was Marius King, I'd say it's game over. That guy has only ever been interested in women for their bodies. I'm pretty sure he wouldn't know intelligence if it bit him on the ass. But this isn't that King. This is Ronan, and he loved how smart you are. Remember that."

As my sister returns to devouring potato chips, I look down at my phone. I can't put off reading his message for any longer. I've never been one of those people who can freeze others out. I don't have the gene for that, I guess. It's probably because I'd hate it if someone did that to me.

Swiping across the screen, I press on the notification as my heart begins to pound in my chest. What I see isn't anything like what I thought he'd say.

Kate, I called twice but you didn't answer. I need to see you today. Will you come over to the house?

I look up to see my sister waiting for me to tell her what's going on. The problem is I don't know.

"That's from him. We weren't supposed to get together until tomorrow, but he says he needs to see me today. What could be wrong?"

She gives me a big smile. "Why does it have to mean something's wrong? Sounds like he's dying to see you. Text him back and tell him you'll be over this afternoon. Then you can show him the kind of fun you can offer."

Immediately, worry sets in, and I feel even more despondent than before. "But what if he wants to see me to say he's not interested anymore?"

"Then I say good riddance. He must have lost his mind when he lost his hand. I don't think that's what he wants to say, though. This is Ronan. Your Ronan. Time to let anyone who believes they can step in and replace you know that's not going to fly."

I know a lot of what my sister's saying is for her and not me, but I'm going to use it to bolster my confidence anyway. Ronan did love me once, and he loved me for how smart I was, among other things.

Now I just need to remind him of that, in case he's forgotten.

I quickly text him back that I'll be over right around two. Instantly, my hands start shaking, and I begin to doubt I can do what Kelly said I should, but I push those fears away.

It's time to show the man I love that I'm the kind of person he can love in return.

# CHAPTER TWENTY-FIVE

onan

AFTER ONE FINAL LOOK IN THE MIRROR AND WISHING I had something other than the t-shirts I always wear, I walk downstairs, checking the time on my phone. 1:50. Almost time for Kate to arrive.

Today, there's no food to show her I remember what she loves and no plans so she and I can spend some time alone. There's just me and my intention to tell her how I feel.

Then hopefully, assuming Marius wasn't exaggerating about what he claimed Kate said to him last night when he saw her, she'll know once and for all that I'm crazy about her. All I've wanted after seeing her was for us to get back together. It's just that I wasn't sure it could ever happen because I felt so messed up after what happened to me.

Now after that fight with Marius this morning, I feel like I'm back to my old self. Yes, I'm still missing my hand, but Kate doesn't seem to care about that anyway. I do, but I can see I'm the same Ronan I've always been.

The same Ronan a beautiful and smart woman like Kate would want to be with again.

Eleanor is in the kitchen when I walk in to grab a water since my mouth seems to have forgotten how to make saliva today. "Have you decided what tomorrow's menu will be?" she asks as she stirs something sweet-smelling in a pot on the stove.

I shake my head. Tomorrow's lunch may not happen if Kate doesn't like what I have to say today.

"Not sure it's going to happen yet. I'll know later, though."

Worry settles into Eleanor's features. "Why? I thought it was all planned out and all you needed to do was decide what to eat."

"It still may happen. I just won't know until after this afternoon."

She nods and returns to whatever she's making. "Okay. Just let me know."

As I try to calm my nerves about talking to Kate in a matter of a few minutes, Sabrina comes rushing into the room. Flustered, she flails her arms around but doesn't say anything. I look over at Eleanor, but she doesn't understand what's happening any more than I do.

"What's wrong?" I ask, unsure what could make her act like this.

In a frantic voice, she says, "Matthias and Ava

went out for a little while, and I'm watching the boys. Matty's taking a nap, but when I went to take Theo out of his crib, I couldn't find him."

"Couldn't find him?" Eleanor says, echoing Sabrina's exact words.

The nanny covers her face with her hands and sobs, "I couldn't find him! He's nowhere in the house!"

Jesus! What the hell could have happened to Theo?

I jump up, nearly knocking over my bottle of water. "He's got to be here somewhere. He's a baby. It's not like he can go far. He can only crawl, right?"

Sabrina nods, dropping her hands from her face. "Yes."

Eleanor quickly turns off the stove and pushes the pot to the back burner. "Oh my God! That sweet little baby. There must be some explanation for where he is, right?"

I don't know who she's asking. All I know is my heart's racing a hundred miles a minute.

"You check downstairs here. I'll check upstairs," I say to Sabrina.

"Oh, I'll look down here too," Eleanor says in a teary voice.

"Then I'll go upstairs with Ronan," Sabrina says, following me out of the kitchen.

Racing toward the front stairs, I take them by two to the second floor, not bothering to wait for her. "Theo! It's Uncle Ronan. Where are you, little guy?"

Behind me as I walk into the first bedroom that used to be Kellen's, I hear Sabrina practically sob as she reaches the top of the stairs, "Oh, Theo! Where are you? Come out so I know you're okay."

After quickly rushing through Kellen's old bedroom and bathroom, I don't find the baby. Where could he be? The kid couldn't have made it that far. How he got out on his own is another question. Isn't Sabrina supposed to be watching him at all times?

I move to Matthias's old room next, but a fast look in here and the bathroom shows Theo isn't here either. With each second I can't find him, I start to really worry. If something happened to little Theo, I don't know what my brother and Ava will do.

Sabrina stands in the center of the hallway calling his name while I go into my room. Since I just walked out of here not ten minutes ago, I doubt he's in here, but it can't hurt to give it a check. As I suspected, the baby isn't in this room either.

Heading out to the hallway, I yell downstairs to Eleanor, "Did you find him?"

The fear in her voice is palpable when she calls back to me, "No! You don't see any sign up him up there?"

"No! Keep looking, and I'll keep looking through the bedrooms."

Now I'm really scared, so I storm into Marius's room and find him kicked back on his bed wearing only a pair of black shorts watching some war movie. He gives me a look like he plans to tell me exactly where I need to fuck off with barging in on his private spot, but I immediately shake my head.

"Not now, Marius. Little Theo is missing. Sabrina

said she couldn't find him when she went in to get him from his crib."

Horror fills his expression, and he jumps up off the bed. "What do you mean she can't find him? He's barely a year old, for Christ's sake! He can't even walk. Where could he go?"

I march into his bathroom and scan the room. He's not here either.

When I walk back out to the bedroom, Marius is standing there like he can't believe what's happening. "What the fuck is going on? Theo can barely crawl. How could he have gotten away? Snails fucking move faster than he does."

Already tired of listening to him, I snap, "How the fuck should I know? What do I know about babies? All I know is he's gone. Not where he's supposed to be. Now suit up and help us look for him instead of asking me stupid questions!"

I don't give my brother a chance to say another word before I run out to the hallway. Sabrina leans against the wall with her hands over her face crying. Feeling like I should say something comforting, I walk over to her on my way to the nursery.

"It's going to be fine. We'll find him."

Behind her hands, she sniffles. "I don't know what happened. How could he have gotten out?"

"I don't know, but he's here. It's not like someone walked in and took him."

Even as I say that, I have to wonder if that's a possibility. Matthias refuses to have any serious security at the front gate of the estate. They simply open it with a damn button to anyone who wants to drive in. None of us worry about locking the doors here either. We never have. The estate has always been safe, so why would we? And most of the bedroom doors are wide open since nobody's using those rooms.

Sabrina drops her hands from her face to reveal utter horror in her eyes. "Took him? How? A house like this has to have the best security in the world."

We don't have time for me to explain that's not exactly the case, so I say, "Yeah. Well, go look in the nursery one more time while I check Matthias and Ava's room."

She nods and hurries off as I see Marius walk toward the stairs while he finishes slipping a green t-shirt over his head. "I'll look down on the first floor."

"Eleanor's doing that, so find her and see where she's looked already," I say before running to the master bedroom.

It only takes a few seconds for me to find the little guy. Lying on his back on the floor in front of Ava's closet, he stares up at me and then smiles as if to say, "It's okay, Uncle Ronan. I'm just relaxing for a little while. No need to get all upset. I've been here the whole time."

I scoop him up and set him on my left hip, checking to see if he's got any bruises or cuts. He seems fine. In fact, he seems sort of confused why I'm carrying him at all. I guess that's not surprising since I don't think I've held this nephew since last Christmas.

Calling out to everyone in the house, I let them know I found him. "Got him! He was in the master bedroom just hanging out."

Sabrina comes running out of the nursery and stops

dead right in front of me. "Oh my God! He's okay! How did you get out, Theo?"

Of course, he doesn't answer. All he does is stick his entire fist into his mouth and then pull it out again covered in baby spit.

As she takes him from me, she smiles. "I can't thank you enough. I don't understand how he got in there. I'm so happy you found him safe and sound."

I nod, just relieved he's okay. "No problem."

Marius and Eleanor rush up the stairs, and just as they reach the second floor, Sabrina steps forward and hugs me, wrapping her one free arm around my body as little Theo presses against my other side. "Thank you so much, Ronan. Thank you."

Perhaps she's just overwrought about the thought of the baby missing, but she seems really emotional right now. I want to pull away after what Marius said about her liking me. I don't want to encourage her to think I feel the same way, but that feels shitty to do to someone who's so upset.

So I put my arm around her and softly pat her back. "It's okay. He just likes to roam, I guess. We'll have to keep a closer eye on him from now on."

Just as I finish, I hear Marius clear his throat. I look up at see it's not just him and Eleanor standing at the top of the stairs.

It's Kate too, and the expression I see on her face tells me what my brother said earlier about what she told him last night was one hundred percent true. And here I am with Sabrina in my arms and the two of us looking like some happy in love couple.

Fucking fabulous.

Gently, I push Sabrina off me and tap on the tip of the baby's nose. "Time for this little guy to get a nap," I say, hoping to God Kate isn't thinking what I think she's thinking.

"Thank you so much, Ronan. You're a hero. Really," Sabrina says, sounding more like a fan than someone working for my brother and sister-in-law.

I wave that whole hero thing off and turn to walk over to where Kate is standing so I can explain what happened with little Theo, but Sabrina stops me and plants a kiss on my cheek. I look down at her, stunned for a moment, and then out of the corner of my eye, I see Kate turn away and disappear down the stairs.

Fuck! Now I know she's got the wrong idea.

Eleanor follows her, leaving Marius standing at the top of the stairs giving me a look that screams, "Told you so."

As I pass him smirking at me, I grumble, "I don't need whatever you want to say right now, okay? I need to find Kate."

"Well, I'd look for her walking in the direction of her car."

I swear he's not helpful at all.

Once more, I take the stairs by two so I can catch up to her. I find her just as she's walking out the kitchen door, pretty much like Marius said.

"Kate! Wait for me!" I call after her, but she doesn't even turn around.

"This was a mistake. I knew it was, and still I couldn't not come after you texted you needed to see me."

I catch up to her right before she reaches her car.

"That isn't what you think. I swear. The baby got lost and I had to help find him. That's it."

She spins around, and I immediately see her eyes are filled with tears. "Last night, I decided this wasn't going to work between us. I'm not what you want, which is fine. I just didn't need to have how much I don't belong here acted out in front of me. Goodbye, Ronan."

What is she talking about? I don't have a clue, so I put my hand on her shoulder to stop her from getting into her car and possibly driving out of my life forever.

"It's not like that. Sabrina was just happy I found Theo. I guess he had crawled into the master bedroom."

That gets me a look that says I'm either a complete idiot or I don't understand what the hell is happening. Right now, I may be both, to be honest.

"What? I'm not lying."

"I don't think you are, but here's a little fact for you, Ronan. Babies Theo's age don't just get out of their crib and walk to their parents' room."

"No, he didn't walk. He crawled," I explain, sure now that I've offered her a reasonable explanation that she won't be so upset.

I couldn't be more wrong. Her expression changes from telling me I'm an idiot to telling me I'm the dumbest person she's ever met.

"Ronan, I'm okay with not being sexy or bubbly, but please don't insult my intelligence."

Shaking my head, I say in all honesty, "I don't understand."

"He didn't crawl anywhere. Seriously. You live

with that child and don't have a clue about him. She put him in there and then waited for you to find him, which is exactly what you did. Then she took that opportunity to kiss you, coincidentally or not just at the moment I showed up. You're not a stupid man, Ronan. Figure it out."

It takes me a few seconds to process what Kate is saying. Marius did tell me Sabrina was into me. I guess it makes sense.

But that doesn't mean I'm to blame for any of that.

"Okay, even if she did, why are you angry at me?"

Kate opens her mouth to tell me but then she closes it again. She does that a second time before hanging her head.

"I'm not angry at you, I guess. I just don't think I'm ever going to be enough, so that's a me thing. I just need to go."

"No, stay. Please. I want to talk to you."

She lifts her head to look into my eyes, and all I see is sadness in hers. "Why? I can't compete with her just like I couldn't compete with Amanda. It's always going to be this way because you're you and I'm me. You may not play ball anymore, but you have that special something women want. I'm just that same nerdy girl I've always been. The one that people like your brother make fun of because I'm not sexy or bubbly. I can't change that, Ronan."

"I don't want you to change that! I've always loved how smart you are. For the first year we were together, I was sure there was nothing I loved doing more than watching you study or helping you with getting ready for tests. Then I was sure you'd leave me because you'd realize I wasn't smart like you. I love that you're smart, Kate. And if you think you're not sexy, you're crazy."

None of that makes her smile, though. If anything, all I say seems to make her even more unhappy.

"Then I'm crazy. Add that to the list of things women like Sabrina aren't. Let me go. I want to leave."

"No. I want to talk to you. I asked you to come over today because I couldn't wait until tomorrow."

Kate sighs. "There's nothing to talk about. We are who we are. That's never going to change. Just let me go."

Jesus, I'm losing her for a second time. I can't let that happen. I can't let the only woman I've ever loved walk out of my life again.

"No! I love you, Kate. I've always loved you. Don't go."

Her eyes are filled with surprise, like she can't believe I just said that. "You still love me?"

"Yes. I never stopped. You broke up with me, and I couldn't stop loving you. I wanted to talk to you today to find out if you think you could ever love me again. I know I'm not the person I used to be because of the accident. I get it that my issues might seem like a lot. But I swear I'm getting better with them every day. I see a therapist, and she's helping me see I only lost my hand. I still have everything else I need to be happy. She's wrong, though. I need you to be happy. I need you, Kate."

# CHAPTER TWENTY-SIX

ate

I CAN'T SEE CLEARLY BECAUSE MY TEARS ARE MAKING everything blurry and Ronan seems like some kind of watery dream standing in front of me. He loves me? I thought there was a chance I was coming here to listen to him tell me he can't see me anymore, and now he's saying he's always loved me?

"So you don't want Sabrina?"

He shakes his head. "No. It's always been you, Kate."

"It sure didn't look like it."

Ronan doesn't answer for a few moments but finally sheepishly says, "I admit I liked having someone interested in me. It stroked my ego, and I guess I needed it. But there's never been anyone but you, Kate."

"You cheated on me, Ronan, and while I thought I forgave and forgot, I can't forget because she was just like Sabrina. Pretty. Sexy. The kind of girl everyone wishes they could be."

Ronan leans down and softly presses his lips against mine before whispering, "You should have never wished you were like that. I didn't."

I look up into his dark eyes and see he clearly has no idea how much I've wished I was like those girls. "All my life I wanted to be like them. You have no idea. You've always been like them—gorgeous, popular, successful. I've always been on the other side. You have no idea how much guys don't like brainy girls, and when we grow up to be brainy women, they like us less."

He smiles down at me, and I swear it's like stepping out from the shade into the sun. "I don't care what those guys like. They can have those other girls. All I ever wanted was you."

Looking down at the ground, I try not to be embarrassed when I admit the truth of how I've been feeling. "I thought you liked her because of how she looks. All those insecurities came rushing back, and I decided I couldn't do this anymore. That's why I didn't answer your calls."

"So you really were thinking you didn't want to keep seeing me?" he asks, and I hear so much hurt in his words.

I lift my head to see that hurt written all over his face. "Only because I was sure at any minute you were going to tell me you decided since you have a new lease on life that you want someone different. Someone like Sabrina."

That makes him chuckle. "The new lease on life I have is because of you. You don't know how many times I wanted to call you since my accident. Talking to you has always helped me put things in perspective, but I wasn't sure you'd want to be around someone who isn't whole anymore."

For the first time, I lift his right arm and look hard at where his hand used to be. The hand that knew how to catch a baseball when he played shortstop and could throw a ball on a frozen rope. The hand that he would use to cradle my face in his when we were alone. The hand that I know meant the world to him.

"This was never all you were, Ronan. I know it's been hard accepting that your dreams won't come true now, but there are a million other things a person with only one hand can do. This doesn't make you disabled. What makes a person that is if they won't keep living because one part of them is gone. I don't care about your missing hand. I care about you. All of you."

He smiles again, and I breathe a sigh of relief. I practiced that speech all the way over in the car, just in case he was planning on telling me not that he wanted Sabrina but that he didn't think I could want him since he lost his hand.

"You sound like my therapist. You'd like her. She's smart like you and doesn't let me slack off with my bullshit, just like you never did."

"Well, then I hope you're listening to her because she's right. I've always loved how strong you are. I'm smart, but I don't have that strength you have. I'm glad to see it's still in you."

Ronan pulls me to him in a hug unlike any other I've ever received. He clings to me, and I hold him tightly to me, utterly content that he loves me and I love him. We've been through a lot since the last time I felt this good.

"So what do you want to do?" he asks, confusing me.

I lean back and look up at his face, hoping to find some clue as to what he means. I can't decipher his words, though, so I ask, "Do? When?"

"I haven't left this house since I got here, except to go to my therapist's office every week. What do you say to the two of us going out for a bite to eat?"

Relief washes over me. So that's what he meant.

"Oh, okay. Just tell me where we're going, and I'll get us there."

As I move around him to open my driver's side door, he puts his hand on mine, stopping me. "I'd like to drive."

Just like the first time we were together. "Okay. The keys are inside. Lead the way!"

He settles in behind the wheel, and I sit down beside him in the passenger seat. Turning his head, he looks at me and says in a quiet voice, "Kate, I haven't driven since the accident."

"Then you have some miles to make up for."

Ronan hesitates before starting the car and says, "Thank you for trusting me."

I reach over and touch his right elbow just above where they amputated his hand near the wrist. It feels like he needs to see I'm not afraid of what he's dealing with. We can handle this. He's strong, and I'm smart, and maybe I'm a little stronger than I ever thought.

"Always. Now let's get going because all of this emotional stuff has made me hungry."

He leans over and kisses me, and unlike a few minutes ago, this one is full of all the passion I know he has inside him. My stomach flips, like it always has when he kisses me like this. When I was a teenager, I wondered if I felt like that because I hadn't been with many guys.

Now I know my stomach didn't flutter just because I was young. It was because it was Ronan kissing me.

I sense his trepidation as he starts to back the car out of the driveway to the road that goes around the estate. He doesn't have to be afraid. I trust him, and no matter what happens today on our drive to get food or any time in the future, I'm right beside him.

"They say it's like riding a bike," he jokes as he reaches over with his left hand to shift the car into drive.

Nudging his right shoulder, I smile at him. "I think that's what they say about most things after you don't do them for a while."

I feel my cheeks get hot from a blush because there's something else I haven't done in a while. Ronan picks up on my hidden meaning instantly and grins.

"Then I can't wait to see if something else is like riding a bike too."

Shaking my head, I can't keep the smile off my face. He is the same boy I fell in love with when I was a nerdy teenage girl. Maybe not entirely, but all the things I loved about him are still here.

"First we eat."

He presses his foot onto the gas pedal and we begin moving a little faster. "Good to know I still have it."

I'm sure he does, and I can't wait to find out. Maybe lunch should wait for later.

# CHAPTER TWENTY-SEVEN

*M*arius

I SIT OUTSIDE WATCHING AVA AND MATTHIAS SPLASH around with little Theo as Sabrina sits with Matty in the stroller. He seems to love sleeping in that thing, so they keep it on the patio whenever they bring him outside.

It's good to see my brother and Ava enjoying parenthood. They've had a lot on their plates these past couple months. A baby nearly a year old. A newborn. Ronan moving in with his own issues. And as always, problems at King Industries for Matthias to deal with. Kellen helps, but the weight of the crown rests on the head of the company, so there's only so much he can do.

"Marius, stop sitting on the sidelines and get in

here! Theo is almost to the point that he's swimming," Matthias says with pride.

I've got other things in mind for today, so I wave him off. He's too busy having fun to care that I seem more interested in hanging out with the nanny than spending time with my family. Good. I don't want to explain myself about that.

Sabrina stares down at her phone as I look over at her, and when she realizes someone is paying attention to her, she begins pushing the stroller back and forth. How nice of her to remember one of her charges need attention.

"So, do you like your job watching my nephews?" I ask, not interested so much in her answer than what I don't hear.

She perks up, but I sense it's merely to make me think she's something she's not. "Sure! Ava and Matthias have been great, and I don't think I've ever lived in such a nice place."

"So you like your room down near Eleanor's?"

This girl is no dummy. She knows what I'm implying not as deftly as I could but exactly as I intend. She seems to think she's part of the family like Eleanor is, but that's nowhere close to being true. Eleanor has been with the King family for my entire life and even longer. Before any of us King boys were born, she was here already working for our parents.

Eleanor is family. This person, on the other hand, is someone who works for my brother. There's a difference, and I don't think she should forget that.

Especially after the bullshit she's been playing on Ronan.

Her chipper way fades a bit, but she keeps the show going. "Yeah, sure. She's so sweet."

Good. Sabrina picked up on what I was really saying. Now she needs to remember it.

"So you and Ronan seem to be getting close," I say with a flatness that doesn't give away that I know what she's been up to.

Once more, she perks up. "Oh, he's so great. I'm so happy he found Theo. For the life of me, I can't imagine how he got into the master bedroom. But Ronan saved me, so I owe him big."

I lean in toward her side of the table and fix my gaze on her. "Don't you mean he saved little Theo?"

That throws her off, and for the first time since we started talking out here today, she stumbles. "Oh, yeah, I mean, sure. My focus was always on Theo. I'm just so happy he's all right."

"Uh-huh."

I let her stew in that for a few minutes as I listen to Theo squeal with delight in the pool. Like the brother he's named after, that kid is one big bundle of life. He's also not even a year old and still hasn't mastered standing, even in his crib.

That's how I knew less than thirty seconds after Ronan came rushing into my room in a panic that there was no way in hell that kid got out of his crib, crawled out into the hallway, and got all the way to the master bedroom. Little Theo was never in any danger because she set the whole thing up to get Ronan to be her savior. That way she could profess her undying gratitude and have yet another tie to him.

My youngest brother is dealing with too much

between struggling with the reality of his new life without a right hand and how he feels about Kate to figure it out. That girlfriend of his is smart, so I bet she knew the truth, though. That's why she ran out of here so upset.

Hopefully, Ronan explained to her in that kind way of his that Sabrina is just the nanny and nothing else in his life. If I know him, he found a way to reassure Kate. Those two are meant for one another, so I think they'll figure out how to get past what this little minx has been up to lately.

She doesn't look at me as I sit here pretending to enjoy this beautiful sunny day. Like Ronan said, at first glance, it seems odd that she didn't latch onto me instead of him.

He's too good a person to understand why she wouldn't, but I know. Sabrina saw him as an easy target. She must have thought it would be like shooting fish in a barrel. He's struggling with what he lost and was barely hanging on. All she had to do was flash him a pretty smile and walk around here pretending like she was Miss Helpful. Ronan was so lost in his misery he didn't see her trying to ingratiate herself with him.

But I did. It didn't take a day from when I arrived to see what she was trying to do. Now she's going to find out her plan is blown. Let's see how she takes that. Something tells me Matthias and Ava are going to need a new nanny pretty soon.

"I saw Ronan and Kate leaving right after he found Theo. They've been in love for a long time. Did you know that?" I ask Sabrina but don't directly look over at her.

No need to look into her eyes to see her reaction. All I need to do is stare straight ahead and catch how her mood changes in my periphery.

Unlike my youngest brother, I'm not kind nor am I nice. Now she's dealing with a King who knows how to manipulate as well as she does.

"Sorry. I didn't hear you. What did you say?" she asks, and now all her sweetness is gone.

Interesting how different she sounds when she isn't pretending to be the sweet, young thing. She almost seems like a much older, much more jaded version of herself.

After nearly a minute of making her wait, I turn my head to look at her and smile. "Just shooting the breeze. I'm happy for Ronan that he and Kate are back together. They've been in love since high school."

She's practiced at controlling how her emotions show on her face, but I can see in her eyes she's disappointed the King brother who seemed like such an easy target isn't anymore. That only leaves me if she's looking to snag her a man with money in this family, but that won't happen.

"Can you watch Matty for a few minutes? I need to visit the little girl's room," she says, her perky act back in full force as she stands up to go inside the house.

"Take your time."

She disappears behind me, and I hook my foot onto the front of the stroller to pull it toward me. Leaning down, I tickle Matty and make him giggle.

"Can you believe she thought she could pull that nonsense off without anyone noticing?" I say to him.

Of course, it might have happened if I didn't show

up. Matthias is swamped between work and everything here, and Ava has her hands full with two children under a year old. Eleanor is too sweet, just like Sabrina said, so she may not have figured out what she was up to.

And Ronan? Until Kate started coming around, he couldn't see any future that included love and happiness for him ever again. He was like a sitting duck primed to fall for Sabrina and all the attention she was giving him.

I knew the second Matthias mentioned to me when I called a couple weeks ago that Sabrina and Ronan were getting close that something felt off. Not that he wouldn't have a woman interested in him, but knowing how difficult he'd been with everyone since he moved here, something wasn't right.

It only took one day to see Sabrina had set her sights on Ronan for reasons that had nothing to do with actually caring for him. I couldn't let that happen to him. He's my baby brother, and even though I enjoy busting his balls about nearly everything, it's my job to protect him like we all did for his entire life.

So just like that day I found him bleeding out and close to death, I did what I had to do. A well-placed word or two with Kate that night at the restaurant when I knew neither she nor Ronan would move fast enough to ensure Sabrina didn't sink her claws into him and that's all it took.

And to think my entire family just thinks I'm a jaded misanthrope. Well, maybe I'm jaded, but I love my family.

Matthias swims up to the side of the pool and lifts

himself out. Grabbing a towel to dry off, he looks around and asks, "Where's Sabrina? I thought she was watching Matty."

"Change of plans. She had to run inside, so I'm in charge of my nephew. I'm telling him all the things he needs to do to have a good time without you guys being any the wiser."

My older brother looks nervous for a moment before he realizes I'm joking. "Well, thanks. You don't mind?"

I shake my head and look down at Matty who's wide awake now. "Not at all. He's family, and you know how I feel about that."

Matthias nods. "If you want to swim, I can come out and hang with him."

"Nah. I'm good. I accomplished what I wanted to do out here, so now I'm just hanging with your little guy. Enjoy yourself, Matthias. You deserve it. We'll be fine out here."

He jumps back into the pool, and I smile down at the baby. "We're just two guys hanging together, right, little guy?"

Matty kicks his legs excitedly, so I tickle his belly again before checking the time on my watch. "I need to make a call, buddy, but no worries. I've got my eyes on you, so you're safe."

Taking my phone out, I press four and the number comes up on the screen. No name since I'm not interested in having people know my business.

"Hey, you!" she says in a playful way. "Right on time."

"Always."

"Are you still at the estate?" she asks.

"Yeah. I've done what I needed to do, so I'll probably be leaving soon."

"When are we meeting?" she asks, and I hear the impatience in her voice.

I've been consumed with watching out for Ronan lately, so we haven't seen each other much in the past couple weeks. Since things are better for him now that he and Kate are together, I can devote one hundred percent of my attention to her, just like she deserves.

I look down at Matty and smile. "How does seven sound?"

"Make it eight and you have a deal."

"Deal. Are we staying in tonight?" I tease, knowing we can't go out on the town. Not yet.

"Of course. It's not like we can go around letting everyone see us. How would we explain it?"

I laugh at the way she says that. "Indeed. I've never liked explaining myself when it comes to this kind of thing. Everyone can find out when we decide they can."

"So eight o'clock?"

"I might be a little late," I say, looking toward the pool as Ava hands little Theo up to Matthias on the deck.

"I'm tired of waiting. Shame on you for making me wait this long."

"Mmm...I do love a woman who knows what she wants."

"Eight o'clock, Marius. Don't be late. Bring something good to drink for after. We'll order dinner in."

"Eight o'clock, Duck. You should wear the little black dress you wore to that party last year. I love you in that."

She laughs at my demand. "I don't plan to be wearing clothes for very long."

"Fair enough, but I'll enjoy seeing you in it for the thirty seconds before I rip it off you."

"I love that dress, so don't you dare rip it. Just for that, maybe I'll wear shorts and a t-shirt," she scolds.

As much as I enjoy seeing her in anything, I do love her in that dress. "If I promise not to ruin it, will you wear it? I'll make it worth your while."

"Oh, really? How's that?" she asks, teasing me.

Matthias, Ava, and Theo come walking toward me, so I can't tell her exactly what I plan to do that will make her eyes roll back in her head. "Gotta go now. See you at eight. Wear that dress."

"You're so demanding, but I'll wear it."

I end the call just as my brother and his family sit down around the table. Ava looks around and then asks me, "Where is Sabrina?"

With a shrug, I say, "Not sure. She went into the house a few minutes ago and hasn't come back."

She and Matthias exchange glances, and he asks me, "You didn't say anything to upset her or offend her, did you? I know how you can be. She might not get your sense of humor, Marius."

I glance down at Matty still enjoying his time in the stroller and then at my brother. "Trust me. She understood exactly what I was talking about, but no worries. By the way, I was considering sticking around for a little while longer. I know Ronan is good, but I have some things I want to do here. Do you mind?"

Again, my brother and his wife look at each other and then me. "Sure!" Ava answers, and then adds, "Maybe we should have a party since you're in town. Ronan can invite Kate since I hear they're together now."

"You don't mind being the odd man out again, do you?" Matthias asks, referring to my never having a date for their get-togethers.

I grin, knowing the truth even though they don't. "I'm a perpetual bachelor, big brother. I'm fine with being a single in a world full of couples."

"Then it's settled," Ava says full of excitement. "You know my friend Eden is going to be there, right?"

I shrug again. "As always. She doesn't bother me."

Ava pouts and starts typing into her phone. "Doesn't bother you. It must be nice to have people adoring you and you get to be so blasé about it."

It's good to be me.

# CHAPTER TWENTY-EIGHT

ate

RONAN HOLDS THE STEERING WHEEL SO TIGHTLY HIS knuckles turn white, but I don't want to say anything to him about it. He doesn't need caution now. If he's ever going to truly be himself again, he has to conquer any fears he has about driving.

He could have chosen anyone to do this with. I'm sure his brothers have been hoping he'd try driving again, so they would have jumped at the chance to be sitting beside him as he gets behind the wheel for the first time.

But he chose me to accompany him, so I want to support that decision as best as I can.

We've only driven on side roads until this point, but I see him look at the sign for the Taconic as we pass it. I don't know if he's ready to tackle that yet. He needs to know I'm here for him for that too.

"Feel free to drive wherever you want to, Ronan."

He pulls the car off to the side of the road and puts it in park. I can't tell if what I said upset him, but it can't be good that we've stopped.

As much as I want to ask if he's okay, I don't. I just give him time to say what he needs to. If that means sitting here all day in silence, then that's fine.

Whatever he needs, I'm here for him.

Finally after a minute or so of complete silence, he turns to look at me. His voice low and unsure, he winces like he's in pain when he says, "I don't know if I'm ready to drive on that road yet."

I smile and lean over to kiss him softly on the cheek. "It's your call. Wherever you want to go, I'm good."

"I'm just not sure…"

He stops and takes a deep breath before continuing. "What if I screw it up? I'd never forgive myself if you got hurt, Kate."

Fear fills his dark eyes, making me wish I knew what to say to make that disappear. I can only imagine the terror he experiences whenever he remembers that horrible night that changed his life forever. I want to help, but I don't know what to do.

"It's okay, Ronan. I don't think I'm going to get hurt, but if this isn't something you want to do, then we don't have to do it."

A slow smile lifts the corners of his mouth, and he leans over to kiss me. Against my lips, he whispers, "Okay, I think it's time. I want to do it."

My heart starts racing at the thought that he's about to try to conquer his biggest fear. I know he can do it. Ronan can do anything he puts his mind to. I know I won't get hurt either. I'm just worried it will be too much for him. Returning to the very place where you nearly lost your life and where your dreams ended has to be the hardest thing in the world.

"Okay, I'm right here with you."

He turns back to face the road ahead of us, and I slide my arm around his right arm. Waves of fear radiate off him, but he sets his jaw and leans over to shift the car with his left hand.

Once we're in drive, he takes his foot off the brake. At first, we're barely rolling down the road, but then he steps on the gas, and we're off!

I don't think I've ever been this nervous or excited all at the same time. Even when I was walking into that job interview for my teaching position I didn't feel this way.

Ronan's right arm tenses as we move up the on-ramp to the highway, so I gently pat his shoulder and say, "It's all good, Ronan. You've got this."

He tries to smile, but it never really materializes into much more than another bout of cringing for him. His left hand tightly grips the steering wheel so his knuckles turn white again, but he's determined to overcome his fear of the highway where he lost so much.

Cars stream by us going seventy and eighty miles an hour, and for a few seconds, I'm not sure we're going fast enough to merge onto the highway. Normally, I'd say something to warn the person driving that we need more speed, but I bite my tongue and let him handle this. I can't overcome what he's feeling for him. He has to do that all on his own.

I look back as he gets into the lane, and I swear it's like some higher power has cleared the road for him so he could get on at a slow speed. Ronan nervously checks the rearview mirror and then focuses his attention on the road ahead of us.

"Never in my life have I ever seen the Taconic look like that when I came onto this highway."

"I was thinking the same thing!" I say excitedly. "It's like someone up there is watching out for you."

He turns his head to look at me with a strange expression, causing the car to veer toward the breakdown lane. When he moves to get the car back into the right lane, he overcompensates, jerking the car and us, and for a few seconds, it feels touch and go.

But he gains control again, and it's like I see the fear drain away from him. I don't think I could be happier.

"Sorry about that. I've got to get used to things. I didn't mean to scare you. It's just what you said about someone up there. That's what I wanted to tell you about Sabrina."

As much as I don't want to be miserable whenever I hear that person's name, I can't help it. I'm still jealous, even though he told me he has no interest in her.

I don't want to ruin this for him, though. This drive means too much to Ronan for me to be petty about the nanny.

"What about her?" I ask through gritted teeth and a forced smile.

"She's into these signs you can get from people who aren't around anymore. She told me to ask my mother for a sign, and Kate, I know this is going to sound crazy, but I think I got one. It was a rabbit just like the one my mother and I saw when I was a little boy. You probably think it's stupid. I did too, but then that rabbit came out of nowhere, and I swear it nodded at me when I asked my mother to show me she's not disappointed in what I've become."

I rest my head on his shoulder and smile at how unbelievably sweet this man is. Like my sister said, the world is full of clowns. It needs more men like Ronan, though. How could I have ever doubted him?

"Your mother would be so proud of you, baby. Look at what you're doing right now. I bet she was looking down and made sure you weren't under pressure getting onto the highway. It sounds like something a mom would do."

Cars zoom past us again, but Ronan continues to drive the speed limit, oblivious to everything else but how incredible he feels. I even notice he loosens his grip on the steering wheel.

He's going to be okay. I know it now. And I couldn't be happier.

"WE'RE LOOKING FOR ROOM EIGHT FOURTEEN," HE says as we walk down the hotel hallway checking out the numbers on each door.

The two of us pass room eight twenty-five, and I

wonder if we turned the wrong way coming off the elevator. "Does this hotel go completely around in a square? If not, we might be in the wrong hallway."

Ronan looks over at me and gives my hand a squeeze. "No worries. I just handled driving on the one road that used to terrify me. We can deal with this."

I snuggle next to him and press my cheek against his left arm. "I know, but I think I'm sort of in a hurry to get back on the bike, if you know what I mean."

He stops and looks at me strangely for a second or two before a smile lights up his face. "My Kate with another sex joke. I think I like this new you."

"It wasn't a joke."

His eyebrows shoot up into his forehead. "Then we better get moving. There's bike riding to get to."

As we continue to search for our hotel room, he quietly asks, "Kate, why didn't you want to go to your apartment?"

Afraid he may think I'm trying to hide him or us being together, I stop and step in front of him. He looks down at me with worry in his eyes, so I quickly explain why I wanted to come to a hotel for our first time together instead of my apartment.

"I wanted it to be like it was on prom night. Do you remember?"

He smiles and leans down to kiss me. "I do. You were the most beautiful girl there that night in that pink dress."

"Well, that's the only reason why."

We start walking again, turning off the hallway we were on to another one. In no time, we find room eight fourteen, thankfully. I've waited years to be with the man of my dreams again, and some crazy hotel set up wasn't going to stop me from finally getting what I've been thinking about from the moment Ronan kissed me.

The door closes behind us, and I look around the hotel room. It reminds me of the room we had that night after senior prom.

Before I can mention that, Ronan comes up behind me and nuzzles my neck. "I think I should warn you it's been a while for me."

I turn around and look up at him, charmed by his honesty. Most guys wouldn't tell a woman that for fear they'd be seen as odd. Not Ronan, though. I love the way he just says it because it's the truth.

"Well, then that works because it's been a while for me too."

Surprise fills his eyes, which I guess is flattering. "Really? Are all the men around here out of their minds?"

I stand on my toes and kiss him sweetly on the lips. "Either that or I've been giving off some go away signals. The reality is probably the second choice."

Ronan smiles and shakes his head. "Then they're crazy because I'd fight through every one of those signals if it meant being with you."

He's the same boy I fell in love with all those years ago. Yes, some things have changed with him and with me, but the love I felt for him is the same I feel right now looking up into those soulful brown eyes staring down with such sweetness at me.

"I love you for saying that, Ronan."

With a shrug, he begins to slip off his t-shirt over

his head. "It's the truth. I'm glad they're all blind or stupid."

He pokes his head out from under the shirt and smiles in a way that reminds me of a pirate. "Better for me."

Running my hands over his chest and abs, I can't help but adore this man. I push his shorts down over his hips. He's hard as a rock underneath his boxer briefs, and I palm his cock over the thin fabric still covering it.

Ronan groans above me and then eases me back onto the bed. Burrowing his hands under my sundress, he pushes it up over my ribs and stops.

"Arms up. We need to get rid of this dress."

I do as he commands, and a few seconds later, he's got my yellow dress with the daisies on it in his hands. He tosses it onto the other bed and returns his attention to me.

"The woman at the front desk probably wondered what a beautiful woman dressed in that was doing with a guy dressed like me."

I shake my head at how clueless he can sometimes be. "Because you were in a pair of shorts and a t-shirt? You do realize you look like a billionaire even dressed like that, don't you?"

He genuinely looks surprised when I say that. "What's a billionaire look like?"

Amused he truly doesn't realize what he looks like to the rest of the world, I poke my fingertip into his abs and chuckle. "Uh, you?"

That Ronan King actually believes people see him as just another guy because he wears something other than an expensive Italian suit is just another reason I love this man. He has no idea how gorgeous and sexy he looks just being himself.

Smiling down at me, he leans forward and kisses me. "I think you're crazy."

"Only about you."

When he plants kisses down the side of my neck before moving down my body worshipping every inch, I swear I feel like I'm going to explode. In my wildest dreams, I couldn't imagine being with him like this again. I wanted to more than I could say, but after waiting for so long, I didn't know if I'd ever have Ronan back in my life.

He stops at my waist and looks up at me. God, he's so sexy I can barely take it.

"So I think from this point on you should stop wearing underwear. What do you think?"

I laugh at how funny that sounds. "Um, okay. Where did that come from?"

Ronan slides his finger under my panties. "I think we're going to be busy catching up for a while, so it would just be better if you ditched these from this point on."

"Very logical. Okay. I can do that. Let's just hope there isn't ever a gust of wind, or everyone around is going to get a glimpse of the goods."

I'm not sure what about that makes him pause, but he shakes his head after thinking for a moment. "Okay, maybe that's not a great idea."

Curious, I ask, "Why?"

Ronan's expression gets very serious, and he

answers, "The last thing I want is for Marius to get to see you like that, so the underwear can stay."

"I don't think your brother even likes me, so I wouldn't worry."

Moving down to between my legs, Ronan softly kisses the inside of my thigh as he looks up at me. "I think he does. He's always talking about how sweet and virginal you are. I just don't think I want to give him any chance. That's all."

Even though I don't think Marius has any interest in me, I sit up and cradle Ronan's face. "You're the only King I've ever wanted. Let 'em look. It won't matter. I'm yours. Forever."

That's all it takes to make him smile again, and he kisses me long and deep on the lips. "Mine. It's been too long since I could say that. Time to start catching up on all the years we missed."

Ronan slides down my body again and positions himself between my legs as I say, "We don't need to make up for that. We can just make new memories from this point on."

With a devilish twinkle in his eye, he says, "Then I say we start with making you come so hard your eyes roll back in your head."

No woman in her right mind would say no to that with this beautiful man's mouth just inches away from her pussy. Leaning back on the bed, I close my eyes as the first slow swipe of his tongue nearly sends me into outer space. Damn, he's gotten even better at this since we were together.

For a fleeting second or two, I'm jealous from thinking who he was with to make him better at sex, but that's just silly. He had every right to move on after I broke up with him. Now I get to enjoy the benefits of that time away. That's all that matters.

Like he warned when we got to this room, it doesn't take long for me to come. The combination of not having sex for months and his talented tongue expertly lashing my clit makes my orgasm rage not even a minute after he begins going down on me.

When I finish coming and my thighs are still quivering, he sits back and looks up at me. "I don't have to ask if you came. I thought your thighs were going to squeeze my head off."

"Sorry. I told you it's been a while."

He slides up my body again and kisses me on the lips. "No need to apologize. I just like seeing you come. It's the sexiest fucking thing I think I've ever witnessed."

I wrap my legs around his waist and press my heels into the small of his back. To me, he's the sexiest thing I've ever seen. He always has been.

Ronan rests all of his weight on his left hand and slowly tilts his hips forward, easing into me and making my body feel like it's going to explode again. Bigger than any of the other men I've been with, he always made sure to take his time with me, just as he is now. I love how caring he is that he worries about hurting me.

But he never would. I could always trust Ronan. Yes, he made a mistake, but when it's just the two of us together like this, I know he'd never hurt me.

Like before, he fills me completely, nearly taking

my breath away. He falls still and stares down at me, almost as if he's waiting for me to say I'm okay.

I reach up and stroke his cheek before running my hand through his dark hair. "I've missed you so much, Ronan."

He kisses me, and against my lips, he whispers, "Nobody else has ever made me feel the way you do. Like I'm home when I'm with you. I never want to lose that again, Kate."

Burying his head in my neck, he slowly thrusts into me, touching a spot no other man has ever reached. It's like Ronan King was made for me. I never want to be without him again.

We make love in a hurry, almost as if we can't wait to make our relationship again like it used to be. He lasts longer than either of us expected, but when I come for a second time, it makes him come.

Afterward, he gently eases out of me and rolls over onto his side, hiding his right arm. I don't know if he's sensitive about it, but I decide now's the time for us to acknowledge the truth of who he is.

"I want to talk about your arm, Ronan."

With a big smile, he lifts up his left hand. "This one?" He tries to joke, but in his eyes, I see he understands what I'm saying.

I roll him over onto his back and kiss him. "No, the other one. You don't have to hide it anymore. It's nothing to be ashamed of. I just wanted to tell you that."

He looks over to his right arm and winces. "It's taken me a long time to come to grips with it. I can't tell you how many mornings I woke up and looked down at it, hating how it looked and felt, and all I wanted to do was pull the covers up over my head and hide away."

I look at it too. Yes, it's hard to see knowing what he used to look like and how much his right hand meant to him, but that's only one part of the whole person I love.

"It's who you are, and because of that, I love it just like I love the rest of you."

For another moment or two, he stares at what's left of his arm and then turns to face me. "I don't know if I'll ever love it, but I accept what my life is with it now. My therapist says that's a big step in the right direction."

"It is."

"I told her about you too," he says with such sweetness I can't help but kiss him.

"Oh, yeah? What did she say?"

Ronan hesitates for a second but then answers, "She said to take things slowly. I think I'm going to have to tell her that plan is out the window."

"My father said pretty much the same thing. I told him he didn't have to worry."

Pulling me to him, he wraps his left arm around me, and I rest my head on his chest just above his heart. "They don't understand. It's us, Ronan and Kate. We never took things slowly, did we?"

I shake my head as I remember how we were barely dating for two weeks before we said I love you the last time. "No. We've been in love since about ten minutes after our first date."

He squeezes me to his body and presses a kiss to

my forehead. "You've always been the one for me. My Kate."

I close my eyes as a feeling of complete bliss washes over me. I'll always be his Kate.

And he'll always be my Ronan.

"So, I have a surprise for you," I say softly against his chest.

"For me?"

Lifting my head, I look at him and smile. "Yeah. Just tell me when you want it."

He thinks about it for just a brief second. "Now's good."

"Okay. We have to go into the bathroom for it, though."

Ronan cocks an eyebrow and looks at me strangely. "The bathroom is where my surprise is?"

I get up off the bed and hurry over to my bag. "I got it when we stopped at that store on our way here."

Still unsure what I'm doing, he sits up. "Since this is the first time we've been together in years, it's not a pregnancy test. Or do they have tests that show you immediately after you had sex that you're pregnant?"

I grab the white plastic bag and start walking to the bathroom to set the bag of goodies in the sink. "No, I don't think they have those yet. Follow me."

He gets off the bed and comes into the bathroom behind me. I point to the toilet and say, "You can sit on either the toilet lid or the bathtub. Your choice."

Ronan stands in the doorway naked deciding where he wants to sit for a moment before walking over to the toilet. I quickly grab a towel and throw it over the seat to cover it.

"Just in case they don't clean well enough all the time."

As he sits, he says, "You know, I would have never thought of that. Guys just sit their naked asses down anywhere."

"Ready for the surprise?" I ask as I eagerly wait to show him what I secretly bought.

"Sure! I'm sitting in a hotel bathroom, so why wouldn't it be a good time for a surprise?" he says with a chuckle.

I lift out a can of shaving cream and a men's blue disposable razor from the bag. "Ta-da! What do you think?"

He gives me a big smile. "I think one of my fantasies is about to come true."

Relieved he's pleased with my idea, I get everything ready and then walk over to stand in front of him. Once I have a dollop of shaving cream in my palm, I rub my hands together to coat them and then rub them over his jaw and chin.

I hold the razor up in front of his face and tell him the truth about what I'm about to do. "I've never shaved anyone, so forgive me in advance if I cut you. I promise to be careful."

He's so sweet and lifts himself up to kiss me, getting shaving cream on my face too. "You're going to do great. It's easy. If a fifteen-year-old boy can do it, you can too."

"Okay. Let's do this!"

As I run the razor over his stubble that's a few days old, he watches me like every move I make is important and he doesn't want to miss even a single one. I'm focused so I don't cut his face to ribbons, but I see in his eyes he likes me doing this for him.

"You know, Kate, she never meant anything to me. Sabrina, I mean. I only let her shave me because I wanted to look nice for you."

I smile as relief fills me. "I know that now. I'm sorry I got jealous."

One final sweep of the razor under his chin and I'm done. Tossing the razor in the sink, I step aside so he can stand up. "Take a look and let me know if it's okay."

He leans against the vanity to inspect his face in the mirror and then looks over at me. "You did a great job! Thanks!"

When I start to clean up, he takes me in his arms and kisses me, getting what's left of the shaving cream still on his face all over mine. Grabbing a washcloth, he wipes off my face and then does the same to his.

"For future reference, any time you want to shave me, I'm all in."

I throw everything back into the plastic bag and take it out to my purse as he lies back on the bed. He beckons me over to him, so I curl up beside him, loving how warm his skin feels against mine.

This is what I've always dreamed of but never found with anyone but Ronan. Other people can have nights out at bars. I have all I want right here.

We lie there silently as I revel in how happy we are, and then Ronan breaks the silence in that adorable way only he can do. "By the way, that fantasy I have of you shaving me. We only got it half right."

I lift my head off his chest and look up at him. "Oh? You said it turned out great."

He smiles and shakes his head. "You definitely did great, but for it to really fulfill my fantasy, we have to have sex while you're shaving me. So, technically, that didn't count."

"You should have told me."

Shrugging, he says, "Next time."

"Would it count if we had sex now?" I say with a tiny giggle.

Ronan looks up at the ceiling. "I'm not sure the judges would say that's the same."

I lie back down next to him and set my head on his chest. "Oh, well. Then I guess we won't."

Of course, I don't mean that. Being with Ronan is one of my favorite things in the world. I do like teasing him, though.

He rolls me onto my back and kisses me long and deep. "I told the judges to fuck off, so it counts."

"To hell with the judges anyway. We decide what counts, right?"

"Right."

It's been nearly five years, but it feels like no time has passed at all when it comes to us. Ronan is still the same boy I fell in love with that first night when we talked for hours and he kissed me in the park.

And I'm still madly in love with him.

# CHAPTER TWENTY-NINE

onan

My heart racing, I pace back and forth up and down the hallway as I try to calm down. I stop for a moment to listen to the people downstairs at the party, but it's no use. I'm a nervous wreck.

On one of my passes in front of my bedroom door, I consider going inside and closing the door behind me, letting tonight go by without following through on my plans. It's not like tonight is anything special. Just one of Ava's parties. I can do what I want any other night.

Busy talking myself out of what I couldn't wait to do earlier today, I don't hear my brother come up behind me until he taps me on the shoulder. I jump, startled that I'm not alone.

"What are you doing up here?" Marius asks with a look on his face like he thinks I'm some idiot.

"I'm not ready to go downstairs yet."

His expression morphs into one of complete confusion. "Why?"

It's no surprise he doesn't understand why I'm a mess and standing up here in the hallway while everyone else is downstairs having a good time. Marius has never a day in his life worried he was going to make a fool of himself. I swear he was born with all the confidence he'd ever need and likely some for me.

I take a deep breath in and let it out slowly, trying to calm myself. It doesn't work.

"What if I screw this up?" I ask him, silently hoping he understands now is not the time to bust my balls about anything.

Knowing his nature, he won't be picking up any of the signals I'm sending about that, though. He wasn't just born brimming with confidence. He's also been the world's biggest bust ass from the moment he entered this world.

And right now, that's the last damn thing I need.

He sets his hands on my shoulders and squares me up in front of him. I wait for him to say something snide or stupid, but this time, he disappoints me, thankfully.

"You're not going to screw anything up. You've got this, Ronan. It's a done deal. Trust me."

But that doesn't convince me as much as it should.

"How? How do you know? You have no idea what Kate's like."

That gets me a big smile. "True, but you've said

time and again that she's smart and sweet, so that tells me she's going to love what you're doing tonight. Don't worry. She's crazy about you, dude. This is going to be a cakewalk."

God, I hope he's right.

"If I was like you, I wouldn't even worry. It would be a done deal."

He laughs at that and says, "If you were like me, you wouldn't be doing this. You aren't like me, though. You're your own man, Ronan. You've been through hell these past eight months, but that's all changed now. Just take a deep breath and do this."

"I guess if someone who hates love as much as you do is egging me on, I should do this."

Marius nods and starts pushing me backwards down the hallway toward the stairs. "First of all, I don't hate love. I just don't think it's all it's cracked up to be like everyone else. Now come on. There's no time like the present."

Even though I don't say it, one horrible question fills my brain. What if she says no?

I don't mention that to my brother since he would think that's the most ridiculous question in the world. Instead, I turn around and slowly walk down the stairs with him following behind me.

"She got here five minutes ago, and I told her I'd come up and find you. Better hope she's not pissed you left her to fend for herself with all these people. Shy girls don't like that, little brother."

Spinning around halfway down the stairs, I glare at him. "Why are you doing this now? Can't you see I don't need another thing to worry about?"

Marius walks past me, smiling as he says, "You don't have anything to worry about. She'd have to be crazy to say no to you."

Maybe he's right. Kate loves me as much or maybe even more than she did when we were together the first time. I love her like I always have—completely without reservation. She's the only woman I've ever loved, and I hope tonight she's ready to make it official.

I reach the first floor, and my stomach does a full flip when I see her standing alone in the living room near the door to the patio. Damn, she probably is going to be upset I left her down here alone.

She looks so incredible in that pink sundress she's wearing. It wouldn't matter what she was dressed in, though. To me, Kate's always beautiful.

When she sees me, her face lights up, like I've made her day. Nobody else in the world has ever looked like that when they see me. Maybe my mother, but I don't remember it's been so long without her.

I hurry over to her and pull her aside. "Sorry I'm late. I had to take care of something."

"Was it with Marius? I saw him come down just a few seconds before you. He was nice enough to say he'd go up and tell you I was here."

Not wanting to explain what I was actually doing, I take another deep breath and nod my head toward the door. "Let's go outside for a few minutes, okay?"

"Okay. Is everything all right, Ronan?" she asks as I guide her out to the patio, making sure to close the door so we have some privacy.

"Yeah. It's just a little busy in there."

Concern fills her expression. "If you don't want to hang out here for long, that's okay. I understand if you're feeling uncomfortable around so many people. You know me. I'd be fine if I never had to be in a crowd again."

When we get to where the table and chairs are near the pool, I stop and silently ask whoever is watching to help me not screw up the next minute that's likely the most important sixty seconds of my life. A sudden calm washes over me, as if my mother saw how nervous I am and is silently making me understand everything's going to be okay.

"So I wanted to talk to you about something tonight, Kate," I say, my voice quivering when I say her name.

She looks up at me, her blue eyes wide. "Okay."

I hear the fear in her voice and know she's probably worried it was like that night all those years ago when I told her we needed to talk and then I confessed to cheating on her. She has every right to worry about that. I fucked up. I hurt the most wonderful person I had in my life, and I deserved to have her leave me.

That's how I know what we have now is even better than what we were before.

My hand fumbles with the tiny box in my pocket for a few seconds, and then I slowly bend down on one knee. I see her stare down in shock as she realizes what I'm about to do.

When I pull the black velvet box out, it tumbles out of my hold, bouncing across the concrete patio. I hurry to grab it, hating myself right now for ruining what was supposed to be the moment we'd remember forever.

"I wanted this to be perfect," I say, disgusted with myself.

Kate crouches down to stop me, picking the box up and handing it to me. "It's okay, Ronan. You don't have to be nervous. My answer is yes."

"I wanted to do this the right way. I'm sorry I messed it up," I say, hanging my head. "It's just that sometimes my left hand and my brain don't seem to want to work together."

She kisses me softly on the lips and whispers against them, "Oh, baby, it's okay. Nothing got messed up."

Opening the black jewelry box, I show off the engagement ring I bought when Marius and I went shopping a couple days ago. The diamond isn't huge like I can afford because I know Kate isn't flashy like that. It's a simple ring with a round two carat diamond and a gold band. As soon as I saw it, I knew it was the perfect ring for her.

"Kate Abbott, will you marry me? You're the only woman I've ever loved. Do me the honor of saying you'll be my wife."

Tears fill her eyes as she nods and wraps her arms around my neck. "Yes, of course, I'll marry you, Ronan. You're the only man I've ever loved. You were my first everything. I never stopped hoping that some day this would happen. You've made me the happiest woman in the world!"

I let out a sigh of relief as I hold her in my arms. My Kate, the first and only girl I loved, said yes to becoming my wife. I thought I'd lost everything all those months ago as I lay in that hospital bed wishing I'd never survived the crash. In my wildest dreams, I wouldn't have been able to see I could be this happy just eight months later.

She leans away from me and looks down at the ring as tears roll down her cheeks. "It's so beautiful, Ronan. How did you know that's exactly the kind of ring I'd like?"

I carefully lift it out of its velvet home and slip it on her ring finger. It's even more perfect seeing her wear it.

With a smile, I answer, "Because I know you."

Kate sniffles and throws her arms around my neck again. "Thank you for making me the happiest person in the world right now."

"Thank you for saying yes."

When we finally let go of one another and stand up, she slips her arm through mine and looks up at me with a smile. "Please tell me you weren't nervous about this tonight."

"I was. I didn't want to mess things up."

She stands on her tiptoes and presses a soft kiss to my lips. "You were perfect, just like you've always been."

My days of perfection, if they ever existed, are long gone after last New Year's Eve, but that doesn't mean I don't want to try to be the kind of man who deserves someone like Kate. I knew how lucky I was the day she first said yes to going out with me back in the spring of junior year. That Ronan doesn't exist anymore, but maybe that Kate doesn't either.

What matters is who we are now.

"Kate, I want to do something with my life. I don't know yet, but maybe start a foundation for people like me. I haven't figured it all out, but I was given a second chance with life and with you. Now that you've said you'll marry me, I want to be worthy of being your husband."

She smiles, and it's like my whole world lights up. "Ronan, you're already worthy, but whatever you choose to do, I know you're going to be great at it. I'll be by your side every step of the way."

I let out a heavy sigh and take her hand in mine. "I guess we better get inside before someone comes out to find us."

As we walk toward the door to go inside, she asks, "Did you tell anyone in your family that you were planning to propose tonight?"

"Just Marius. He went with me to buy the ring."

Kate looks up at me like she can't believe what I said. "Marius?"

"Yeah, go figure. I think he's warming up to the whole idea of love these days."

"Now that's a sentence I didn't think I'd ever hear," she says with a laugh.

The moment we step inside, the entire party cheers, "Congratulations!"

Marius stands near the door with a drink in his hand. Raising it in the air, he says, "To Ronan and Kate, may they have all the happiness they deserve."

Once more, everyone cheers. Ava and her friend Eden rush over to hug Kate and see the ring, so I step off to the side and Marius hands me a glass of whiskey on the rocks as Kellen and Matthias walk over to where we're standing near the window.

"Did you tell everyone what I was doing out there?"

Marius laughs and shakes his head. "No. I just told a few select people that they might want to look out the window."

"Let me guess. Ava and Eden."

He shrugs and hands Matthias and Kellen glasses. "Of course. I wasn't about to go telling everyone at the party. I knew those two would handle spreading the word better than I ever could."

"I can't believe you didn't tell me you were doing this tonight," Kellen complains as he lifts his glass in the air to toast me. "You beat me to the punch. Thank God this guy here will never get married, or I'd be the last one."

The three of us look at Marius, who's rolling his eyes at the mere thought of him getting married. "Don't look at me. I'm not the one proposing to the love of his life tonight."

Matthias laughs and shakes his head. "Love of your life? I'd be surprised if you had a love for the night. But tonight is all about Ronan and Kate, so congratulations, baby brother. When's the big day?"

"No idea. I couldn't even get the proposal right without nearly losing the ring. We'll have to talk about when the wedding is going to happen."

From behind us, Ava says, "Well, it has to be here. It just has to be. The grounds are big enough to handle all the guests you could want to invite, and no matter what the weather is, we can do it. Oh, please say you'll have your wedding here!"

Kate walks over to where I'm standing and smiles. "I'm happy to have our wedding here if you are."

The idea of us getting married where I grew up and had some of the best times of my life is fine with me. I want to believe my parents and Theo will be able to see things turned out okay for me, even with all that's happened.

"Then here it will be!" I say before kissing her.

Matthias raises his glass and loudly says to the entire room filled with guests, "To my brother Ronan and his beautiful wife-to-be, Kate, all our love and congratulations! As soon as they tell us when the wedding is going to happen, we'll all be back here to party once more!"

Everyone cheers again, but the only person I care about being happy tonight is the only woman I've ever loved. When I was as low as I could get, she made me see I had things to smile about again.

As my brothers and all the other guests get back to enjoying themselves, I pull Kate aside and whisper to her, "I love you, Kate. It's always been you. It always will be."

"And I love you, Ronan King. I've been in love with you since the first time you kissed me. Remember that night? We went for a walk after we hung out at the coffee shop? I knew that night I'd met the only boy I'd ever love."

Smiling, I hold her to me as I remember our first date. I couldn't believe she'd said yes to going out with me. Kate was smart and sweet and gorgeous, and I was a guy who's biggest claim to fame was my four older brothers and playing baseball. She had no idea I'd been crazy about her for weeks before I asked her out.

And now she's going to be my wife. There's not a luckier man on this planet now that she said she'd marry me.

It's been a hard road for me to get to this place, and many times I wasn't sure I'd ever survive after the accident. I don't know if I can say I wouldn't change a thing that's happened in my life, but if I had to go through it all so I could have Kate in my life, then it was worth it.

**LOOK FOR BOOK FOUR IN THE KING BROTHERS SERIES, LONE KING, MARIUS KING'S STORY!**

# ABOUT THE AUTHOR

K.M. Scott writes contemporary romance stories of sexy, intense, and unforgettable love and edge of your seat thrillers. A New York Times and USA Today bestselling author, she's been in love with romance since reading her first romance novel in junior high (she was a very curious girl!). Under her Gabrielle Bisset name, she writes paranormal and historical romance. She lives in Pennsylvania with a herd of animals and when she's not writing can be found reading or feeding her TV addiction.

Be sure to visit K.M.'s Facebook page at **https://www. facebook.com/kmscottauthor** for all the latest on her books, along with giveaways and other goodies! And to hear all the news on K.M. Scott books first, sign up for her newsletter today and be sure to visit her website at **http://www.kmscottbooks.com**

## BOOKS BY K.M. SCOTT

HEART OF STONE SERIES

Crash Into Me (Heart of Stone #1)

Fall Into Me (Heart of Stone #2)

Give In To Me (Heart of Stone #3)

Heart of Stone Volume One

Ever After (Heart of Stone #4)

A Heart of Stone Christmas (Heart of Stone #5)

Return To Me (Heart of Stone #6)

Forever With Me (Heart of Stone #7)

Heart of Stone Volume Two

Hard As Stone (Heart of Stone #8)

Set In Stone (Heart of Stone #9)

Silent As A Stone (Heart of Stone #10)

Heart of Stone Volume Three

All of Me (Heart of Stone #11)

CLUB X SERIES

Temptation (Club X #1)

Surrender (Club X #2)

Possession (Club X #3)

Satisfaction (Club X #4)

Acceptance (Club X #5)

Complete Club X Series Box Set

PROJECT ARTEMIS SERIES

In The Darkness (Project Artemis #1)

After The Storm (Project Artemis #2)

Behind The Scenes (Project Artemis #3)

Project Artemis Box Set

FINDING THE ONE SERIES

Hard Work (Finding The One #1)

Big Love (Finding The One #2)

DIRTY BOSS SERIES

Sweet Things (Dirty Boss #1)

Private Secretary (Dirty Boss #2)

Play Date (Dirty Boss #3)

Dirty Boss Volume One

THRILLERS

Now You Know How It Feels

The Neighbor

K.M.'S BOOKS ARE IN AUDIOBOOK TOO!

# BOOKS BY K.M. SCOTT WRITING AS ANINA COLLINS